when the night stood still

m a r i l y n   j a y e   l e w i s

a n   e r o t i c   r o m a n c e

First Magic Carpet Inc. edition February 2004

Published in 2004

Manufactured in the United States of America
Published by Magic Carpet Books

Magic Carpet Books
PO Box 473
New Milford, CT 06776

Library of Congress Cataloging in Publication Date

When The Night Stood Still by Marilyn Jaye Lewis
ISBN 09726339-7-9

Book Design: P. Ruggieri

For Andrea

AUTHOR'S NOTE

The Oscar® and the Academy Award® are registered trademarks of the Academy of Motion Picture Arts and Sciences.

PROLOGUE

There were two ways the world defined John Shay. As the media did, with awe; he'd been one of America's leading men of literature for the last twenty years. Or as most women did, with desire; they called him 'Johnny' and his reputation among them for being hot-tempered in bed was nearly eclipsed by the rumored size of his bank account.

When John Shay considered himself, however, as he did on this cold evening in late November, he was merciless. He privately cursed his inability to stay sober when he got bored, and these days boredom had become a full time occupation.

Stinking drunk on expensive scotch, he sat barricaded in the bar, his favorite room in the house. Upstairs, Jacqueline, his latest girl du jour, was packing. John Shay was a coward when it came to breaking up with a lover. He relied on his drinking binges to get the woman to come up with the idea on her own. Jacqueline had proven to be tenacious, however. It had taken her two solid weeks to dredge up enough self-respect to leave the famous Johnny Shay, and in that time, John's liquor bill had gotten outrageous.

'I'm still young, you know,' she spat. Her bags were packed now and out in the foyer. A taxi was waiting but she was giving him one last chance to beg her to stay. 'I'm not even near my prime. There are plenty of other men out there to choose from; successful ones who aren't drowning their impotence in booze.'

'Virility,' he countered, 'is highly overrated, my dear, when the choice comes down to another roll in the sack with a social climber like you, and an evening alone with a good bottle of scotch.'

To add a bit of injury to his insult, he refused to see Jacqueline to the front door, or even carry her suitcases out to the cab for her. He kept his drunken ass planted firmly on the bar stool in hopes that Jacqueline would be so infuriated with him that she wouldn't look back, wouldn't be on his doorstep again some lonely evening down the road. Out-and-out rudeness was the only foolproof tactic John Shay had come up with over the years to permanently sever all ties with a girl du jour. They had an annoying habit of reappearing, wanting another shot at it, hoping it would lead to an engagement ring this time. As if he would consider marrying again, after his life with Amanda, and all things decent, had turned to dust.

A blazing log crackled suddenly in the fireplace. It fell noisily against the heavy grate, sending a rush of embers up the chimney and distracting John long enough to grab his glass of scotch from the bar and move to a more comfortable chair.

He slid into a deep-cushioned leather lounger. With a convenient flick of a switch, the lights in the room dimmed consolingly. And where only a moment ago an impressionist painting of Paris had hung, a large, flat movie screen was revealed on the wall in its place.

John pushed the PLAY button on the remote and the same

movie he'd been watching every night for the last two weeks began again. The familiar credits rolled, fusing his drunken attention to the screen.

It was Master of the Storm, Hollywood's version of his best-selling novel from two years earlier. John himself had written the screenplay, or one of the many versions of it. He was credited with the writing of it, at any rate, and had been paid handsomely for it, too. Produced and directed by the legendary Jared Warren, the film starred John's favorite actress, a flickering gem of celluloid beauty, Lillie Diver.

There she was now, barely dressed in a slip of sheer silk. She looked wistful, standing alone on a stone balcony somewhere in the Mediterranean. It was a night shot, and the black sea was laid out below her; the dark waters dotted with the winking lights of countless boats rocking gently in the harbor.

The opening theme swelled. John knew every frame of the film by heart, and not just because he'd written it. Hollywood had come up with an interpretation of Master of the Storm that John barely recognized as the story he'd written anyway. It was more his fascination with Lillie Diver that had caused him to commit the entire movie to memory.

He watched her move across the screen, lithe and delicate. John took a sip of scotch. The smoky heat of it lingered in his mouth. The pleasurable aftertaste blazed across his tongue. His eyes filled with the splendor of this perfect fantasy, Lillie.

The sensations melted together as they'd done every night for the last two weeks; the taste of his favorite booze and the sight of this ethereal woman had become entwined in his brain, one insep-arable from the other.

This is my only comfort, he thought; it's come down to this. My brilliant career has been distilled to a flickering image of a woman adrift on a sea of scotch. And whose fault is it? Mine. I can't seem to do anything anymore except get drunk off my ass and watch this movie. God knows when I'll ever finish the next book.

Still, he reveled in the failure, as lonely as it was; at least he was feeling something he could identify. So much of his life nowadays had become a blur. Things happened too quickly. The world seemed to glide over the surface of his awareness, he couldn't feel passion for it anymore – an emotion upon which he'd founded an entire career.

Passion… a sobering spark of life shot through him, but it was a memory from long ago, the world he'd known with Amanda. There was no recapturing that world, he knew, so he let the spark drown in another sip of scotch, once again fusing that pleasurable heat in his mouth with the idea of Lillie.

Lillie Diver's career was on a trajectory through the stratosphere, or so it seemed to the uneducated eye. She was one of those actresses who came along only once in a generation. The camera loved her fine bone structure. It was easy for the lighting crew to make her skin look like porcelain. It was translucent, made all the more fragile-looking by her dark eyes, her dark hair. Her body moved with grace; the camera never caught her looking awkward. Dialogue never came out of her mouth sounding artificial or forced. Lillie had that intangible quality that was meant to be captured on film, and audiences everywhere loved to dream on her, as if her image were so bewitching it drew the viewer into a better world.

Even John Shay, who had years of experience with Hollywood and with selling dreams to the masses, had succumbed to the spell of Lillie Diver along with everyone else. For all his fame and money, there was still something ordinary about him. He was just another lonely man who had fallen in love with a face on a movie screen.

'And how common is that?' John drunkenly cursed the screen.

'Anyone can write that scene. Anyone can have it all and lose it in a crap shoot, with nothing left but fantasies to grasp at. Holding on to the brass ring in the first place,' he railed, 'that's what sets a man apart!'

Above all else, John needed to be recognized as special. Now all he was, he told himself morosely, was a drunk.

John took another sip of scotch but the taste had turned bitter.

A cigarette might help, he thought. And for a moment he missed Jacqueline; she was always one to jump up and fetch him a cigarette so that he wouldn't have to get up off his ass and get it himself.

'She was a halfway decent cook, too,' he reminded himself. John could do with a good meal right about now.

It was too late to lament Jacqueline, though. She was probably boarding some chartered jet at JFK, off to who cared where. John would be better off just hiring a new housekeeper who knew her away around a kitchen, and forget all about the debatable merits of Jacqueline.

Besides, Amanda had always been an excellent cook, and look where that had gotten him. Good food had filled his gut when he was married to her, but it had done little to stem the rising tide of his other cravings. There was always the lust for new places yapping at his heels, the temptation to travel light and to keep moving; the blackjack tables and roulette wheels of the casinos down on the islands; and finally, the siren call of booze. How splendid it had been to feel the warmth of a swig of good scotch slipping down his throat while the night air had been alive with magic, the kind of magic that only a mind like Johnny Shay's could pounce on and turn into something more extraordinary, capturing its magnitude with words and somehow squeezing it into a best seller.

The fire in the fireplace had died down to mere embers when

Master of the Storm approached its denouement. John had to make a choice; would he surrender to all-out sloth and pass out right here in the chair? Or would he summon a final ounce of dignity and drag his drunken body up to bed?

Lillie's parting shot showed her ascending a grand stairway on the Riviera, a look of steadfast determination on her lovely face. She was resolved to see it through, this labor of love, whatever it was – at least until the director shouted 'CUT!' and Lillie was returned to the world of mortals.

But all that 'living' stuff happened off-camera. What mattered at this moment was that John felt moved by Lillie's on-screen determination. After all, it was his pen that had provided her with these celluloid emotions. He ought to be able to feel them, too. Under a thick haze of booze, his brain seemed to be shouting to him that there was still something worthwhile in it, this idea of dignity, of having resolve. He forced himself out of the chair and up the stairs, where he collapsed into a dreamless sleep in the safety of his own bed.

It's going to be okay… his heart consoled him as he slept. The morning sun will be in the window soon and life will be waiting with a fresh, sober beginning…

John's mind was lulled by this encouraging news but the following day, he drifted still farther from sanity's shore on the ever-returning waves of booze.

CHAPTER ONE

F our months later… It was Oscar Day in Hollywood. The sun that usually beamed down so brightly all over Los Angeles seemed to shine just a little brighter on the trendier neighborhoods on this exciting day in late March. Every house in the Hollywood Hills crackled with palpable electricity. For those few as fortunate as Lillie Diver, who was nominated for one of the coveted awards, today felt like Christmas with all the frayed nerves and chaos in the air, not to mention the piles of gifts – they'd been arriving all morning by special messenger until the front hall was overflowing with them.

Slowly, Lillie raised herself up from the pink silk chair in the living room. It was only a practice run. Her strapless evening gown fit her tighter than a corset. If she couldn't get out of a simple chair in the privacy of her own home, she didn't know how she'd manage to get out of the limousine in front of that merciless crowd or out of her seat in the Kodak Theater, if it turned out to be her lucky name written inside the Best Actress envelope.

'Stunning,' Jared Warren declared. 'You look graceful as all hell, honey. I mean it, Lillie, you worry too much.'

'I can't breathe!'

'It's just nerves.'

'No, it's not nerves. The dress is two sizes too small, I tell you. Why did they even bother with the fitting if they were just going to arbitrarily choose a size at the last minute? I can barely move in this thing!'

'Lillie, honey, calm down. You look flawless, you really do. And you're not blue yet so you must be getting oxygen somehow. I promise I'll be the first to rip that dress off you at the slightest hint of suffocation.'

'That's very reassuring, Jared. You've really boosted my self-confidence.'

Jared looked at his watch. It was two thirty; the limos would be arriving within the hour. It was a perfectly respectable time to open the bottle of champagne.

He was up for an award himself, for Best Director of *Master of the Storm* – the same film that had grabbed Lillie her nomination for Best Actress. But unlike Lillie, Jared Warren had been down this road too many times to count. He had forty years of filmmaking under his belt that had garnered him a lot of nominations. Some years he won, other years he watched the golden statuette slip through his fingers and land in someone else's lap. Jared's experiences of both triumph and defeat in Hollywood had at least taught him how to arrive at the Oscar ceremony without looking as if he were coming apart at the seams – and looking in control, whether or not you actually were, counted for everything in this business.

He poured them each a tall glass of champagne. 'Here, my little lovely, drink this. It'll calm those nerves.'

'You sound like a mad scientist.' Lillie reached for the glass, a chunky diamond bracelet slid down around her delicate wrist.

Normally, she didn't wear ostentatious jewelry, but the bracelet and the matching diamond earrings were gifts from Jared. He'd given them to her the week before, one evening after they'd made love. In those brief moments before he hurriedly threw on his clothes then headed for the door, he'd pulled the box out of his coat pocket and shoved it at her. It was tied with a simple white bow.

'From now on, no more rented jewels,' he'd announced before she'd even had a chance to open it.

'These are beautiful,' she'd said, thinking that a pair of diamond earrings suddenly solved the dilemma of how she would wear her hair on the big night; it would be pulled up and away from her face.

Lillie noticed now how dazzling the bracelet looked, sparkling around her wrist in broad daylight, how it complimented the bubbles bursting wildly in her glass of champagne. She imagined that late in the evening, by candlelight, the jewels and the bubbles would look even more hypnotic; maybe she would drink champagne all night. But who would notice, really, or care? Jared was still a married man; he'd be expected to keep up appearances no matter how many Oscars they might win.

'When I was a little girl,' she recalled, 'my mom used to love to watch the Oscars on television. She'd plant herself in front of the TV set, and on that shabby little sofa we had, she'd drink martinis and smoke Bel-Airs, jumping up and down and carrying on like a teenager whenever her favorite actors won like they were her best friends. She had all their pictures taped to the kitchen wall, torn out of movie magazines. My mom was what made the movies seem glamorous to me, you know? It wasn't Hollywood; it was my mom's reaction to it. I never even noticed back then that all the actresses were wearing evening gowns that my mother couldn't have afforded in a lifetime. To me, my mom seemed more glamorous than all of them, in her little rayon nightgown from Penney's.'

Jared cut her off. 'Why do you always have to be so morose, Lillie? Does everything have to remind you of your impoverished childhood? You're up for an Academy Award, for chrissakes. What more do you want – and don't bring up Abby,' he warned her. 'I don't want to hear it anymore.'

'I wouldn't dream of bringing up Abby,' Lillie assured him, taking a large swallow of champagne. 'Abby couldn't be further from my mind. I was talking about my mother, who wasn't married, either, I might add. I guess I'm following in her lofty footsteps.'

'I mean it, I don't want to fight.'

'I'm not fighting. I'm merely pointing out that I'm not married and neither was my mother. You have a guilty conscience, that's all.'

'Abby, come on –'

'My name's Lillie. Abby's the one with the ring on her finger, remember? I'm the one with the bracelet and the earrings.' She shook her jeweled wrist for emphasis.

'Jesus, Lillie, it was a mistake, all right? I apologize. A simple slip of the tongue. I think we're both a little too tightly wound today.'

Jared paced over to the window, hoping that by some miracle the limousines had arrived early. But there were no limos parked in the circular drive. There was only the small army of personal assistants stationed by their cars in the bright sunshine, comparing lists and screaming into cell phones. Jared took a deep breath and a quick gulp of champagne.

'It'll all be a breeze,' he sighed, 'you'll see. I can feel it in my bones, honey; you're going to win that award. I'm not so sure about me, but I know that tonight you're going to be a winner.'

Lillie set aside her champagne glass and tried once again to sit down in the painfully tight dress and get up as gracefully as possible, her full body weight teetering precariously on her stiletto heels. 'God, I'll be glad when this night is over.'

'Don't say that,' Jared said, turning to her in all seriousness. 'Don't ever wish it away. It flies by quick enough on its own. Before you know it, you're going to be as old as I am, Lillie Diver, and all the good roles will be going to the newer, younger versions of you.'

For a moment, Jared had that look on his face that Lillie adored – passion. Here he was pushing sixty already, and still managing to feel passionate about Hollywood and all its inequity, its insanity.

Lillie wanted to ask him, why do you do it? How do you stand it? How can you put up with it, decade after decade? She knew he would take it as an affront, but they were real questions that Lillie was anxiously seeking answers to. She was barely twenty-eight-years-old and already she felt fed up with it, the constant nipping of the world at her heels, everyone waiting for her to make a misstep, waiting to see her fail. She felt like she was floundering. Her career was never fun anymore, and it was hardly what she'd call glamorous. It may have been a couturier gown she was wearing, a gift from the designer – an original, no less, a dress that her poor mother would have laid down and died for – still Lillie couldn't fully appreciate it. Not on a night as demanding as this would be. It was hard work, trying to seem untouchable and enchanting and then staying that way for ten or twelve hours under the unforgiving glare of the strobe-lit media.

'You're going to have plenty of time for regrets if you're not careful.' Jared was going on as if she were in rapt attention. 'We all get old in a heartbeat; trust me, I know about this. One day you'll look back on these nerve-wracking nights and realize they were the high points of your life and that they vanished in the wink of an eye. They seem overwhelming now, but they're just fleeting moments. You'll wind up like all the rest of us, wishing you could re-capture everything.'

'Talk about morose,' Lillie cried. 'You've got me living at the old actors' home already.'

He chuckled softly, realizing it was true. 'All right,' he relented. 'I guess maybe I'm more nervous than I thought. Come here.'

Lillie went to his open arms. 'I hope you win,' she said, feeling herself relax for the first time in weeks. 'You did such a marvelous job on the film, you deserve it.'

'Don't kid yourself,' he told her quietly. 'You made the film what it was. All I did was try to help the scenery keep up with you.'

Lillie smiled weakly and wondered if he was serious, with a man like Jared it was hard to tell. Sometimes he revealed his most intimate feelings with what sounded like a passing remark. Other times, his mean-spirited intentions were only thinly veiled by sarcasm, especially on a movie set, where his wit could get brutal.

'I wish we could spend the night together,' she said. 'It would mean so much to me to be with you tonight, especially if either one of us wins.'

Jared's chest tightened. It was so hard for him to deny Lillie anything. 'I've made myself as available to you as possible, honey, this whole week. I've done the best I could. I've been here since eight o'clock this morning. I've made love to you twice already, which is pretty damn good, for my age. I've told you all along that I can't stay with you tonight. But come to the party. Reconsider.'

Lillie pushed away from him. 'And do what?' she wanted to know. 'Always stand with at least two people between us? Be part of your entourage? No, thank you. I'm getting really tired of that routine. You're supposed to love me the way I love you.'

'Don't be childish,' he warned her. 'You know what my situation is, you've known from the beginning. You came into this with your eyes open, Lillie. Why is it that women always want to change the rules when the game isn't going exactly the way they want it to?'

'I'm not trying to change the rules. I'm just getting fed up.' But then Lillie shut up before she made a complete fool of herself. Jared was right. She was trying to force his hand. How pathetic am I, she wondered. The damn woman is in a wheelchair. Her looks are gone, her youth is gone, her career is over, her health is poor; and I need to take her husband away, too? Am I really that shallow? With everything I have in my life, is it really going to kill me to spend another night alone?

Lillie drained the last of her champagne from the glass. She felt helpless. Why did she have to be so in love with him?

'Patience,' he told her, reading her mind. 'One of these days we're going to be together twenty-four, seven. I promise. But I can't just forget about Abby on such a big night. She used to be the one who stood beside me at these awards. She was with me when I won my first. It would kill her to see the pictures of us in the paper. Not to mention that there are the children to think about, and my grandchildren. They read the papers, too. They watch TV. Too many photos of you and me together gets hard to explain, even on a night like this.'

'But Abby knows about us, or at least that there's someone you're spending all this time with-'

'Lillie, knock it off. I told you I don't want to discuss it.'

She felt slapped when he took that tone with her. Well, I guess this is it, she resigned herself; I'm sleeping alone tonight. She felt humiliated. Needlessly, she straightened her dress with a quick tug and ran a hand lightly through her coiffed hair. 'Thank you for this morning,' she said coolly. 'I appreciate it, you know. I always enjoy making love with you. I wish we had time for one more, it helps take the edge off my nerves.'

'Really? Sex works better than champagne?'

'Yes, it works better than champagne and it's less fattening.'

He took her in his arms again, pressing her body up close to his. Her curves always felt inviting; even more so now, squeezed into the tight evening gown. God, she made him feel so young. 'Can I at least kiss you,' he asked, 'or will Eduardo be in here screaming about ruining your lipstick?'

'We mustn't make Eduardo scream again, he's already hoarse from screaming at you all morning. Kiss me later.' Lillie tried to pull free from his embrace, but he held her more tightly.

'We have time for a quick one, you know. I promise not to mess your hair.'

'Jared, the cars will be here in a minute.'

'Trust me, I can do it in a minute if I put my mind to it.'

* * *

Enclosed with Jared in the small guest bathroom, Lillie tried not to think about feeling a little cheap. It was another chance to be close to him, she told herself instead. It will make up for not being able to be with him in bed tonight.

Jared unzipped his trousers and pulled out his cock. He was already hard. 'How do you manage to do this to me?' he whispered urgently. 'It's like I'm nineteen again. I'm always hard for you!'

Lillie fumbled with her evening gown, trying to tug it up past her hips without destroying it. She leaned her ass unceremoniously against the sink. Her long legs were sheathed in very expensive stockings. They stayed put by themselves. The tight gown left no room for even a garter belt. Her body was squeezed inside a one-piece girdle that held every ounce of her flesh in a vice grip. She deftly unhooked the crotch of it while Jared slid on a condom. He never seemed to be without one. There was always at least one in his pocket. As usual, Lillie privately wondered if it really was because of his unpredictable lust for her, as he said, or if the condoms were always on hand because he was the famous Jared Warren, the powerful producer and director; a man who could, if he felt like it, dole out stardom in a heartbeat in exchange for a myriad of favors.

Jared stood very close to Lillie, not yet touching her, his mouth wanting to devour her glossy red lips, his teeth wanting to sink into the translucent flesh of her neck. But all of it was off limits now. Her image would soon be televised world wide and she had to look like a winner. He couldn't so much as touch her breasts, her perfect, excitable breasts; they were his favorite part of her anatomy and were among the rare tits left in Hollywood that were actually real. Normally, just the sight of Lillie's tits pushed Jared into ecstasy. But now they were only hinted at, squeezed seductively into two soft mounds that were mostly concealed inside the snug-fitting strapless dress.

'God, you look gorgeous, even like this, sweetheart,' he insisted. 'I wish I could ravish you with absolute abandon.'

He fell to his knees instead and lavished his kisses between her legs. She held the material clear of herself, exposing everything to her lover's mouth. Jared was surprised to discover that she was already wet. The idea that her arousal was due solely to her lust for him, only increased his passion. He licked her, sucking her pussy ravenously, his ego tied inextricably to his cock.

Lillie let it all happen even though she thought it was tacky. This is not how I want to make love to a man, she thought. Why am I always like mush with him? Whatever he asks me to do, I do.

She looked down at his head of sleek, silver hair and wanted to run her fingers through it, push his mouth impossibly close to her aching clit. Her desire for him, her love for how he made her feel between her legs, temporarily overpowered her needling propriety. But she couldn't touch him. Every one of his perfect silver hairs needed to be in place for the cameras. Instead, she spread her legs wider, giving him unhindered access to her, reveling in the sensation that was building under the constant pressure of his tongue against her clitoris.

Suddenly, though, he rose to his feet. 'What am I thinking of?' he whispered hoarsely. 'We don't have time for this.'

She'd been so close to coming. 'Jared, honey, please.'

He positioned himself between her legs and instantly, as if he could do it in the dark with his eyes closed, his solid cock was thrust deep in her hole. 'Oh God,' he exulted through clenched teeth.

He was going at her more roughly than usual. It was hard to believe, but she could tell he was ready to come. Lillie wished she could throw her arms around him and get lost in the fiery, crazy moment, but she held tight to the edge of the vanity instead, letting him pound into her, the sink behind her easily taking the force of his rapid, relentless thrusts.

'Jesus,' he sputtered repeatedly. 'Oh, Jesus. You are incredible, Lillie.'

She grunted softly in rhythm to his climax until it was over. It had all happened so quickly, neither one of them had broken into a sweat.

* * *

Eduardo's Spanish accent was always more pronounced when he was upset. He could be heard all over the first floor of Lillie's enormous house as he stood in the front hall and rapped impatiently on the bathroom door. 'Little love birds, come out of there! I am going to kill you! The limousines, they are here now!' He rapped louder, growing more agitated by the sound of their muffled laughter. 'Lillie Diver, you are a naughty girl! Eduardo knows what you do in there! After all the hours I spend on your hair and all that lovely make-up! How could you do this to your good friend, Eduardo? Is it that you want all of the world to think I am no longer an artist? Do you want me to be laughed at, your trusting friend, Eduardo, who tries to make you look so stunning for less money than he charges everyone else?'

Startled inside the bathroom and giggling like children, Lillie tugged her gown back in place while Jared tucked himself quickly into his tuxedo pants and zipped up. As he wiped his face with a wet hand towel, she offered quietly, 'After all this shouting, do you really think there's anyone left in Hollywood who doesn't know that we're lovers?'

Jared kissed her; a light peck on the cheek so as not to smear the lipstick that was still perfectly in place. 'Just bear with me, Lillie,' he pleaded. 'You know I love you.'

'I know you do,' she relented.

She pulled open the bathroom door and watched Eduardo's look of despair turn into astonishment. Lillie still looked spectacular; in fact, she positively glowed.

'Oh,' he sighed rapturously. 'You look like a princess! This is a good sign!'

Outside, the front portico was alive with a flurry of personal assistants, scrambling to get Mr. Warren and Miss Diver into their separate limousines, then down through the hills and off to the theater at Hollywood & Highland. The countdown to Oscar destiny had finally begun and it was what personal assistants lived for.

CHAPTER TWO

'Amanda.' John looked up from the TV set in honest surprise. 'This is decent of you.'

Amanda Shay, dressed as usual in a stylish but conservative suit, hesitated before entering her ex-husband's private hospital room. 'Denmark is a long way to come from Connecticut, John, especially in the dead of winter. You didn't really think I'd fly all this way with Selena, speak to your doctor, and then leave without bothering to see you?' When he seemed to be considering an answer, she added, 'I'm not that petty, John, please.'

He switched off the TV set, her tone of voice helping him feel like a fumbling fool. He'd interacted with very few people in the last three months. 'I'm sorry if I – come in, Amanda, sit for a few minutes. How's Selena?'

'She's better. She's with Rick at the hotel. I think after she visits with you tomorrow, sees for herself that you're okay, that you're sober at any rate and that you're in a very nice hospital, she's going to adjust. She'll be fine. But you gave her quite a scare, John. That wasn't a smart thing you did. How are you feeling, anyway? Your doctors say you've been making good progress, now that the initial detox is over.'

'Amanda,' he sighed, too overwhelmed by all he'd been through to say anything more coherent.

She sat down on one of the two chairs available for visitors, keeping her heavy winter coat in her lap. She wasn't going to get comfortable. 'It's a nice room,' she said. 'A bit heavy on the Danish Modern though, isn't it?'

'Well, we are in Copenhagen.'

She managed a smile. 'Doing any writing?'

He shrugged. 'Making notes now and then. There's a story brewing. I'm not really focused yet.'

'I'm not surprised. That was quite a bender you went on. You outdid yourself.'

A flood of disconnected memories rose in John's now sober brain. He remembered Jacqueline and knew that she was gone, but he had no memory of when she'd actually left his house. She'd been there one minute, and he was alone the next, wandering the empty house in a stupor. It seemed as if it was suddenly Christmas and his daughter, Selena, was spending her school vacation with him. His memory of Selena's visit was sketchy, at best; his primary occupation throughout the New Year seems to have been keeping the bar well stocked with scotch. There was his fixation with Lillie Diver, he recalled that. It hovered over his memory of the drunken holidays like a specter in his psyche. In flashes of painful lucidity, he sometimes gained perfect recall, mostly of how regrettably he'd behaved toward Amanda and Selena when they'd staged the intervention that had landed him here in the Lindegaard Institute, a posh sanitarium in Copenhagen.

Amanda watched John's distracted silence uncomfortably;

divorced six years now, intimacy was not their style anymore. She turned her mind instead to trivial things. His hair had finally begun to turn gray, she noted. It made him look even more handsome, but then she'd always assumed it would. Nothing could make John Shay an unattractive man, on the outside, anyway. That mohair sweater, though – where had he dug that up? she wondered. It seemed incongruous to the Johnny Shay she'd always known. The sweater made him look resigned somehow; softer, less dynamic, maybe even defeated.

It's probably this environment, she cautioned herself. It's chic here, pricey and exclusive, and it's practically run like a private resort. Still it's a rehab, plain and simple.

'Amanda,' John began, his voice faltering.

'Yes?'

'I just wanted to say…' But his nerve failed him.

It embarrassed her, this sudden display of weakness from the literary lion himself. 'What is it, John? Just say it.'

'Well, I appreciate what you did to get me in here. I know I wasn't very civilized about it at first, but you did the right thing. I, well, I wanted to say it was very kind of you… after everything.'

She dismissed it. 'You're still Selena's father.'

'Yes, that's right. I'm that, if nothing else anymore.'

'Don't be so morbid, John. You're up for an Academy Award tonight, and how many other people in this sanitarium, regardless of how chi-chi it is, can say that?'

He made no reply.

'You're a winner, John. You always have been. This is just a midlife crisis or something, a setback. It's temporary; you're already on the rebound, I can tell. And face it, you wrote a good story. I think you're going to win that Oscar.'

'That movie is not my story, Amanda.'

'I know that,' she conceded. 'But who really reads anymore? In everyone's minds, Master of the Storm is your story and that's what matters, right?'

'I suppose so.'

'Are you planning to watch the show? It must come on in the middle of the night over here.'

'It does, but I don't sleep too well in this place. I'm usually up until all hours anyway. What time is Selena coming tomorrow?'

'Dr. Christensen said that I should bring her after you've had lunch.'

'Yes,' John nodded, 'lunch, I'm always in such good spirits after lunch. They feed us like kings here, you know. The food is incredible.' Then he sat quietly and thought about the lunch he'd had that day.

Amanda sighed. What was there left to say? Did she really want to talk about the meals in a sanitarium? Yet, when the polite conversation between them dried up, it left ample room for the old bitterness to surface. Surely, any talk about what had sent him on that bender in the first place would only bring up memories of how his reckless behavior, in her opinion, had torn apart their marriage; it would get them nowhere fast. She stood up to leave. 'Speaking of food, we have dinner reservations over at the hotel, so I'd better get going. I'll be by tomorrow with Selena in the early afternoon,' she promised him. 'And John, good luck tonight. I hope you win.'

He smiled faintly; it was just an award. What he really needed was a renewed lust for life and that seemed infinitely harder to come by. 'I'll walk you out,' he said.

The hallway was lushly carpeted and very quiet, adding to the feeling that this was a luxury hotel, not a hospital. The visible staff on hand was minimal, along with any signs of other patients.

Almost everyone had migrated to the dining facility for their royal feeding, where the opulence of the Lindegaard Institute's decor was even more pronounced.

'Good evening, Mr. Shay.'

Like almost everyone else in Copenhagen, the guard at the front door used perfect English when speaking to Americans, like John and Amanda. 'You might want your coat; it's a little chilly out for just a sweater,' he offered cheerily. Nevertheless, he rose to escort John out to the parking lot; patients went nowhere unaccompanied by security guards.

Beyond the glass doors, John could see the guard was right; it was a typical March evening out there, cold and bleak. Slight traces of leftover snow clung to the edge of the parking lot, blackened by car exhausts. The tall trees dotting the surrounding landscape were hauntingly bare; branches like bony fingers scraped against the low-hanging sky. On clear evenings, Copenhagen in winter could be dazzling, but this was a night for staying indoors.

'I'll say goodnight to you here, Amanda. You can get to your car okay, can't you?'

Parting at the door in full view of the guard was in fact a relief for Amanda; she didn't want intimacy rearing up its ugly head between them. 'I'm fine,' she assured him, slipping into her winter coat and putting on a brave smile that only made John feel more like a fool. 'My car's right there.' She pointed to a German luxury car in the parking lot, a rental not more than ten steps away. 'If the coast is clear, I think I'll make it.'

'It was decent of you, Amanda,' he said, repeating his earlier sentiments. It was all he could think of to say as she waved a quick goodbye. It was what he felt in his heart, it was decent of her. She had once again come to his rescue, this time with Selena in tow. Who else but Amanda had ever had the courage to come between

Johnny Shay and his bottle? Now his daughter had followed in those unfortunate footsteps. It had to end, that cycle; it was unacceptable. There was no doubt in John's mind.

This is that moment of clarity, he realized. Booze isn't going to turn my daughter into my caretaker. I won't allow it. It's something I can control.

The guard unlocked the door for Amanda and let her out, bidding her a friendly good evening.

John watched her through the glass as she crossed over to the freedom of the outside world. It would be his again soon, he told himself; the pearl, the oyster and the whole shebang. Not Amanda, she'd moved on to someone else; to Rick, an architect ten years her junior. But somehow John would grab the brass ring again, he would find someone new to love and make it work this time. He had it in him, he knew it. And no matter how fast the world spun him around, he would hang on tight. This time, he wouldn't let go of the magnificent prize.

* * *

'Lillie, over here!'
'Miss Diver, this way, this way!'
'Smile, Lillie!'

The shouts, the strobe flashes, seemed to come at Lillie from all quarters as she tried patiently to pose for the bank of cameramen lining the red carpet. At this pace, the walk from the curb to the Kodak Theater was going to be endless. For now, though, the towering stiletto heels and the gown's stranglehold on her vital organs were the last things on Lillie's mind. She'd had several years to perfect a look of calm, to cultivate a dazzling smile that didn't betray the awkward insecurity burbling just beneath the surface of her mask. She was a pro now – even in situations where the crowds and the paparazzi threatened to surge out of control. However, she'd never been at the center of a storm that was quite like this one.

The sheer numbers of people calling her name at the same time had a dizzying effect. She couldn't possibly look in all directions at once. Jared and his people had gotten far ahead of her. As much as she wanted to search the crowd for him, she had cameras flashing in her face, reporters thrusting out microphones. Every nuance of her mood would be captured and magnified by the media and plastered around the world by tomorrow morning. Lillie tried hard to keep her heart a complete blank. She didn't want it showing on her face, this hopeless love affair she was having with a married man.

Lillie's assistants had been sucked into the chaos of the crowd. Was she on her own here? A sudden urge to panic gripped her. She took a deep breath, as deep as the dress allowed. Where was Jared now, with his promise to ensure that she wouldn't turn blue?

'How does it feel to be walking up the red carpet?' a reporter shouted.

I feel utterly invaded, she wanted to say. She flashed a broad smile instead. 'It's wild!' she cried above the noise of the crowd. 'But for an Oscar nomination, I could get used to it!'

'You look stunning, Lillie!' another reporter called.

'Thanks!' She smiled again and the strobes tore blindly across her field of vision.

'Whose dress are you wearing?' A woman's voice rang out.

My own, you idiot, she wanted to say. 'It's an original Machard.'

'And what about the diamonds?' came a booming inquisition; a man's voice, a foreign accent.

With a knowing twinkle in her eye, one Lillie had rehearsed a thousand times, she shot back in the direction from which the voice had come, 'A gift!'

'From the designer?'

'No, an admirer.' A pause, a sly grin. The perfect photo-op; a coy looking Lillie in her priceless diamond earrings, her tokens of love. The cameras went wild. Then she moved slowly on to the next surge of photographers, another dazzling smile barricading her heart, perfectly obscuring the wretched condition of her dignity.

* * *

The volume on the television set was turned down low. It was one o'clock in the morning in Copenhagen. Wearing a warm cashmere robe and flannel pajamas, John sat propped against his pillows in his private hospital room, one of the few patients on the floor who was still awake. But that wasn't unusual.

A shot of Lillie Diver took over the small screen. John's heart lurched at the sight of her. She looked sensational tonight as she walked the red carpet, smiling, working her way toward the theater. The Oscar countdown had begun.

'She's quite beautiful, isn't she, Mr. Shay?'

One of the night nurses, Ula, was making her rounds. She'd popped into John's room just as Lillie's name and face lit up the screen. A commentator noted in English that Lillie Diver was a 'nominee for Best Actress for her role in Master of the Storm.'

'That's your picture, isn't it?' Ula inquired. 'Master of the Storm?'

'Yes,' he replied, leaving out the part about how Jared Warren had turned it into a story John barely recognized.

'Good luck, Mr. Shay. We're all hoping you win,' she said quietly. 'Buzz us when it's time for your award. I'll slip back in and watch with you if I'm not too busy.'

'I don't know if I can stay awake that long, Ula. It'll be hours from now.'

'You'd fall asleep before they announced your Oscar? I can't believe that, Mr. Shay.' She smiled comfortingly and returned to her rounds, leaving him alone in the room.

John hadn't smoked in months but he craved a cigarette now.

It's better than craving a drink, he told himself – although he generally only went about sixty seconds without craving one. Still, having neither, he fingered the sash of his robe absently, his attention glued to the TV set, his mind thousands of miles away in sunny Los Angeles where it was still the previous day.

Lillie was somewhere in the thronging mass of tuxedos, jewels and gowns. Another actress was on the TV screen, Adele Crown, an aging movie goddess who hadn't won an award in decades. She was a trooper, though, John gave her that much; one of the rare few that Hollywood couldn't kill. Try as they might, she simply refused to die. She chose facelifts instead.

'Give 'em hell, Adele,' he said under his breath.

He knew what it was like to go head to head with Hollywood. It took a kind of emotional armor (venom-proof skin was more like it, he thought) to hold a job there for even a year.

'Best Director nominee for Master of the Storm,' the announcer was saying. Jared Warren's serious face flashed on the screen.

Now there's a man who looks unhappy and preoccupied, John decided. 'Probably busy cooking up some new scheme,' he muttered under his breath. 'Trying to keep himself employed. Even on a night like this. Can't relax and just let life happen; has to try to pull the strings. A man like that is always running, he's out there ahead of his own life.'

John Shay had always been one to talk to himself, but three months of seclusion in the unnatural environment of a rehab had made this tendency in him more pronounced.

Jared Warren's face was gone from the screen but John's thoughts lingered over the legendary director/producer.

'Fantastic book, Shay! Just fantastic. What more can I say about it? What hasn't been said, right?'

Those were Jared Warren's first words to John Shay when the pair met for drinks at Manhattan's famous La Belle Saison hotel bar. It was more than two years ago and Master of the Storm crowned the nation's bestseller lists. Outside, powdery snow fell gently on the hard concrete grid of midtown. Christmas was just around the corner.

The snow wouldn't last, it never did in New York City when it fell before New Year's Day, but even the slightest promise of a white Christmas brought out the best in hardened New Yorkers. There was nothing quite like a New Yorker at Christmas to help one feel the full effects of faith, hope, charity, and brotherly good cheer. The late-afternoon bar was humming with glad tidings. The warm glow of flickering votive lights amid the blond wood veneers and honey-toned leather seating seemed all the more cozy with fat snowflakes falling steadily outside the hotel's tall, narrow windows.

Jared Warren rose to vigorously shake John's hand, setting the power play in motion. Every single one of his sleek, silver hairs was perfectly in place. 'I read the book on the plane from L.A. Couldn't put it down. It's gonna make a great film, you know that? Of course, with a more compact focus. Sit down, Shay. What're you drinking?'

'Scotch,' John replied, unfazed by the bowled-over enthusiasm of Jared Warren. He'd seen it too often in every meeting he'd ever had with any production or development person from Hollywood. Post-meeting enthusiasm was the only emotion that actually counted.

'Neat? On the rocks?'

'On the rocks.'

'Scotch on the rocks. My kind of guy,' Jared extolled, though he himself was drinking vodka, top shelf. 'Scotch on the rocks,' he told the waitress. 'I want you to write it, Shay,' he continued. 'How long before you can pull a script together, give me something to get going with?'

'Then you're offering to buy the rights?' John asked patiently.

'Offering? What offering? I already did. Didn't your agent tell you?'

'No.'

Jared thrust his cell phone at John, 'Then call her and ask,' he advised John. 'Go ahead, I can wait.'

It didn't seem likely – not that Jared hadn't already bought the rights to Master of the Storm, but that he could wait for anything. John took it on faith for now that the rights had been secured by Jared's company. Calling his agent in full view of the Belle Saison bar's clientele would be like tripping over the rug on his way up to claim an Academy Award; it would blow his shot at seeming self-possessed and in control.

'I could get something workable to you in two weeks. Let's say, just after the first of the year. Does that sound good?'

'That sounds spectacular,' Jared enthused. 'Now, let me tell you a little about how I see it.'

The rest of the conversation had faded now. It had all been talking in the wind anyway, until John's name was on the dotted line. What remained in John's memory was the man himself; the indelible impression of Jared Warren that existed separate from the conversation. How it had felt to sit across from a powerful man like him, a man whose over-the-top energy was infused with an undercurrent of desperation.

He'd worn L.A. casual – expensive but subtle – and a perennial tan, making the winter coat draped over the back of a chair seem as if it were left behind by a previous patron. Jared didn't smoke, and the way he abstained from joining John in a second round indicated that he wasn't much of drinker, either. His sole occupation seemed to be securing the next project and staying in Hollywood's power elite, which meant making blockbuster movies, working out in his gym, and doing little else.

John had barely sipped his second scotch when Jared glanced at the gold Rolex around his tanned wrist and said, 'Okay. We're set, then. I gotta go, but I'll call you. You have a good Christmas, Shay. And plan to come out to L.A. in early January.'

'You have a good Christmas, too,' John said. 'Are you here with your family?' he asked, in no hurry to move yet.

'No,' Jared said as he slipped into his coat. 'My wife's dying. It's tough. She can't travel. She's in a wheelchair now. I'm here with a friend, but we're heading back to the West Coast tomorrow night.'

A friend… the tone of Jared's voice made the friend sound female and probably quite young. But that was his business.

John watched him sail out of the bar, in an obvious hurry to meet his paramour. He has to be pushing sixty at least, thought John, taking in the full effect of Jared's silver hair; but his 'friend' is keeping him young, whoever she is.

When John had finished his drink, he left the hotel in a buoyant mood. Quickly dusted by the lightly falling snow, he walked down Fifth Avenue in the black-purple twilight, deftly maneuvering through the oncoming throng of office workers, just released from their cubicle-hells. John hadn't seen this year's tree yet and now seemed as good a time as any to kick off the season. He headed for Rockefeller Center. He rounded the corner and there it stood, New York City's magnificent Christmas tree heralded by rows of silver angels blowing celestial trumpets. The tree towered in the swirling flakes of white, lit up in a festive array of colorful lights. Making a silent toast to the start of a perfect holiday, John pushed his way through the tourists and realized that he felt happy.

The air was crisp and just cold enough to feel like Christmas. In a wink of an eye, he told himself, he'd be in L.A., the bright white town awash in sun, and all of this would be long gone. He leaned against the railing and watched the skaters below. The ice rink was a frenzy of glinting skates and pompoms bouncing on knit hats. An occasional straggler with weak ankles slipped and slid and struggled to stay upright as the rest of the skaters went slicing past.

How many years had it been, John wondered, since Selena was small and he'd brought her here to skate for the first time? She was fourteen now; an honor student at a private girls school in Connecticut but floundering emotionally. John knew it, he recognized the signs in Selena because he'd been on it himself countless times, that roller coaster ride between elation and despair. There wasn't much he could do for his daughter besides stand back and let her life happen to her. If she needed him for guidance or reassurance, or as a confidant, she didn't let on anymore. Since the nasty divorce, she'd become more Amanda's daughter. Only time would tell if she'd come back around to trusting him.

Now how unlikely is that, he thought. On the other side of the ice rink stood Jared Warren. His silver hair and Hollywood tan made him stand out from the crowd by a mile. Jared's arm was draped over the shoulder of a laughing, dark-haired beauty, obviously the 'friend' he had mentioned earlier. John knew he had seen the woman in a movie recently. She was an actress. He couldn't place the name, but who could forget that stunning face? Everyone near the couple gawked at her.

John smiled at the spectacle the actress was causing and his thoughts turned to Cassie, this year's girl du noÎl. They had a date to attend a Christmas party that night. He should call her and touch base. He pulled out his cell phone and turned away from the crowd.

* * *

The snow had slowed to barely noticeable flurries. John strolled leisurely in the direction of Central Park. At the fountain in front of the Plaza hotel, a fountain now outlined in bright white Christmas lights, Cassie stood waiting for him.

'Hey stranger,' she said with a smile. 'That didn't take too long.'

'What were you doing when I called?'

'Shopping. You want to come up with me while I change?'

Cassie had a room in the Plaza. She was a writer, too; well known but not as famous as John, and from out of town. John couldn't remember what town. They'd met a couple nights ago at a party his publisher had thrown at a trendy downtown restaurant.

'Sure, I'll come up,' John said happily, hoping for a quick roll in the sack before they headed out for the evening. 'You want to skip the mini bar and order up some serious drinks?'

'The last time we tried that,' Cassie admonished him, 'we didn't get any farther than my bed for the rest of the evening.'

'But what a memorable evening it was.'

Cassie smiled. 'Yes, that it was.'

Together they walked up the steps to the Fifth Avenue entrance and inside, the lobby gleamed with warmly lit crystal chandeliers. In keeping with the Plaza's staid reputation, the Christmas décor centered on evergreen boughs and lots of red velvet trimming. The sound of a string quartet emanated from the Palm Court, where high tea was winding down. Well-dressed, conservative rich people were milling about in small groups.

John and Cassie headed toward the bank of elevators.

'How did the meeting go with Jared Warren?' Cassie asked. 'If you don't think I'm being nosy?'

'You're not being nosy. It was brief but I guess it went well. Assuming my agent really did hear from Warren, it looks like I'll be out in L.A. in a few weeks. He wants to make the picture and he wants me to do the adaptation.'

'That's great, isn't it?'

'Yes and no. It means I have to come up with a reasonable fac-simile of a working script sometime during the holidays.'

In the elevator, John pulled Cassie closer to him. They weren't alone, but he kissed her on the cheek, trying to make the kiss seem casual yet suggestive. He was determined to order cocktails and get between her legs before they went anywhere else that evening.

'What possessed you to agree to write a script at this time of year?' she asked quietly, not moving away from him, liking him near her. 'Nobody works during the holidays.'

'I do,' he said. 'Sometimes, but not tonight, tonight I'm all yours. That much you can count on. Hollywood's going to have to wait.'

'You're so gallant.'

Everyone in the elevator was openly eavesdropping on their conversation. It was obvious to John that they were trying to fig-ure out who he was, was he in TV or the movies?

The elevator doors opened on Cassie's floor. 'After you,' John said.

*　*　*

Cassie came out of the bathroom looking flawless, fresh from the shower, her light-brown hair fluffed pertly around her bare shoulders. She smelled expensive, like something out of Bergdorf's. She wore one of the hotel's thick white towels and nothing else.

True to his word, John had ordered up cocktails from room

service and they'd arrived in record time. He was well into his drink when Cassie came out of the bathroom.

'I've been making merry,' he confessed. 'I started without you.'

Cassie didn't mind. 'That's okay,' she said. 'But I'm warning you, we're not camping out here for the whole evening like last time. I want to go to that party. I want to get out and into the spirit of everything. I'm leaving the day after tomorrow, and who knows when I'll get back to New York.'

John conceded, 'Point taken. We'll go to the party, I promise. But first, let me relieve you of that cumbersome towel.'

Cassie's breasts were full and ripe-looking, her belly comfortingly rounded, in keeping with her small waist and wide hips. She wasn't tall, still her bare legs seemed long; John's eye traveled from her manicured pink toenails, up her luscious thighs, to the thatch of brown hair trimmed into a neat triangle below the tiny exclamation point of her navel.

He tossed the damp towel to a chair and pulled her into his arms. 'You're such an inviting lass,' he told her playfully. 'I'd love to find you in my stocking on Christmas morning.' She would be long gone by then so he knew it was safe to say that. 'I couldn't wait for tonight to get here. I've been thinking about you all day.'

Whether or not it was true was irrelevant. Cassie put her arms around him and kissed his lips, tasting the scotch, feeling the slight scratch of his beard. 'You seem over dressed,' she said. 'Why don't we do something about that?'

Both in and out of his clothes, John Shay was a near perfect specimen of masculinity. He'd always been diligent about working out, though never obsessive about it. He kept in shape mostly to stave off for as long as possible the aging effects of cigarettes and drinking. Consequently, he was now in his mid-forties and even better looking than he'd been as a younger man.

He returned Cassie's kiss with passion, urging her toward the bed. He was already hard. There was no reason for him to take his time with her; they both understood that this encounter was meant to be a quick one. He found the condom he'd tossed on her night table while waiting for her to get out of the shower. He opened it and slid it on.

The hotel bed was comfortable, the kind that invited amorous activities. John fell onto his back, pulling Cassie on top of him.

She straddled him eagerly, lowering herself down on him, her tight hole opening around the thick shaft and taking it all the way in, until the head of his cock was in so deep, it made her cry out. She rode him vigorously then, her full, warm tits bouncing enticingly close to his face. He grabbed them with both hands, getting an erect nipple between his lips and sucking it hard.

Cassie moaned. She ground her tender clit against him while his cock impaled her. Within moments, she'd reached that level of ecstasy where there was no turning back. Her hips worked the penetrating cock harder, back and forth, she moved; rubbing her clit against him in a frenzied rhythm.

His mouth worked her nipples, first one, then the other and back again; sucking the stiff little buds with mounting pressure. He wanted to devour her she was so responsive to his fervent sucking. He squeezed her tits tightly, grabbed them in real handfuls right in front of his face. The stiff nipples were red and extended. He flicked them with his tongue, his fingers; his ears filling with the sounds of her exquisite pleasure. Her little cries and groans of lust charged the room. He pushed his hard cock straight up into her and let her squirm around on it with abandon. She was obviously coming. Her vagina quivered noticeably and squeezed his cock, her whole body seeming to tremble.

He gave her only a moment to thrash around on him before he

expertly flipped her over on to her back, without uncoupling, and pressing her already spread thighs down close to her tits, he fucked her open hole with all his power.

Cassie's orgasm mounted and enveloped her in delirious waves. Her swollen pussy lips were pushed open wide by John's relentless pounding, keeping her sensitive, climaxing clitoris in constant contact with his grinding pelvis.

She tugged on her aroused nipples, twisting them manically in her efforts to keep her orgasm crashing through her. When was it going to subside, she wondered. She couldn't remember ever coming like this.

The sight of Cassie pulling on her own nipples triggered John's climax. He cried out sharply and surrendered to its fire. And even before his orgasm had completely subsided, he knew he wanted her again.

'Maybe we can find a cozy nook at that party,' he whispered down at her, panting slightly. 'I've got to have you again, Cassie, as soon as possible. I'm so hot for you.'

*   *   *

The Christmas party was thrown by a wealthy socialite, Mag Gunther, in her duplex high atop an apartment building on Fifth Avenue, not far from the Metropolitan Museum of Art. Serviced by a private elevator that opened directly into the duplex, Mag Gunther's home was designed in jaw-dropping proportions meant to show off her impressive collection of modern and contemporary art – paintings, sculpture and ceramics of all colors, shapes and sizes.

John and Cassie were greeted in the foyer by two pretty, young coat check girls. (Actresses in need of cash, John thought.) They were then shown to the bar. It was decked with elaborate poinsettias and candles and Christmas greenery, and offered every sort of

booze imaginable, but it was already at least three-deep ᵢ
guests. Beyond the crowded bar was the living room, with it's
tacular views of Central Park and Upper Manhattan. It
jammed with party-goers in a festive holiday mood.

Almost immediately, something silver caught John's eye. He
spied Jared Warren and his actress friend across the crowded
room. Why was he surprised to see them there? He should have
expected it, he told himself; Mag Gunther's Christmas parties
always drew a wide circle of the rich and famous. John wondered
if he should bother to say hello to Jared. He didn't want it to lead
to shop talk. John was in no mood to think about work right now.
All he wanted to do was get Cassie alone in a secluded, out of the
way corner of the noisy, overflowing duplex and try to persuade
her to let him fuck her again.

He couldn't get his cock to calm down and behave. Cassie was
wearing black high heels, shimmering black stockings and a trim
black skirt that showed off her pretty legs and flattered her ample
behind. And to show off her gorgeous breasts, she'd worn a soft
pink angora sweater with a deep V-neckline. In her cleavage, a tiny
diamond and sapphire pendant glinted.

'What are you drinking?' John asked.

'Champagne,' she said.

'Champagne it is, then.' He managed to hail a passing waiter
carrying a silver tray of freshly poured flutes of champagne. He
handed a glass to Cassie and took one for himself. 'Don't look
now,' he told her, 'but Jared Warren is across the room.'

'Should we say hi?'

'No,' he said, turning his back to Jared and his friend. 'Not
unless he gets closer and it becomes impossible to avoid him. I
don't want to think about work right now.'

Cassie's eyes surreptitiously searched the room for the famous director. 'Oh look,' she said under her breath. 'He's with that actress, Lillie Diver!'

'Is that who that is? I knew I recognized her.'

'They look awfully chummy together, don't they? Isn't he married?'

'Yes, but his wife's incurably ill and unable to travel.'

'Well, that's chivalrous of him.' Cassie took a healthy sip of champagne. 'Uh-oh,' she warned him. 'He's spotted you, John. He's making his way over.'

'Should we run, or is that too conspicuous?'

'Way too conspicuous,' she advised reproachfully.

'Shay!' Jared called out. 'Imagine running into you again!' He slapped John on the back good naturedly. 'Lillie, this is John Shay, the guy who wrote Master of the Storm. Lillie's got the lead in that.'

'Already?' John asked, not really surprised.

Lillie extended her hand to John. 'Already,' she said. And she flashed one of her dazzling smiles.

Up close, John was instantly smitten by her porcelain beauty. He understood what all the commotion had been about back at the ice rink in Rockefeller Center. 'This is Cassie Gravas, the novelist,' he said. 'Cassie – Jared Warren and Lillie Diver.'

'This is quite of view of New York, isn't it?' Jared asked Cassie, indicating the enormous plate glass windows all around them but his gaze lingered lewdly over the jeweled pendant snuggling in Cassie's cleavage.

'Yes, it's quite breathtaking,' she replied politely, wanting to give him a good kick in the balls. How rude, she thought; staring so openly at another woman, in plain view of his date. Cassie tried to ignore him. 'I saw you recently in The Lover's Charade,' she told Lillie. 'You were great in that.'

'Thank you,' she replied graciously.

'That's where I saw you, in The Lover's Charade!' John blurted without thinking. 'I knew that I knew you from somewhere. I noticed you earlier today at Rockefeller Center. You outshone even that enormous Christmas tree.'

Lillie dodged the compliment. 'Wasn't the snow wonderful?'

'Yes. It was perfectly timed for the season.'

'I rarely get to see snow anymore, living in L.A. Least of all, at Christmas.'

Cassie nudged John, tired of Jared Warren's unwavering leer. John took her hint. 'Well, we need to go in search of the food. We're famished. It was nice meeting you. Enjoy your stay in New York.'

'Nice meeting both of you, too,' Lillie said, while Jared simply nodded.

Cassie took John's hand.

'I guess we'll see more of each other in L.A.,' Lillie added. 'I loved your book, by the way.'

'You read it?' John was shocked.

'Yes, I read it. I do read.' Her smile was pleasant, but her tone, patronizing. 'I'm the one who told Jared about it, that he should secure the rights. I was born to play that role, Mr. Shay. I promise I won't disappoint you.'

'I'm sure you won't, Miss Diver.'

'Lillie,' she insisted.

'Lillie. It was very nice meeting you.'

As John led Cassie politely away, he couldn't help but feel impressed. 'Well,' he said, 'that went better than I expected.'

'Lillie Diver seems like a good egg,' Cassie said. 'She's so well-mannered. I wonder what she's doing with a man like Jared Warren? He's old enough to be her grandfather.'

Spying a buffet table across the busy foyer in a room that appeared to be an all-out art gallery, John said playfully, 'Ours is not to reason why, my dear. Ours is to see if they've got any good caviar around here and grab some more of that free champagne.'

* * *

D o you always behave so disgracefully?' Cassie whispered excitedly, feeling dizzy from all the champagne she'd drunk. They were in a darkened upstairs bedroom, standing alone by another impressive plate glass window. All around them the duplex vibrated with the sounds of deejay Christmas music and happy partiers. 'We don't do scandalous things like this in Des Moines, you know.'

John kissed her cheek, her nose, her lips. 'You're not from Des Moines,' he scolded her. 'I can't really remember where you're from, but I know it's not Des Moines.'

Cassie giggled quietly. 'Atlanta,' she admitted.

'Well, I know darn well they do things like this in Atlanta.' John had the back of Cassie's skirt tugged up just enough to get two good handfuls of her fleshy ass. 'Aren't you wearing any panties?' he asked hopefully.

'It's a thong.'

'Ah yes, one of those. Well, that's just as convenient.'

'Convenient for what?' she asked, one arm draped around him, pulling him close. Her other hand was down between his legs, checking the progress of the erection growing steadily inside his trousers.

John kissed her again. 'Convenient for looking out the window and taking in the spectacular view. Turn around,' he said.

Cassie turned and looked out the window. It really was breathtaking. From where they stood, it seemed that all of Manhattan was on display. Beneath them, Central Park was lightly blanketed in the snow that had fallen earlier that evening. Colorful Christmas lights dotted various apartment buildings in the distance for as far as the eye could see.

John snuggled against her, suggestively pressing the hard-on straining inside his trousers against the exposed flesh of her ass. His hands slipped under her angora sweater. He gently squeezed her warm tits through the silky material of her bra.

Cassie's nipples stiffened immediately and her rear end arched up high against his crotch. John knew that she was feeling aroused already.

He kissed the nape of her neck. 'We could wait until we get back to your hotel room, you know. I don't have to behave like a complete cad.'

'I know, but I don't want to wait,' she urged him quietly.

'I'm not going to lie to you,' he whispered. 'I'm very happy to hear that.'

Cassie pulled up her angora sweater in front and tugged down the cups of her bra. 'There,' she whispered back. 'Now work your magic on me.'

The plate glass window was ice cold and Cassie's bared breasts were close enough to the glass to respond to the chill. Her nipples stiffened to hard little points.

John groaned quietly in her ear. The sight of her tits exposed in front of the window like that, even in the dark, made his desire surge through his cock. He sank his teeth into the flesh of her neck. She squirmed and moaned.

'I feel like we're going to get carried away,' he warned her, squeezing the ample mounds of her naked tits in his hands.

'Me too,' she said. 'Is it all that champagne?'

'I'm not sure what it is,' he said. 'I think it's just you.'

'There's no way anyone can see this,' she encouraged him. 'We're too high up and the room is dark.'

'You never know who's watching who in this town,' he said. But it had no effect on Cassie. She pulled her sweater off over her head and tugged her bra down around her waist. The diamond and sapphire pendant around her neck swung as free as her healthy tits now.

John smiled. 'You're crazy.'

'No,' she corrected him. 'I'm on vacation.' She tugged her skirt up higher, up over her hips to around her waist, and slid her thong down to her ankles.

'Whoa,' John sighed, feeling suddenly breathless. He fished in his pants pocket for a condom, trying to keep pace with her. Cassie unzipped his fly, feeling inside his boxers for his erection and pulling it out. Before he knew it, she'd squatted down and taken his cock in her mouth.

He gasped. It felt so good. There was more than enough light from the huge expanse of glass in front of them for John to see her perfectly. Her white skin made her almost glow in the dark. John could easily make out her gorgeous tits. She sucked his cock ravenously, as if she'd been waiting to do that all evening. It made him feel weak in the knees. He had to grab hold of her hair to steady himself.

Her mouth felt soft and warm and wet, and her tight lips riding his shaft applied just enough friction to make him feel like coming. 'Stop, Cassie,' he urged her quietly. 'I don't want to come yet. Please.'

But she kept at him for a few more moments, her cold fingers teasing his hot balls while she sucked him.

He nudged her head. 'Cassie, please.'

Laughing playfully, she spared him at last and he helped her to her feet.

She kissed him aggressively and he squeezed her fleshy breasts, then her ass. His hands were all over her. 'Bend over for me,' he finally gasped. 'Right in front of the window. You want to do that?'

Cassie's black stockings stopped at the tops of her thighs, creating a dramatic line between her dark sexy legs and her naked white ass. When she bent over for him, John thought he'd come from just looking at her rear end; it seemed huge in that position. As if he were on a mission, he knelt down abruptly, pried her ass cheeks apart and slid his tongue into the musky folds of her pussy. She was slippery wet in there. The lightly haired lips were swollen fat with arousal. She smelled incredible. John pressed his face in deeper as if starved for her sex. Her scent was quickly all over his mouth. He probed his tongue up in her hole while his fingers reached around and felt for her clitoris. He found the erect little hood and rubbed it.

Bent all the way over, she steadied herself against the window. 'God, that feels good,' she chanted softly, her face against the icy glass. 'Oh, Johnny, yes…'

He licked and sucked her until his lips and chin were a slippery mess. He couldn't get enough of her taste, her smell.

'Let's fuck, Johnny,' she said, begging him; not caring at all if they could be seen or heard. 'Fuck me, please.'

John rose in an instant. With fumbling fingers, he undid his trousers and let them fall around his knees. Then he managed to squeeze his eager cock into the tight condom. Cassie was still bent over, her ass thrust up high in anticipation.

'Oh my God,' he gasped. 'Your ass looks incredible. Don't move.' Quickly, he directed the head of his cock to her hole. He held tight to her hips and then shoved it right in.

'Oh yeah,' she groaned, spreading her legs farther apart, steadying herself in her high heels and bracing herself for his luscious assault. 'Fuck me… that's right… oh yeah.'

John gave her all he had, his thick shaft pushing easily in her to the hilt. She was so wet, so open for him that he fucked her vigorously, without restraint.

She was pressed against the window, her tits hanging down in full view of all of Manhattan – if they only knew, John thought. He fucked her harder, and harder still, while she cried out with each renewed thrust, encouraging him to fuck her, yes, fuck her, fuck her, just like that, oh God...

One hand was down between her legs, rubbing her clitoris like mad, bringing on her climax in a cacophony of her cries and whimpers.

When John finally came, they were both sweating, panting heavily. 'Oh my God, that felt good,' she sighed. And when he helped her stand upright, she sputtered, 'Oh shit.'

'What?'

John turned and discovered that their lewd spectacle had attracted quite a little audience in the open doorway.

'Sorry,' he offered lamely, the booze in his veins keeping him from feeling utterly humiliated.

'Don't apologize,' someone spoke out. 'That deserves a round of applause. What do you do for an encore?'

* * *

John stared blankly at the small color television screen beside his hospital bed. The Oscar ceremony was in full swing now but his mind had been miles – no, years – away.

He wondered what had ever become of Cassie Gravas. Hadn't he heard somewhere that she'd gotten married? To a journalist or something. A newsman. Someone who'd won a Pulitzer Prize? He was one lucky guy, whoever he was. And here was John, at his very nadir in a fancy rehab.

When had it come to this, he asked himself, still staring blankly at the TV screen. When did the booze start meaning more to him than his life did?

CHAPTER THREE

The nominees for Best Actress are…' Lillie's bowels clenched as she tried to appear serene and nonchalant. Never in her entire life had she wanted to hear the sound of her own name more than at this very moment. Was she sweating profusely? She felt like it, but she couldn't be sure. Was that television camera, now trained on her face, revealing her to the world with make-up running from all the sweat, or was it merely her vivid imagination? Somewhere, Eduardo was planted in front of an expensive television set, surrounded by his worshipful entourage, and either gasping in ecstasy or livid with outrage.

'And the winner is…'

Carly Matthews and Reese McNaughton were fumbling like fools in formal wear and taking an eternity to open the damn envelope. Lillie thought she would spontaneously combust from sheer anticipation. In the row ahead of her, Jared was craning his neck around to see her, smiling broadly and mouthing, 'good luck.'

'You need a little assistance there, Carly?' Reese McNaughton joked. The audience laughed on cue.

'My fingers don't want to work!' Carly Matthews giggled. 'I'm more nervous than the nominees!'

I seriously doubt it, you crazy nut, Lillie wanted to shriek. Open it already.

'Lillie Diver for Master of the Storm!'

The applause was thunderous. Startling cries of joy emanated from the balcony. Until now, Lillie hadn't realized just how many of her fans had crowded into the upper levels. They sounded as excited about her win as she did, their cheers nearly drowning out the wild thumping of her heart.

Here it goes, she thought in a flurry of excitement as she stood up from her seat. Would she split open every tight seam of her original Machard gown?

God smiled down on her and the gown stayed intact.

Everyone around her was applauding her. People smiled. Jared rose from his seat, clapping crazily. 'Congratulations, Lillie!' he called out warmly. He was bursting with pride.

Lillie told herself in a daze, why shouldn't he be proud? He's old enough to be my father. And it suddenly struck her like slow motion lightning. A dazzling smile taking over her face, she was on her way to collect her Academy Award, and she wondered perversely why it had never occurred to her until this very moment: Jared Warren looked just like her father. Funny, that she shouldn't notice it until now.

'Go for it, Lillie!'

'Great job!'

'Congratulations!'

All around her, people were joining in her thrilling moment as she made her way down the aisle; urging her on, up the stairs to claim her prize. The television camera was tracking her now, keeping pace with her, making her feel like she should hurry. She hoped she wouldn't break her neck tripping over her impossibly high heels.

At the top of the stairs, she knew she would never forget these golden twins, these angelic messengers, Carly Matthews and Reese McNaughton. They stepped aside, smiling, applauding her, as she came up to the podium. And the prettiest creature of all, probably some starlet with larger than life talent and a bright future ahead of her, handed Lillie her Oscar.

Lillie leaned into the tiny microphone, clutching the golden statue to her breast. She wished her mother were still alive to witness this moment. She'd be in her nightgown from Penney's, jumping about wildly on the sofa, spilling her straight-up martini in her childish enthusiasm. 'I'd like to thank Jared Warren,' Lillie said breathlessly. 'And every one at Opus One who made this picture such a success. Of course, it couldn't have happened at all without the incredible talent of John Shay. I'll never forget this night! Thank you, everyone!'

* * *

John craved a cocktail, a cigarette – anything celebratory that he could hold in his hand and ingest through his mouth somehow; something to signify his happiness was part of him. Twenty minutes ago, he'd won his own Oscar for Best Screenplay with Master of the Storm. Jared Warren had accepted the statue on John's behalf. However, the truth was that too many people had had a hand in the final draft of the movie, that it didn't seem fair to single John out as having produced the definitive version worthy of an award. The value of it didn't register with him. But this did, Lillie winning an award, too. And thinking enough of John to let the sound of his name come out of her mouth on a night like this.

'God, I want a drink,' he confided breathlessly to Ula.

The night nurse smiled knowingly, as if she'd been expecting him to say it. She'd been sitting in the room with John for the last half hour. She'd been with him when he won his award in absentia. Ula had administered to many successful, accomplished, and sometimes famous people at the Lindegaard Institute, but she'd never sat next to someone while they won an Academy Award. It would be a highlight of her life for years to come.

'Try to enjoy your happiness for the gift it is, Mr. Shay,' she said. 'It doesn't take something outside you to make happiness any more real.'

'You're right,' he said, trying like hell to convince himself. 'You're right.'

'Well, I guess my breaks over, Mr. Shay.' Ula got up from the chair to resume her rounds. 'Why don't you try to get some sleep now? You've got a big day ahead of you tomorrow.'

John clicked off the TV set with the remote. He laid his head on the pillow and stared into the dark room. A big day tomorrow? He tried to remember what it was that made tomorrow a big day.

It came to him. 'Selena,' he said quietly. 'Tomorrow I'm seeing my daughter. She's visiting me in a rehab, a veritable nut house. My little girl is going to see me like this.'

* * *

From seemingly out of nowhere, Lillie's people met her backstage and in a flurry of excitement, directed her to the press room. A long line of award winners and award presenters waited ahead of her. The room was a boisterous riot of chaotic enthusiasm. When it was finally her turn to pose with her Oscar for the press, the deluge of flashes and shouted questions overwhelmed her. The best she could do was smile her famous smile and say whatever came into her head first. Judging by the press's jovial response to her answers, Lillie, in her lightheaded delirium, seemed to be holding her own. She'd know better in the morning, when she saw everything laid out in the news.

Afterwards, she consented to so many on-camera interviews with entertainment television shows from all over the world, that when she had a chance to catch her breath, it was time for the winner of the Best Director category to be announced onstage.

Lillie watched it unfold on a monitor in the press room and her heart sank when Jared didn't win.

It's not like he hasn't won an Oscar before, she consoled herself. Still it would have been nice if they could have been winners together.

Now that the torture of the last couple months was officially behind her, the anguish of the uncertainty was over and she'd emerged a bona fide winner, everything in Lillie's world relaxed, even her dress felt more comfortable. She changed her mind about skipping the post-Oscar party with Jared and his entourage. She could endure being relegated to the background one more time. Being in the same room with him tonight was what mattered. The last thing she wanted right now was to celebrate alone.

'Lillie, honey!' As if on cue, Jared had made his way back to the press room. He hurried to her and gave her a congratulatory hug, crushing her Oscar between them – or what would soon be her Oscar, her name still had to be engraved on it.

The photographers took full advantage of the photo-op. With cameras flashing crazily, Hollywood's powerful Jared Warren kissed Lillie Diver, the year's most sought after actress, right on the mouth, smudging her lipstick. Lillie was beside herself. It wasn't like him to be so familiar with her in public, least of all with cameras practically on top of them.

'I insist that you come to the party with me, Lillie. I'm not going to let you be alone on the biggest night of your life!' Then he added, for her ears only, 'I'm not letting you off my arm for the rest of the night, either, so you just keep smiling that beautiful smile.'

'But what about Abby?' she whispered, her nervous fingers wiping her smudged mouth.

'What about her? She's been around this business long enough. She'll understand. By now, she knows I didn't win this year, so what? You did and you're my star, Lillie. To me, that's just as good as winning the award myself. My place is with you tonight.'

This was quite a change in tone for the always-cautious Jared Warren. Lillie wasn't sure what to make of it. If Abby were going to be so accepting of the relationship between Lillie the star and Jared the director, why hadn't Jared been above board with Abby about tonight from the moment the nominees had been announced? Lillie felt as if it were a last minute career move on his part, being seen with her tonight. After all, she was a winner now and he wasn't.

Still, wasn't this what she'd been longing for – to win the award and celebrate the momentous occasion in public with the man she loved? Maybe she should just gather her riches wherever she could find them. 'Thanks, Jared,' she said. 'I mean that, thank you.'

A bevy of personal assistants surrounded the pair as they headed through the theater lobby to where the limousines waited. Jared took charge of the evening's agenda. The first order was to dispense with Lillie's car and driver; he turned them over to the personal assistants. Lillie would ride alone with Jared to the party, in full view of everyone attending.

Babylon, the ritzy movie magazine from the east coast, was throwing the A-list party at the Bodhi Pavilion, a chic West

Hollywood night spot not far from the theater. Twice as many photographers were waiting outside the Bodhi than had been at the ceremony itself. When Lillie was helped out of Jared's limousine, chaos swarmed around the enormous car. Unsteady on the pavement in her stiletto heels, Lillie clung to Jared's arm, a nervous smile across her face as they pushed through the crowd.

It made for another perfect photo-op for the cameras; the new Oscar winner on the arm of the most famous director in town.

Lillie thought uneasily about the morning yet to come and how these photos would look to Abby, to the children and grandchildren. Why wasn't he worried about that?

Jared held tight to Lillie and hurried her into the Bodhi, far from the ravenous paparazzi. Within moments, they were ushered inside the velvet rope of the VIP area. It already brimmed with party-goers who immediately turned their boisterous attentions to Lillie.

In every way, it was a dream come true for her, being at the center of everyone's awe and envy.

Jared managed to snatch two glasses of champagne off the tray of a passing waiter who was quickly becoming engulfed in the crowd of thirsty VIPs. 'Here, sweetie,' Jared said, handing a glass to Lillie. 'To the future; it's wide open for you now!'

At the very moment that the entire world seemed to be vying for Lillie's attention, Jared was suddenly pushing for center stage. 'Let's think about what we want to do next. A romantic comedy? Maybe a thriller? We're going to be bombarded with scripts now, you know. We should probably hook up later this week and start brainstorming.'

Lillie liked the sound of Jared saying 'we.' She clinked her glass with his and toasted to the future, their future. And as she'd suspected earlier, the seductive lighting of the night club did indeed enhance the allure of her diamond bracelet, her new good luck charm, as she held the glass of sparkling champagne. It tasted particularly pleasing – the victory toast. Was there anything comparable to it? If there was, she had yet to experience it.

'I want to thank you again for the diamonds,' she said. 'In fact, I want to thank you again for everything, Jared. You've given me so many opportunities. From day one, you believed in me more than anyone else did.'

'That's because I've been in love with you since day one.'

'Really?'

'Really.'

'Jared...' Lillie searched his face. His eyes met hers with an unfamiliar openness.

'What is it?'

'Are you going to reconsider? Are you coming home with me tonight?'

'I wouldn't have it any other way.' He lightly kissed her lips in plain view of everyone. 'This is the night you'll always remember and I want to be part of it.'

Lillie's mind was swimming with elated surprise. What was happening here? She was almost afraid to believe it; why was it suddenly so easy? Usually Jared kept her at arm's length, even when they were making love, his commitment to his wife of thirty-five years kept him from surrendering to Lillie completely. Was the award really this important; it could change how his heart felt about her and his wife? Whatever it was that was causing this sudden good fortune, she didn't want to jinx it. 'I'm so glad,' she said quietly, returning his kiss. 'You have no idea how much this means to me.'

'Lillie Diver, congratulations!'

It was Carson Lee, the director who'd won the Oscar, the director to whom Jared had lost. Carson was making his way inside the velvet rope, shouting Lillie's name and pushing his way through the crowd to shake her hand, to kiss her cheek. 'May I say, you looked positively stunning up there tonight? And in my book, no one deserved to win more than you did. You were fantastic in that part – a world away from everyone else. That role was made for you! We should talk soon, honey. I have a part in mind that would be perfect for your next vehicle.'

Jared cut in rudely. 'She's not available right now. We're taking some time off and then she's committed to my next film.'

'Oh really?' Carson regarded Jared with a look of such incredulity, Lillie felt embarrassed for both of them. 'And what project might that be?'

'The next John Shay piece. We're all doing it together. Me, Lillie, John; a sort of return of the triumvirate.'

'I wasn't aware Shay had anything new in the pipeline. I thought he was stuck in some sort of loony bin overseas.'

'He's at the Lindegaard,' Lillie put in tactfully. 'It's a rehabilitation center. It's highly regarded all over Europe. It's not a loony bin.'

'And he's doing his best work ever.' It was another lie from Jared. This was getting ridiculous. It set Lillie's nerves on edge. A man of Jared Warren's stature didn't need to tell lies.

Carson took Lillie's hand again and squeezed it quickly before departing. He seemed in a hurry to get away from Jared. 'You get in touch with me anyway, Lillie. I'm sure we could find a project together somewhere down the line that will blow everybody away.'

'Just move along, Carson.'

'What was that all about?' Lillie demanded before Carson was even out of earshot.

'Carson Lee is a social pariah, always has been. I don't see any reason for you to get involved with him.'

'He just won an Academy Award, Jared. How is that supposed to hurt my career?'

'You've got your own award. You don't need to be anywhere near his.'

Since when did her entire career become Jared's domain? 'Can I ask you a stupid question? Have you really been in contact with John Shay?'

'Why should I be? That's someone else whose reputation is not going to be of any use to you for a long, long time, honey.'

'Of any use to me? Are you crazy? He's one of this country's greatest authors.'

'It's over for John Shay. He's nuts. Everyone knows it now.'

'He's had a little setback, Jared. A lot of people do in this business. I seriously doubt that it's over for him.'

'Why this sudden interest in John Shay? When he was here working on the film, you barely had time to speak to him.'

'That's not fair. I was in over my head with that role and you know it. I had to give it my undivided attention to pull it off. But I did pull it off and I almost had a nervous breakdown doing it. I doubt John Shay thinks I was avoiding him.'

Jared slipped an arm around her waist and drew her closer, switching gears. 'Come on, honey, why are we arguing on a night like this?'

'I have no idea. But I didn't start it.'

She wanted to push away from him and this sudden need of his to be physically attached to her in public. The room was spilling over with everybody who was anybody in the industry, and one thing was certain, they loved to mind everyone's business but their own. They looked oblivious to anything outside themselves but the free cocktails right now, but Lillie knew they had keen peripheral vision and killer instincts. Jared was single-handedly turning their affair into a spectacle, after having spent the last three years doing his damnedest to keep it discreetly in the background. It didn't make sense.

'What would you say about leaving early?'

'What do you mean, early?' he asked, confused.

'Like, right now. Leaving this madness and coming home with me. The night is young. We could spend it alone, spend it together. Just the two of us. It would be incredibly romantic.'

Jared looked puzzled. He didn't reply.

'Or haven't there been enough pictures taken yet?' She grew impatient. 'Is that what the problem is? You want to make sure the entire town sees us together like this – in lieu of winning your own award?'

'This isn't about winning awards, or not winning awards. It's about celebrating and wanting to be with you. Don't blow it, Lillie.'

'Don't blow it? What's that supposed to mean?'

'It means behave, okay?'

'Behave?' She was outraged. 'Who are you to tell me to behave? You know what, Jared? You might look an awful lot like my father, and you might be old enough to be him, but you aren't my father. You're supposed to be my lover – that's it. And you might try taking a bit of your own advice. In my opinion, it's your behavior tonight that could stand a little improvement.'

'I don't remember asking for your opinion.'

Lillie knew this was going nowhere fast – from a spectacle to a sideshow. She wouldn't let her hard won reputation for cool-headedness get torn to shreds in full view of Hollywood's notorious gossipmongers, least of all, on a night as important as this one.

'I'm going home,' she announced quietly, barely keeping her seething anger in check.

'Fine,' he said. 'I'll call for the car. He can take you home and come back here and wait until I'm ready to leave.' Jared flipped open his cell phone and turned his back on her.

'You are a son of a bitch,' she said.

*   *   *

Lillie left the Bodhi Pavilion through the back exit where the limousine stood waiting with its motor running. The back exit was only slightly less chaotic than the front entrance. Lillie put on a brave smile and pushed through the paparazzi alone. Within moments, she was safely sequestered in the back of the large car, the reflective glass keeping out all inquisitive stares.

It wasn't a long drive from the night club on Sunset Boulevard to her home up in the hills. Lillie sat alone in the back seat and fumed. She felt too angry at Jared to cry and too empty to feel anything good about her win from earlier that evening. She needed to get herself together. She had to figure out what was happening. Jared had never treated her like this before. Why had he chosen a night like this to come unglued?

The chauffeur opened the door for her in front of Lillie's house. He waited while she let herself inside. The house was dark. In all the excitement of the afternoon, when Eduardo had left, he'd forgotten to leave a light on for her. She felt her way to the light switch.

Upstairs, Lillie kicked off her shoes and stripped out of the dress, the corset, the stockings, the jewels – everything that had its stranglehold on her, that suffocated her and made her feel imprisoned. The make-up came off next; it seemed to take longer getting it off her face than the hours it had taken Eduardo to apply it. Then Lillie tugged a comb through her stiff, lacquered hair until, at last, she thought she resembled herself again.

In the comfort of her satin night gown, she went downstairs to mix a cocktail. The one glass of champagne she'd had at the party had gone mostly untouched.

What a disheartening outcome to what should have been the most exciting night of my life, she thought.

Then she mentally tossed the thought on to the heap of other thoughts she'd been having lately that made her feel so dissatisfied with her life. She had to forget about Jared Warren for now. But one of these days, she was going to have to figure out what he was doing in her life. Why was she wasting her prime years committing herself to an unavailable, married man?

Lillie poured herself a martini, straight up. She almost never drank martinis but tonight, her mother had been on her mind.

Everything her mother did had seemed so glamorous to Lillie when she was a little girl. Now Lillie could afford real elegance and her life didn't seem half so glamorous. Why was that, she wondered. What was it about making do and scraping by; what was it about being poor that made the little joys of life seem so much more significant? Even the cocktail glass Lillie held – it was made of expensive crystal, the light reflected off it almost magically, and yet it didn't make the martini taste any better, it didn't make her enjoy it more.

In fact, I'm not enjoying it all, she realized.

She set the drink aside and headed out the French doors to her patio, to the serene world that overlooked her swimming pool. It was under a canopy of starlight now. She gazed out at the night's splendor.

'It's no sin to be poor,' she could remember her mother saying. 'As long as you've got someone to love and share your life with, you'll be all right. Look at us. We may not have many nice things, honey, but at least we're happy, right? We have each other. We always will.'

For years, Lillie had blindly subscribed to this theory. She took it for granted that everything her mother told her about life was true and she adored her mother's company, her undivided attention and her devotion to Lillie. But as Lillie grew older, when she was in her teens and her mother's drinking habit had steadily worsened and more often than not, what little money they had was used for buying her mother's booze, Lillie had stopped believing it. It not only seemed like a sin to be poor, it seemed criminal. Especially after Lillie had been told the truth about her father, about who he was and why he wasn't in their lives.

Lillie's father was Samuel Masters Kincaid III. On the outside, he was a well regarded local politician and upstanding citizen of Mountville, the small northeastern town where Lillie was born. Sammy, as he was affectionately called even as an adult, was the youngest child and only son of seven children. He was the namesake of his grandfather, Samuel Masters Kincaid II, a District Attorney who, because of a long line of inherited wealth, had been one of the richest men in the state. Being both the only son and youngest child of such a large privileged family, Sammy had been spoiled rotten by his mother and older sisters. His father, however, had tried hard to rear his son for a life in politics, to help him grow to be a man worthy of the town's respect, but it was often an uphill battle. In his teens, Sammy took to running wild. He became a bully, throwing his weight around, abusing his family's revered status in Mountville to menace his neighbors. He'd even committed a slew of petty crimes.

Sammy's grandfather had been so elated at Sammy's birth, not just by the prospects of having a grandson but of finally becoming Samuel Masters Kincaid II, instead of simply being called 'Sam Junior' for the rest of his life, that many times he'd used his political influence and privately intervened on Sammy's behalf, ensuring Sammy's police record was kept clean. He overlooked all of

Sammy's shortcomings – of which there were many. He greased the palms that got Sammy through law school, and then bought Sammy a career in Mountville politics.

That's where Sammy had been, right smack dab in the fat comfort and luxury of being a Mountville Kincaid, and a confirmed bachelor to boot, when nineteen-year-old Sally Diver had suffered the mixed blessing of crossing his esteemed path.

It was love at first sight for Sally. But it was more like pure lust on Sammy's part.

Their illicit affair lasted three years, until Sally turned twenty-two and thought she'd finally gotten wise, had finally figured out how the game was played. She announced one night to Sammy that she was 'accidentally' pregnant with his baby, thinking for sure this would finally force Sammy's hand and he'd have to marry her – if only to protect his political reputation. What she'd been too ignorant to prepare for, though, was the tenacity of the Kincaid clan.

Although his family would have loved nothing more than to see Sammy finally take that walk down the aisle and produce an heir to his share of the family money – he was forty-one at the time of Sally's pregnancy. They weren't about to let a penniless girl of questionable morals anywhere near the Kincaid fortune, whether or not she was having Sammy's child.

The sad truth was that Sally and Sammy's affair couldn't have begun under less reputable circumstances. Not all politicians in and around Mountville were corrupt. The ones who were – a couple circuit court Judges, a county Sheriff, and Samuel Masters Kincaid III, to name but a few – frequented a social club on the outskirts of town. The club, Montecito's, was run by a woman named Louise Haskell. It's main room featured an imposing seventy-five-year-old solid oak bar that served a wide range of spirits, and a small stage with live music nightly. There were private back rooms for poker games, or 'political fundraisers,' as they were often called, and an upstairs floor that operated as a hotel. Out-of-towners or perhaps even local men who'd enjoyed too much to drink, could for a nominal fee, take a room up there for the night. A female companion to keep the bed warm came at an added cost. Sally Diver was just one of those professional bed warmers that Louise Haskell had on Montecito's payroll.

Sammy had been enjoying his cigars and an unbroken string of highballs the night he found Sally Diver warming his bed upstairs at the club. She was a new girl, one he'd never seen before. She was still unspoiled by the hard knocks of life. She was trusting, exuberant and engaging, although it was clear from the start she was under-educated. But what did that matter? It wasn't as if Sammy were planning to parade around town with Sally on his arm. In fact, none of the things he had in mind for Sally Diver were likely to take place in broad daylight.

'You play your cards right,' Louise Haskell told Sally, 'and you could be Mrs. Samuel Masters Kincaid III one day. I've seen it happen around here more than once.'

The idea was immediately appealing to Sally, but she was clueless about how to proceed. 'Just how do I play my cards right? What does that mean?'

'It means you be as wild as you want to be upstairs, but keep everything dignified in public. That's how it works. That's how you snag these men. Stay presentable. Make sure you look and behave like the kind of woman a man's family can embrace, but keep things exciting for him in bed. Do everything you can think of to please him; become like an addiction to him, a thing he's got to have no matter what, like his private parts are going to burst without you. Become the very blood in his veins.'

It was fine talk and it made Sally's own blood boil to think of it, the things she could do to Sammy in bed to make herself seem more accommodating than most girls might be. And from there, she could become a necessity.

But was this talk of Louise's just that – talk? Maybe she said it to all the girls, to ensure that the Montecito's members were kept happy and satisfied. Maybe a good dose of false-hope ladled out liberally to all the girls was what helped keep Louise Haskell a rich woman until she died.

Whatever it had been, truth or fiction, the advice had kept Sally and Sammy's affair alive for three years, years that had filled Sally Diver with dreams of one day being the top woman in town. The woman everyone stepped aside for, welcomed at odd hours, and eagerly made room for in their lives. She wasn't going to be poor anymore; a nobody. She was going to be Mrs. Samuel Masters Kincaid III. It was her only goal. And to achieve it, she willingly spread her legs, turned over, moved under, and always said yes to anything new, regardless of how unseemly it may have made her look on the surface.

Sally was more than Sammy could have hoped for, he'd never been with a girl who'd been more accommodating than she was to his libido. He had his own dreams of living out his life with her. Not as married people, because Sammy was content in his bachelorhood. But to always have her there available to him... the notion of it gave him comfort. For three years, anyway, after that, when Sally announced unceremoniously that she was pregnant with his child, the dream soured.

At first, he offered to pay for all medical costs and a house for Sally to live and raise the baby in. But that proposal wasn't good enough; it wasn't what Sally was after. It went against everything she'd planned. She held out for an offer of marriage, of holy matrimony. And that was her mistake. That was what brought the formidable force of the Kincaid clan down around her wretched ears. It was one thing to live in sin and ask everyone to politely look the other way; quite another thing to help one's self to even a small portion of the Kincaid fortune.

Soon, the only offer being held out to Sally Diver bordered on blackmail. It involved her picture, her name being smeared in the Mountville Tribune; her true occupation at Montecito's spelled out in black and white. A warrant for her arrest would be issued next – it would then be up to Sally to hire a lawyer who could prove the allegations of prostitution against her were false, and fight the Child Welfare Agency for custody of the baby she was carrying. Really, when it was all said and done, what lawyer in Mountville would be willing to go up against the Kincaids? Their resources were bottomless, they had unfathomably deep pockets – everyone in Mountville knew that.

And so that was Lillie Diver's auspicious start in life. She was born in a charity ward, out of wedlock, to a dirt poor young woman who had no formal education to speak of. There was no mention of a father's name on Lillie's birth certificate. However, Sally loved Lillie with all her heart, kept her fed and clothed and enrolled in the local public school when the time came, and Lillie didn't know enough about anything to be unhappy, not for many years.

* * *

At least he'd been handsome and my mother had been good looking, Lillie consoled herself now.

That alone had opened so many doors; Lillie had inherited the best features of both her parents. It made for a stunning combination.

But he's still a son of a bitch, she told herself; there's no way around it.

Sam Kincaid had spurned Lillie's mother, had publicly denied that the baby Sally was carrying was his. He made no more offers of money or assistance of any kind. He had nothing more to do with Sally Diver for the rest of her life. And her life had ended as inauspiciously as Lillie's had begun. Sally died in a county hospital from the ravages of poverty and alcoholism.

Now that had been more like a loony bin, Lillie thought. Nothing at all like the Lindegaard Institute, or its reputation, anyway.

Lillie had no first hand knowledge of the Lindegaard.

John Shay is a lucky man – or as lucky as any alcoholic can be, she thought. He can afford expert care. He can return to his career if he wants to and be relatively unscathed in the media. It all boils down to a simple spin factor. After all, he's just won an Academy Award.

Then Lillie got an idea.

It was already morning in Copenhagen. She'd put through a call to John Shay and congratulate him. It would probably perk his spirits. She knew how much even the tiniest remembrances had meant to her mother when she'd been committed to the county hospital, anything to feel as if she hadn't been forgotten by the world.

It didn't take long to get a main number for the Lindegaard, and an overseas operator had her call connected within moments.

In the early morning quiet of the nurse's station, Ula was finishing her daily reports. It was almost the end of her shift, almost time for her to go home. Wait until her family heard the news – she'd been right there with John Shay when he'd won his award! Who else could claim anything close to that? The thought of it made Ula lighthearted.

The phone rang and Ula answered it. She spoke in English

since so many of the Institute's patients were from overseas.

The woman's voice on the other end of the phone spoke English, also – American English.

'I'd like to speak to John Shay, please.'

'It's awfully early to put through a call to a patient,' Ula explained.

'I realize that, but I wanted to perhaps be the first to congratulate him on his award. This is Lillie Diver, calling from Los Angeles. He won an Oscar earlier tonight, is he aware of that?'

Ula thought she would burst from the thrill of it all – Lillie Diver, speaking to her from Los Angeles! 'Oh yes, Miss Diver, he's very aware of it. I watched the show with him, in fact, on my break.'

'How kind of you to extend yourself to a patient like that,' Lillie said, remembering the horrible nurses who were regularly employed by the county hospital back home; they left patients like Lillie's mother feeling meek and terrorized. 'I'm sure it meant a lot to him to have someone to share it with.'

'Oh, it was my pleasure, I can assure you.' What a well-mannered woman Lillie Diver is, Ula thought. 'Now, you hold the line and I'll check in on Mr. Shay and see if he's awake yet.'

Ula pulled together a look of dignified professionalism as she walked with purpose down the quiet, carpeted hall to John's room.

She eased open the door. 'Mr. Shay?' she called quietly.

John was awake and staring at the ceiling. But his eyes had only been open a matter of moments. 'Yes?'

'You've got an overseas call from Lillie Diver. She'd like to congratulate you, should I put it through?'

John smiled in unmasked surprise. 'Of course I'll take the call. Put it through.'

It was a bit like being called upon to assist the monarchy, Ula decided as she walked back to the nurse's station; like being needed by Her Majesty Queen Margrethe herself. It wasn't like the countless other phone calls Ula had patched through in her years at the Lindegaard. This was like connecting royalty.

'I'm putting you through now, Miss Diver. Thank you for holding.'

Whenever a phone call came through to John's room, it was more like a beep than a ring. He grabbed the beeping receiver, feeling as if he might still be dreaming. He'd only slept a few short hours and those hours had been troubled. Selena was on his mind.

'Hello?' he said into the phone.

'Hello, Mr. Shay? It's Lillie Diver calling from Los Angeles.'

'For heaven's sake, call me John. What a nice thing to wake up to!'

'Oh, I'm sorry. I hope you weren't sleeping. You know, it's still night time out here.'

'I wasn't sleeping,' he assured her. Her voice sounded clear and distinct, like she might be calling from down the street. 'How did you know where to reach me?'

'Oh, you know. Word gets around. Listen, I called to congratulate you! So, congratulations!'

'Thank you. Congratulations to you, too. You know, I fell asleep before the end of the broadcast, did Warren win?'

'Jared? No, I'm afraid he lost. But it isn't as if he hasn't won before, in the past.'

'True.'

Lillie stood barefoot in her satin night gown, alone in her kitchen, with only a small light burning. She could see her reflection clearly in the kitchen window and the dark night beyond. She watched herself talking on the phone. She wondered what had prompted her to even make this call?

'I hope you don't think I'm being intrusive,' she apologized. 'How've you been?'

'I'm making it.'

'I'm sorry we didn't get to spend more time together when you were in L.A. I hope you don't think I was snubbing you. I just wanted to give my best to the part.'

'And it seems to have worked! I didn't feel snubbed.'

John absently studied the contents of his hospital room, his ear pressed tight to the phone. He didn't want to miss a single sound of her words.

Thank God she can't see me like this, he thought. 'Listen, thanks for thanking me – during your speech, I mean. What a big night for you! It was nice of you to think of me. Hey, why aren't you out at some party or other? Shouldn't you be out dancing until dawn?'

For a fragment of a moment, there was silence, hesitation.

'I was at a party earlier,' she said. 'But then I felt like being alone. So I came home.'

'Well, at least you got in a little celebrating. Now no one can accuse you of being a wet blanket.'

'Yes.' Lillie smiled to herself. He was being so polite. 'So are you working on anything?'

'My relationship with my daughter, it's pretty much in tatters.'

Lillie couldn't stifle the laugh; it came upon her too suddenly. 'I didn't mean it like that!'

'I know. That's okay. I knew what you meant. I'm making some notes here and there. There's definitely another book trying to get out.'

'I can't wait to see it when it's finished. I hope you'll let me be one of the first to read the next John Shay novel.'

'I'm afraid it's far from being a novel for a while yet. I don't even have the first page – or a title, for that matter.'

'I'm sure the moment will come when the words start pouring

out and you'll be scrambling to keep pace with your pen.'

'I sure hope so,' John said.

'I know it will. Well, it was nice to get a chance to speak to you, John. I really do hope I didn't wake you. Congratulations, again. Keep in touch, okay?'

'I will,' he said. 'I'll do that. Thanks for calling.'

John hung up the receiver, still feeling as if he were in a dream. What a considerate person, he thought. And then he wondered if Lillie Diver had any demons whatsoever.

Lillie hung up the phone. The clock on her microwave oven informed her that it was after three in the morning. When had that happened, she wondered.

Lillie went up to her room and got in bed.

Perhaps she'd been a fool to storm out on Jared like she had. Here she was sleeping alone on the biggest night of her life, after Jared had finally agreed to come home with her. What was the matter with her these days? So what if Jared had wanted to be part of her success? He had directed the movie, after all. He was part of it – if not the largest part of it. Wasn't he entitled to be happy for her?

Still, maybe her tired mind was playing tricks on her now. She wouldn't have gotten angry at Jared if she hadn't been pushed into it. She never got angry on a whim, she wasn't like that. She didn't jump the gun. There was something about the way he'd treated her tonight that didn't sit well with her, plain and simple.

Let him stew in it awhile, she decided. Jared didn't own her. Maybe her asserting her independence right now was something he needed to experience. And as for herself, winning an Oscar was never a guarantee against going to bed alone.

Lillie slept fitfully for several hours. When she awoke, the first thought that came into her head was of John Shay, how he'd said he was working on his relationship with his daughter. Lillie hadn't realized John Shay was married. On the few occasions when their paths had crossed, he'd always been with a different girl, none of whom had ever struck her as anyone's wife. But it was good that John took an interest in his daughter. Lillie would have liked an experience like that with Sam Kincaid...

Someone was downstairs knocking. Lillie was fully awake now – maybe that's what had roused her in the first place – the knocking. She glanced at the bedside clock. It was only 6:30. Who could be pounding on her front door at this hour?

Then her phone rang. Startled, she reached for it quickly. 'Hello?'

It was Jared on his cell phone. 'I'm downstairs. Come down and let me in. Let's talk.'

'Jared! Have you even been to bed yet?'

'No. And I didn't stay at the Bodhi, either. I must have hit half a dozen parties tonight. I guess I was hoping you might still be out and about; that you hadn't really gone home on a night like this.'

'You could have called me hours ago and found out.'

'I know. Come on, just come down and let me in.'

Lillie threw on her robe and headed downstairs. She couldn't make up her mind whether or not she was happy he'd come.

She opened the front door for him and was surprised to see him looking so self-possessed, his tux hardly looking the worse for wear. 'For someone who's crashed half-a-dozen crazy parties in a matter of a few hours, you're looking pretty darn good.'

'Thank you,' he said, stepping inside and then giving her a quick kiss.

It was a kiss of familiarity, not a kiss of apology, or a kiss that called a truce. It was merely a peck on the cheek between two grown people who knew each other well.

'Were you sleeping?' he asked.

'Of course, I was sleeping.'

'You want to go back up there?'

'You mean, alone?'

'No, I guess I meant, do you want to have some company up there? I told you I wanted to come home with you tonight – last night, whatever. I meant that.'

She sighed. It all came back to her. It wasn't so much how he was treating her; it was his sudden decision to turn his back on his usual concerns for Abby. Lillie couldn't understand this.

'What's wrong?' he said. 'You're not going to stay angry, are you?'

'I don't think so.'

'Well, what's going on with you?'

'I guess I'm just confounded by the whole 'Abby' thing.'

'You're not going to start on that again, are you? You won a huge award tonight, why are you harping about marriage?'

Lillie bridled. 'I'm not harping, Jared. I wasn't even thinking about marriage – or at least, not about getting married. I'm just trying to figure out why my winning this award has made you change your mind about Abby, that's all. I'd hardly call that harping.'

Lillie started back up the stairs.

'Can I come with you?' he asked. 'Or are we still fighting?'

She stopped on the stairs and looked at him; why was he so hard for her to resist? More and more, she was coming to the conclusion that this relationship was no good for her. It may have helped her career, it may have given her opportunities that other actresses never got, but emotionally, her relationship with Jared Warren was stunting her. She knew it. How long was she going to kid herself? 'Come on up,' she relented.

He followed close behind her. It had been a long night. He was feeling his age but he wouldn't admit it, not even to himself.

As soon as a man admitted that he felt old, he was no longer vital – to himself or to the industry. That was like being condemned to, well, maybe not death, he thought, but to the ranks of the terminally unemployed. Jared wouldn't join those ranks willingly, not without one hell of a fight. His career was the very blood in his veins. It's what kept his heart beating, his lungs breathing. He'd been a success in Hollywood since he was twenty-nine years old and he was now sixty-two – although, publicly, he was still only sixty. Without his career, what was there? He was not interested in finding out the answer. The mysteries of death were of more interest to him than the mystery of life without a career to tend to every day.

Lillie slid back in bed. The sheets were still warm. She watched Jared undress. He looked tired and yet still managed to look incredibly handsome. It had something to do with the bright silver hair – it was always so impeccably groomed. And his posture was flawless. Jared didn't carry himself like a man defeated by the onset of age. He kept himself active. He had his own private gym that took up an entire wing of his home. Of course, Lillie had never actually seen this fabled gym, she'd never been invited inside, but he'd told her about it numerous times.

'So you managed to survive the vice grip of your dress, I see?' He draped his tuxedo jacket over a chair and then removed his trousers with care. Meticulously, he removed each stud from his shirt, then the gold cuff links and his Rolex, and put them in a safe place on top of Lillie's bureau, in a Porcelain dish where Lillie had placed the diamonds he'd given her.

'There were moments when it was touch and go,' she kidded him, 'where it seemed like the dress might win. But in the end, I was victorious.'

'You were victorious in so many ways last night. Everyone was talking about you everywhere I went. Saying nothing but good things, which you know, is unheard of in this town on a night like this, a night that's usually drowning in sour grapes. But everyone talked about how stunning you looked and how you deserved to win. Now what do you think of that?' Jared got into bed beside her. 'Don't you regret leaving the festivities so early?'

'Not really,' she said quietly. 'It was kind of nice being alone thinking about things. You know what I did?'

'No what?'

'I called John Shay in Copenhagen to congratulate him. I think I woke him.'

'You did what?'

'I called John Shay.'

'They let him take calls in a place like that?'

'Jesus, Jared, it's not an asylum or anything.'

'Why did you want to talk to him? You don't even know the guy.'

'It seemed like a kind thing to do in light of my mother, and all. I know how hard it is, when people feel like they've been locked away from the world.'

'It's my understanding, honey, that he's been locked away from the world for a reason. That guy went off the deep end.'

'Maybe he did, but he sure sounded sane enough tonight.'

Jared settled into the pillows and stared up at the ceiling, giving this new scenario some thought. 'Is he writing anything? Did you ask him?'

'Actually, I did. And he is, or at least, he's starting something.'

'Well, perhaps the triumvirate really will return after all.'

'He didn't mention that he was working on a vehicle for you and me, Jared. He just said he was working on something.'

'You have to choose how to interpret these things, honey, otherwise you'll never come out on top.'

Jared pulled her over to him. 'Speaking of being on top, how tired are you?' he asked.

She smiled incredulously. 'Are you serious? You've been out all night. You must be exhausted.'

'I couldn't feel more energized at this very moment if I'd had a whole eight hours of sleep. I've been craving you all night.'

'Is that so?'

'That's so. What do you say, are you up for it, even a quick one?'

'I hope not as quick as the one in my bathroom this afternoon. I could live without another experience like that for a long time.'

'Aw, you were spectacular, kiddo, even totally dressed in the half-bath. Come on,' he coaxed her, easing up her satin night gown, 'admit it, you were enjoying yourself. I saw the look on your face.'

'If I remember correctly,' she answered promisingly, 'you owe me an orgasm.'

'Do I?'

Lillie's night gown was all the way off. It landed in a delicate heap on the floor beside the bed. She was naked. 'Yes, you do.'

He fished in the drawer of her night table for a condom. He knew full well where she kept them. 'And how does a woman as regal as you, a bona fide Oscar winner, get her randy little rocks off now?'

'I'm no different than I was before the award,' she baited him. 'I'd say you've still got your work cut out for you.' She turned over for him, raising her ass up, steadying herself on spread knees, her face sinking comfortably into the feather pillows.

This was the kind of challenge Jared enjoyed, making Lillie come. It was by no means an easy task, it never had been. When he first met her, she was twenty-two, relatively virginal, and unaccustomed to climaxing in the mouth of a much older man. Back then, she'd been shy; a fledgling actress from a small town, trying to make it in New York City. She almost seemed too young to carry off the weight of her exceptional beauty but Jared sensed upon first seeing her – that she was going to grow into it gracefully. He could tell that about a young woman, he'd seen enough of them over the decades of his career to get a feel for it, for how a woman would age. He'd watched enough of them either blossom into true beauties or age into something hard-edged and brittle looking. Film, especially, magnified both those outcomes.

When Jared laid eyes on Lillie Diver, she was trying out for a bit part in a movie he was producing, not directing; one that required her to recite two or three lines at the most. A casting agency had sent her to him with high praises. He could immediately see why. Her beauty was photogenic. It translated well on film, the camera loved her. Her voice had an appealing quality to it; both naïve and seductive. It was a magic combination for a Hollywood career.

Lillie was cast in the film, but more importantly, Jared made a note of her phone number. He didn't call her until he'd flown back to L.A., and though he lavished her with praise and attention when she came to town to shoot her brief scene, he didn't actively seduce her until after the film was in post-production and had relocated back to New York City. There was something about being on her turf, rather than his own where Abby, before her illness had worsened, was as much a fixture on the scene as he was, that aided him in his seduction.

Their first night together, Lillie's naiveté, which played so appealingly on screen, translated into all out eroticism in the bedroom. She was an inexperienced lover; the proverbial blank canvas for Jared to create on and then unveil. What attracted him most was how without guile she stroked his ego. Lillie seemed to genuinely worship Jared Warren – the man, not the Hollywood legend. He felt Lillie's attraction to him came from her very soul, that her heart was honest. She wasn't in it for a shot at furthering her career; she adored being with him in bed, adored learning what their bodies could do for each other. The more than three-decade age difference between them seemed, to Jared, to border on being an aphrodisiac for her. And that turned him on, being in the role of father figure to such a promising young ingénue.

In the six years they'd been together, she'd come a long way as a lover.

Look at this, he told himself now; his eyes drinking in the spectacle of the goods being offered so openly to him. Her taut, smooth thighs planted wide enough to reveal the lightly-haired lips, pouting at him from dead-center. The wrinkled inner lips glistened. The opening of her hole was slick. How can it be, he wondered, that she's already this aroused? Could it be that just being in this posture – offered up for his pleasure – still excited her after all these years?

He didn't wait to find out what her answer might be to these questions.

Eagerly, he pressed his face into her musky, beckoning crevice, a familiar delirium rising in him, quickening his breath as his tongue tasted her, as his nostrils filled with the scent of her arousal.

He pulled the outer lips wider apart, forcing her clitoris to erect attention, its protective hood pulled back. His tongue felt for the stiff, tiny exposed tip of her clit, found it, and then caressed it unmercifully.

'Oh God, Jared,' she cried into her pillow.

Her thighs stiffened; her ass arched up higher for him.

Her tender clit was caught in a ceaseless barrage of quick, firm tongue strokes. Over and over, his tongue flicked the stiff little nub without stopping; pleasure upon pleasure was forced up through her nerve-endings, centered between her legs.

'Oh God,' she cried again, her fingers gripping the pillow tight, her ass lifted impossibly high now, until the small of her back ached. 'God, that's good. That's so good.'

He released his hold on the captive hood, sucked the tender area between his lips and, while two of his fingers dipped into her hole, he lavished the swollen hood with deep, sucking kisses.

His strong, steady fingers probed her. The slick hole opened easily to accommodate them. She moaned deeply now, her pelvis writhing, pushing her mound more fully into his mouth, pushing her hole down around his fingers.

Her momentum was increasing. Jared pulled his face away. 'Fuck daddy's fingers, baby. Come on, fuck daddy's fingers. You know you like it.'

It was an unspeakably erotic display, the way Lillie so eagerly assumed all fours for him and pushed her snug hole up and down on his fingers. Those gorgeous tits hanging down, bouncing from the force she exerted in the fucking.

In his opinion, she looked just as beautiful like this; lewdly undulating, pushing herself open to accept his thrusting fingers. She was entranced by her lust, and Jared knew that when she was like this, she grew increasingly accommodating to all his whims.

He used it to his advantage. It was hard not to; it was a heady experience, being serviced by such a beautiful, attentive woman.

He positioned himself behind her, his cock ready for her hole. 'Fuck daddy,' he said quietly. 'Work it, baby.'

In the same position for getting her finger fucking, Lillie took on the challenge of his thick cock. She fucked her hole hard against him. Pulled back, until she could feel the wide head of the cock just at her opening, then she fucked the full length of it again, until her mound was grinding against him. Over and over, her pelvis worked vigorously to ride the cock penetrating her.

'Oh daddy, yes!' she cried.

He was ecstatic. He knew that whenever she called him that, when the word 'daddy' came out of her mouth, she was really in a swoon. If he played his cards right, he might even coax her to talk dirty to him while they fucked. He loved this more than anything, since it was a gift she bestowed on him only rarely.

In his exuberance, he took over the action. Grabbing her hips, he heightened the force of the thrusts. The impact of his cock pounding in sent ripples through the muscles in her rear-end.

She grunted lasciviously now; over and over, in rhythm to the thorough fucking her hole was receiving.

'That's right, baby, let daddy fuck you. You know how he likes it.'

Yes, she knew how he liked it. She'd been pleasing him for six years already; pleasing him and herself in the process. She loved this; it was what she lived for, to feel filled up with him, to feel his power, his force. On nights like this (or was it morning already?) the depths of her arousal confounded her. She wanted to be fucked harder, deeper; she wanted to feel impaled beyond her hole's capacity.

Getting good and fucked – this was how she referred to it in her head. I'm getting good and fucked. Daddy's really fucking me now, fucking me until I'm good and fucked.

It was like a delirious mantra that permeated her brain. It was a signal that she'd reached a plateau; that she wasn't likely to come for a long time; that her body had turned into a fucking machine. She wasn't even interested in a climax now; all she wanted was to keep fucking...

Dazed and exhausted, Lillie lay in bed with her eyes closed, listening to the shower running in the bathroom. Her mind wandered, slipping close to the precipice of sleep. Jared had begun singing in the shower. It was an old song, a standard; a vow of undying love. Jared's voice had a pleasing quality when he sang. The sound of it seemed to be urging her closer to the edge of sleep, where consciousness fell at last into the void.

His silver hair glinted in her brief dream. It was her father again. Or was it Jared? He looked like her father. With a start, Lillie came back from the edge of the void; she lay now between wakefulness and sleep, as Jared's song continued wafting in from the bathroom.

Why hadn't she noticed it before last night, she wondered; what was her problem, anyway? Why was she in love a man so much older than she was, who looked just like her father? And why think of her father at the very moment of her win when she hadn't thought of him in a long time? Could it be that he was watching her, that wherever he was – it was a nursing home, she knew that, but she couldn't recall the name of it – it was just outside of Mountville. Could it be that he was watching her win on TV? That he'd finally made the connection and she'd somehow picked up on his revelation? That he knew now that she was Sally Diver's daughter and he recognized her as the girl he'd taken to the hotel? The one who'd led him on and tricked him? Maybe in his feeble-minded state, unexpected things became crystal clear to him.

Lillie's eyes sprang open, she was fully awake now.

Maybe it really had happened, she thought grimly. Maybe Samuel Masters Kincaid III had figured it all out in his advanced, doddering years. That she was his daughter, his own flesh and blood, and that she was the girl who had nearly seduced him.

Jared was out of the shower now and Lillie felt vaguely ill.

It was a mistake, she pleaded with herself; I was young. I wanted him to notice me, to know I was alive; to love me. I didn't know any better.

When was her conscience ever going to let it go?

CHAPTER FOUR

The sun was shining bright; the sky, a brilliant blue. If it weren't for the barren trees and the brownish color of the sprawling lawn, it could pass for a spring day outside the Institute's walls. Never the less, it was a good omen. In Copenhagen, spring was clearly just around the corner.

John Shay sat down to consume a very promising lunch. Everything so far today seemed to bode well for a good reunion with Selena. It was the first time in months, maybe longer, that John could say he felt on top of things – perhaps even optimistic.

All morning long, patients and staff members had been quietly congratulating him on his win. Amanda had called on the telephone.

'Well? What's the verdict?' she'd asked. 'Did you stay up and watch the show?'

'I won,' John replied, matter-of-factly.

'See? I told you. This has all been a temporary set back. It's not something you can't conquer, John.'

John wanted to tell her that it was decent of her to call, but even he was getting tired of how lame that sounded. Why shouldn't she call? They'd lived together as husband and wife for fifteen years, they had a daughter together. And it's not as if the call had been long distance. She was right here in Denmark, only a few minute's drive away.

Out of all these well-wishers, though, nothing touched him more than the phone call from Lillie Diver at the crack of dawn. That would go down in his memory as one of his nicest surprises.

It was still a mystery, why she'd done it. And was it really that commonly known back in the States that he'd gotten booted into a rehab?

John's memory from the last six months was filled with holes. Had he been out in public acting like a fool, disgracing himself and offending people he would be expected to work with again? He had no real way of knowing the answers to those questions. Too much of it was a blank.

John picked over his lunch with his fork. This was a puzzlement he would have to come to terms with somehow. Could it be that in the fog of boozing over the holidays, he'd actually made contact with Lillie? That maybe she was just being polite and ignoring any alcoholic craziness? He'd been obsessed with her, that much he remembered clearly. Yet he couldn't safely determine now what had been a drunken dream and what had actually happened. He remembered wanting to step inside the movie screen and join her on that balcony overlooking the Mediterranean; he'd wished that *Master of the Storm* could have been real, not just celluloid. Had he said these things to her? He had a dim recollection of telling it to somebody.

'John, you seem a million miles away.'

It was Dr. Andersen, one of John's favorite doctors at the Lindegaard.

'Mind if I share your table?'

'No, please do.'

'So today's the big day, huh?'

'In a lot of ways, yes.'

'That's right, the award. Congratulations. I heard about it from the staff this morning. Does your daughter know yet?'

'I think so.'

'Is she impressed by awards, do you think?'

'To be honest, Dr. Andersen, I don't know the first thing about Selena anymore. I'll count myself lucky if I even recognize her.'

The doctor gave John a quick pat on the arm. 'You'll be all right, John. You're ready for this. Let's face it. You'll be going home soon enough. You're ready for a lot of things. I feel very confident in you.'

John took a sip of water, wishing momentarily that it was a glass of wine. 'Actually, today's the first day I've really felt any confidence in myself. I'm beginning to feel like I can be who I used to be before everything went haywire. But it raises a lot of questions – all those blank spots in my memory. What the hell happened? What was I doing while my mind was away?'

Dr. Andersen managed a weak smile. 'That, I'm afraid, will only become clear to you in indirect ways, for instance, when you begin to interact again with people who might have seen you in action, so to speak, your daughter being a case in point. Some of those other things, John, you know as well as I do; you're not likely to ever remember them. But life goes on. You can make clear choices from this moment forward. That's a powerful place to be in. Keep that thought at the forefront of all these other, perhaps less productive thoughts, that are a necessary byproduct of where you're at in your recovery right now. Isn't this pork loin marvelous?' he added.

'Yes,' John agreed, 'another winner. I'm surprised I haven't put on twenty pounds in this place.'

'Well, confidentially, John, you do look a whole lot better now than when you were first brought in here.'

'It's remarkable what a little solid food can do to a person who's been on a steady liquid diet, isn't it?'

Dr. Andersen felt a private moment of relief. John's mood had improved significantly over the past week, and today he did seem better than ever – even after his encounter with his ex-wife, the woman who'd had him admitted to the Institute. If all went well with John's meeting with his daughter, if he showed continued signs of handling these visitors from the outside world, reminders of a life he could never completely return to; if he can handle these things, Dr. Andersen determined, without sinking into depression or succumbing to too much rage, then the patient really was on the road to recovery.

* * *

John paced the reception area, his concentration split equally between watching the clock on the wall and watching the parking lot through the large window, waiting for a glimpse of Amanda's rental car pulling up the drive.

He tried to keep his thoughts focused on the good memories he had of being with Selena in the past. If he thought too much about the recent holiday debacle, it derailed his attempts to stay calm. He didn't know which was worse, what he could remember about Selena's visit to his house during her school break, or what he couldn't remember at all.

When children are little, he recollected, they can be very forgiving creatures, simply because they don't know any better and their parents are their whole world. But Selena is almost seventeen now, long past the age of innocence and well into those years where parents are held accountable for every disappointment life deals them.

And as far as disappoints go, John was forced to admit that having to confront a parent's alcoholism had to rank up there with the worst.

At last, there it was, Amanda's rental car pulled into the Institute's parking lot. Amanda wasn't driving this time, though, Rick was behind the wheel. Amanda was simply a passenger and Selena was in the back seat.

A happy family, John told himself. They look right together. That used to be me.

Selena got out of the car and so did Amanda. But at the front door, where the guard greeted them, they parted company.

'You take care, honey,' John could hear Amanda saying as the glass doors opened. 'We'll be back for you in an hour.'

An hour, is that all? An hour is only a heartbeat.

'Selena.' He welcomed her with a warm smile. He wondered if he should hug her.

She was taller than her mother now. He hadn't noticed it before. He never saw them in the same place and time anymore.

'How are you, honey? I'm really happy you could come.'

She looked relieved. Was it because he was sober, safe, controlled?

'Hi, dad.'

'Hi. Well, come here.' He took the initiative and gave her a hug. He could feel the tension in her thin, young body. He could feel her reluctance. 'You look great,' he said, ignoring her resistance. 'Have you been having a good time?'

'Good enough. We go shopping. We go out to eat. We could be anywhere doing that.'

John smiled. What was there to say to a remark like that?

She took off her coat. 'Mom says you're almost better, that they'll be letting you go soon. Congratulations on your award, by the way. She told me this morning.'

'Thanks, honey. Did you happen to see the movie?'

'Dad, please...'

'What?' He led her into the large, airy day room. It was mostly empty, but the television was on.

'I think I must have seen it a zillion times at your house, at Christmas. Don't you remember? That's all you wanted to watch.'

'Ah, Christmas. Yes, I guess I forgot.'

Silence suddenly honed in on the pair and dropped like a thick tarp over them. They sat down near one of the windows overlooking the deep ravine. The ice had melted completely and the shallow stream was running freely over the rocks, the decomposing leaves, the dead twigs.

I have to say something here, John knew. It's up to me, not her.

'How's school going?' he ventured.

'Okay.'

'You're on your spring break now?'

'Uh-huh.'

'Your grades are still fantastic, I take it?'

'I guess so.'

'Well, you were always such a smarty. I don't see any reason for things to be any different now.'

She rolled her eyes and he took it as his cue that he was speaking to her as if she were still a child.

But it was only five seconds ago that she was a child, he thought.

'I'm sorry about what happened at Christmas, that you had to see me like.'

The words came out suddenly, brazenly, as if of their own volition, as if John had had nothing to do with it. The sound of his voice in the room shocked him.

'It's okay,' she said.

'No, it's not okay.' The words continued on, in spite of him. 'Take a look at this place, Selena. If it were okay, then I would-n't be here, and you wouldn't be here talking to me like this – like we barely know each other.'

Selena looked now as if she would cry. He wished his words had chosen a different way of escaping; that he hadn't been so abrupt. He didn't want to see her cry, least of all on his wretched account.

'Honey, don't cry.'

'You know you could have been in Hollywood last night,' she spat accusingly. 'You could have been part of everything and gotten your award the right way, like everybody else does – even if it was a stupid movie! We could have watched you on TV and been proud of you!'

He didn't reply. She was crying now, she was angry. A nurse was coming toward them. He motioned to the nurse that it was okay. He would handle it.

'Why don't you just get married, anyway?' Selena blurted.

'Married?' That was a baffling remark. 'I don't understand, honey.'

'Let somebody else worry about you and make sure you're all right!'

'Oh, honey.' John sighed. 'That's not what marriage is for, and that's not what our relationship is for, either. I'm going to be all right. I'm promising you that, right now. You're not going to have to worry about me when I get out of here. You won't have to worry about coming to stay with me again, either. It'll be different next time. I promise. I have to get back to work, don't I? I have to have a clear head to do that. If I don't keep working, how can you keep shopping?' he added playfully. 'How can you stay at that great school?'

'I hate that school. I've always hated that school.'

'No, you haven't, Selena. You've had some great times there, I know it. My memory's not that bad.'

John wished they were in a cocktail lounge somewhere far, far away; that he could be helping himself liberally to his favorite beverage, scotch on the rocks. But it was not an option anymore. He was simply going to have to learn to endure these conversations without the taste of booze on his tongue, without the rush of hot comfort in his veins.

'Hey,' he offered jovially, trying to switch gears. 'Guess who called me this morning at the crack of dawn?'

'Who?'

'Lillie Diver.'

'The actress?' She seemed impressed.

'Of course, the actress. She won an award last night, too, for that stupid movie, as you so eloquently put it. What do you think of that?'

'I didn't know you actually knew her. The way you were talking at Christmas, it sounded like you guys had never met. Why don't you marry her, dad?'

John was momentarily aghast. 'Why would I marry Lillie Diver, sweetheart?' His mind raced around in circles; what had he revealed to his daughter about Lillie Diver while he was in his drunken stupor?

'You love her, don't you? That's what you kept telling me.'

'Well,' he fumbled for a reply. 'I meant that in an artistic sense. I loved her in that movie. And see? I was right, she won the Oscar. So there you have it. Everybody loves Lillie Diver.'

*   *   *

When Lillie awoke, Jared had already left the bed. She retrieved her night gown from the heap on the floor and slipped it on. She ventured downstairs and to her disbelief, there was Jared in her kitchen, mostly naked but partially wearing one of her short kimonos, making them breakfast.

'What did you get, about three hours of sleep?' she asked. 'Look at you. You're a bundle of energy this morning.'

'I'm always a bundle of energy, and you know it. '

The television in the kitchen was on with the volume down and the morning paper was spread out on her kitchen table.

'Take a look at yourself, why don't you?' Jared said, pointing with a metal spatula in the direction of the newspaper. 'Has anyone ever told you, you're very photogenic?'

'To be brutally honest? Once or twice. In fact, you may have even brought it to my attention before.'

'So, how does it feel to wake up a winner?'

She gave it some thought. 'It feels pretty good.'

'I was thinking we could take a trip together. Are you ready for a nice vacation, just the two of us? How about some place exotic? We could take my boat.'

Jared's boat was in fact a 147 foot yacht. It slept thirteen adults, comfortably.

'Aren't you a little worried about being away from Abby that long? Are you forgetting that she's not well?'

'This is business, Lillie. We need to relax and do some brainstorming about our next project. I've been thinking,' he said, flipping a pancake with ease. 'What if Shay can't cut it anymore? We should get a backup plan.'

'A backup plan? Jared, John Shay doesn't even have a title yet.'

'I'll get a title out of him, that's not a problem.'

'How are you going to do that?'

'The same way you did. I'm going to call him in that rehab. I'll congratulate him. Then I'll feel him out for his next project before anyone else does. You know, plenty of people in this town get that urge to help the underdog – they want to try and save the needy, save their souls. I think I should be first in that line, don't you? I mean, all things considered?'

Lillie was appalled. It all sounded so mercenary. John Shay was more than likely still in a very unstable place, emotionally. He would probably see right through Jared's phony concern. Lillie felt like calling John again and warning him that she had nothing to do with this new overture on Jared's part.

But that's so high school, she thought; all that scrambling around behind someone's back.

Still Jared's idea made her feel cheap. It made it look like her phone call to John was just a way of testing the waters so that Jared could move in for the kill.

'Don't do it, Jared,' she said. 'Give the man some peace – a little space. At least until he's back home.'

Jared flipped the remaining pancakes onto a plate and set the plate down. He stared at her. 'It almost sounds if you're telling me what to do.'

'Jared come on, be reasonable. It's not like the man is kicking back somewhere, letting the offers roll in. He's in a rehab, for chrissakes.'

Jared grew silent as he considered the situation. Finally, he spoke. 'What gives with you two, anyway?'

'What is that supposed to mean?'

'I mean, you two are so chummy all of a sudden. What gives?'

'Jared, you're crazy. We're not chummy. I barely know the guy.'

Jared's cell phone began vibrating wildly on the counter top. He grabbed it and flipped it open. 'What is it?' he snapped tersely.

Lillie watched his face go from tense anger to slack disbelief. 'When? Okay, I'm coming.' He clicked the phone shut. 'It's Abby,' he said. 'Something's wrong. I have to go. That was my son. They're taking her to the hospital.'

CHAPTER FIVE

The hospital corridor was nearly empty at this late hour. There was something almost peaceful about the emptiness, except for the fact that Jared was where he was – just outside the Intensive Care Unit.

His children were in there, hovering somewhere between weeping and that strange euphoria that overcomes people once they know for certain that the person they so loved has gone on to a better place.

A much better place, Jared thought; he was positive about that.

Jared's lawyer was in there, too, in the ICU. He'd brought a stack of official legal documents. They'd been tucked neatly inside that expensive leather briefcase Jared and Abby had bought him two Christmas's ago. Naturally, the choice of the gift had been Abby's idea. She'd been great with the gift-giving. A-list, B-list, it never mattered. Anyone who received a gift from the Warrens always felt like they had been regarded as special somehow. Left to his own devices, Jared's mind always ran to the same unimaginative ideas; booze, gems, cash; once in a blue moon, a fur. But that was a dicey choice these days.

It was those papers coming our of Lazowitz's briefcase that had sent Jared for the safety of the corridor in the first place. He told James, his eldest son, to do the signing for now – anything that didn't absolutely require Jared's signature. The finality of signing his name to a legal document was more than Jared could cope with. Abby had been dead for less than twenty minutes.

It's an omen, he told himself irrationally as he stared blankly down the corridor. First, I lose the Oscar. Now this, Abby leaves me when the chips are down. Lillie is chasing after John Shay, an out and out drunk who's so unbecoming to her. And if I don't get a lucrative offer soon, I'm going to have to sell the house.

This was Abby's payback, he figured, for everything that he'd done to her since she'd gotten sick – pushing her more and more to the sidelines after she'd stuck by him through the lean years. But especially for last night; this was Abby's chance to spurn him for coming up a loser, for being too old. For not coming home to tell her what everyone was wearing. As if he ever noticed that. He wouldn't have even noticed what Lillie had been wearing if it hadn't become the focal point of their entire day.

'Dad?'

It was Gracie, his youngest daughter, and as of last year, a mother herself.

'Are you okay?'

He nodded his head vaguely.

God, he was tired. When was the last time he'd had a good night's sleep? He couldn't recall. If it wasn't the expenses of Abby's illness keeping him awake, it was the expenses of the house, the boat, the two kids who were still in graduate school, the grandchildren and their pricey pre-schools. It never stopped. He needed a damn good project and he needed it soon.

'I'll be in there in a minute,' he told Gracie. 'I just wanted to think about something.'

'Okay,' she said, and went back inside.

Damn it, why hadn't he won last night? Hadn't he courted enough favors from this town full of idiots? Another win would have been the solution to so many of the problems. Not all of them, but a lot of them. His phone would have been ringing off the hook today. How could Lillie be so casual about it? Turning off her phone on a day like today! Wait until the day comes when the work's not out there anymore. She'll be kicking herself. She'll be jumping when the phone rings then, running to find out if the offer's still good or if the whole project's in turnaround.

Abby, he said, addressing her in his weary brain, it's just that you were looking so damn helpless. Some days, I was afraid to look at you, for fear that I would absorb it somehow, all that frailty. I know you were counting on me to stay vital, to give you something to feed on, something to have hope in every morning. But I couldn't risk it anymore. I couldn't come home a loser and see my loss reflected in you in any way – because then it would be real: I'd be a loser. That's why I didn't come home. That's something you can understand, right? That need to be near the person whose glow is giving off the real heat? You remember how that was in the old days? Well, as much as you need it on the way up, you need it that much more on the way down.

'Jared?'

Now it was Lazowitz.

'How are you doing? Can I get a signature? Are you up to it? Then I'll leave you to the privacy of your family.'

'Sure, Laz,' he relented in defeat. 'Thanks for coming at such short notice. You've been an oak for us, you know that, all through this ordeal.'

'I could say it's all part of my job, but you two have always been more than a job, you've been good friends. I'm sad to see her go, Jared. She was a tough, classy lady. But I know how much she was suffering at the end.'

Jared said nothing. He signed where he was told to sign. Then he gave a slight wave and went to join his grieving children in the ICU.

*   *   *

Lillie lay in bed and stared out at the night. The drapes were pulled back and the bright white moon was just visible at the far corner of the window. It had been an exhilarating day. She was wiped out, but her mind was spinning. Did she really think she would sleep?

After Jared had left in such a hurry, Lillie had turned the phone back on. The calls never stopped. One after another – congratulations, or I have the perfect project, or when can we do lunch? On and on and on... it made her crazy but in the best possible way. If only her mother's voice had been in among those calls. It would have been priceless.

'I want it all, mommy,' Lillie could remember saying; 'the moon and the stars, big yachts and fancy dresses and a diamond necklace.'

Lillie couldn't have been more than eight or nine when she'd made that proclamation. It was based on what Lillie had been brought up to think of as success. Her mother had literally raised her on old Hollywood movies. They'd only cost fifty cents to watch at Mountville's third rate movie house, not that Mountville didn't have a veritable palace where the first-run pictures played, because they did. It was a movie palace left over from the thirties' WPA building boom. But it was usually too expensive for Lillie and her mother to go there, especially since it involved an added bus trip across town. But Lillie was content to watch the old black and white movies at the theater near their apartment building, the theater where the floor was always sticky from spilled Coca-cola. All that black-and-white art deco glamour! It was thrilling dressing for dinner, dressing for the yacht. Or those Technicolor tragedies, the dramas, the musicals. They all seemed more real than real life. In fact, Lillie had been waiting a long time for life to take on the reality of the movies.

'And I think now, it's coming pretty damn close!'

She'd watched herself at least a dozen times on television that day, on the entertainment news shows. It turned out that the nightmare of a dress had had a presence of its own. It photographed flawlessly. No one would ever guess what a torture it had been to wear! All that mattered in the end was that she'd looked like a movie star. Even Eduardo had stopped by, raving like a delirious lunatic. Lillie was his new goddess. He worshipped the ground she walked on, and his phone hadn't stop ringing, either. He had appointments booked solid through the rest of the season.

Machard himself had called from his design studio, thanking Lillie profusely for allowing his dress to be seen to its best possible advantage. 'You made it all look effortless, my dear,' he'd said. 'You are one of the originals.'

'One of the originals,' she repeated to herself now. 'I'm one of the originals – what does that mean? It sounds awful good.'

And the food! At last, she'd been able to eat like a normal person. None of that nibbling here, nibbling there, trying to ensure that the damn dress would fit! She'd had a sumptuous day, eating everything that had struck her fancy as she sat planted in front of the television and worked that remote control; she became a channel surfing fiend.

'Am I really that vain?' she chided herself now, laughing in out-right delight. 'I couldn't go a minute without trying to find my face again. I've never done anything like that in my life!'

But then life had never been this perfect before.

Jared was right, she realized. My future is wide open now.

CHAPTER SIX

Seven days passed before Jared was able to give even part of his attention to Lillie again. They were seven momentous days for each of them, days that took them to opposite spiritual shores. Jared focused more acutely on the changes Abby's passing would bring, and on the dismal state of his private affairs. He made a heroic effort to appear stoic for his children's sake, and in the privacy of his own mind, he fought off the depth of his bereavement in the only way he knew how, by turning his thoughts away from Abby and to his career – what could he do to save it from dying, too?

Lillie was shocked by the suddenness of Abby's death – or as sudden as a long term illness can allow. Out of respect for Jared's family, she steered clear of publicly participating in the funeral in any way, and limited herself to a single private phone call to Jared to express her condolences.

This was the crossroads, the turning point, that juncture in the road that, for Lillie, had always seemed hopelessly in the distance; where just as suddenly as their illicit years together had seemed never-ending, Jared was finally an unmarried man.

What would this mean for their future? Would he ask Lillie to marry him now, as he'd always promised he would? And if he did, would Lillie say yes?

Funny, she thought; until so recently, it was what I'd been longing for – Jared to be really available for me, to go out with me in public without having to behave as if we're just friends. To take those vacations together to those exotic places he's always promising, without my having to feel guilty about taking him away from Abby. The poor woman was dependant on him.

Now, however, Lillie had seen a side to Jared Warren that she hadn't bargained for. He was becoming controlling and manipulative regarding her career. As much as she'd enjoyed having someone older to turn to, someone more experienced, who knew the ins and outs of Hollywood from decades of having survived it, someone who could guide her and advise her, she'd still always regarded her career decisions as her personal domain. And now because of the award, she had nothing but opportunities laid out in front of her. How prudent would it really be, she wondered, to narrow them down to only those projects that could involve Jared somehow?

Maybe this is just a passing phase with him, she decided, punching up her confidence. A few weeks from now, a month or two, and he'll be back to normal. Things are going to be okay.

*   *   *

As usual, when John Shay least expected it, the tidal wave of words spilled over into his brain. They originated from only God knew where, but a new novel was on its way to him, there was no denying it. Naturally, he was without his laptop at the Lindegaard, or even a typewriter. When was the last time he'd picked up a pen and a scrap of paper and started feverishly writing?

'Probably not since Junior High School,' he muttered to himself. But he kept writing. It was the last piece of the mental puzzle needed to fully revive his spirits. His doctors continued to note the positive changes in John's attitude, the resolve he exhibited now. The time he allocated to working on the new book left less and less time for John to debate endlessly with himself about the social perils of sobriety versus drinking. More frequently he asked his doctors that all important question, when would he be going home?

He craved the familiarity of his own desk, his own room back in New York. He longed for real privacy, where he could get lost in the new manuscript for those uninterrupted hours on end that were always a sign that a novel had taken on a life of its own.

In the meantime, though, he scoured the Nurse's Station for every available shred of paper. Until one night, Ula was thoughtful enough to bring him a small stack of spiral bound notebooks from the outside world. It was the least she could do to help such a famous author, a man who had inadvertently handed her one of the high points of her life.

'I'm going to remember you for a very long time, Ula,' he told her, in genuine gratitude. 'You're one of the few people who has truly eased my misery over these last few months. You're such a considerate human being.'

What he didn't go on to say was that Lillie Diver was one of those few, as well. In fact, it was because of Lillie that John's new book had come into existence at all. It was in answer to the question he'd repeatedly asked himself after his first visit with Selena: 'What needs to change in this world before a man like me could marry a woman like Lillie Diver?'

In his imagination, John set about creating that alternate world. Of course the names and places were changed to protect the innocent, as it were. But the rest of it poured straight from John's heart.

'This is the world I would give you if I could, Lillie,' he whispered. It was a perfect world, a world where love was requited and conquered all. It was one of John's more magnificent love stories. His aching fingers gripped the pen and kept pace with it, with the story's urgent need to tell itself.

The World I Could Give was well over a hundred pages when a transatlantic phone call came through for John late one afternoon. It was Jared Warren calling from his house in Bel Air.

'Shay? It's Jared Warren. How are you, you son of a gun?'

'Warren, this is a surprise.'

'When are they planning on springing you from that trap anyway? Any ideas?'

John sighed in resignation. The man definitely had a unique way with words. Not exactly the Goodwill Ambassador of Hollywood, was he? 'I'm not really sure when I'm leaving, sometime within the month. Why? Were you planning a visit to Copenhagen?'

'Not on your life. But I was planning on looking you up when I flew back east. You could come into the city and we could meet for a drink.'

'I don't drink anymore, Warren. Maybe you hadn't heard.'

'Sorry. I forgot. We can meet for lunch then, how's that? I want to talk all about your new book.'

How on earth did he know about that? 'What book?'

'The one I know you're writing.' Jared was bluffing, but every conversation he engaged in these days was a crap shoot. 'What's the title, anyway? Got a title yet?'

John admitted it reluctantly, 'The World I Could Give.'

'No kidding, a love story?'

'That's right. How could you tell?'

'The sentiment, that's how. Something for Lillie in it?'

'Why do you ask that?' John felt immediately alarmed; was he really that transparent, his love for Lillie that pathetically obvious, even to a blockhead like Jared Warren, a man not exactly known for his sensitive depth?

'I'm always on the lookout, you know how it is,' Jared explained. 'We're engaged – did you know that?'

'Engaged? You and Lillie?'

'Me and Lillie.'

'What about your wife?' John felt a peculiar ache in his heart. Lillie engaged? The pain was sharp and sudden.

'Abby's gone, Shay. She died. I won't say finally,' but you know, it wasn't unexpected.'

'I'm sorry to hear that,' John admitted. Though just how sorry he was wouldn't thoroughly hit him until hours later, when the night came again and the Lindegaard was tranquil, quiet; the rooms dark except for the occasional comforting glow of a television set left on by a patient now sleeping soundly.

'Thanks for your sympathies,' Jared went on. 'I appreciate that.' Whether or not he did had become irrelevant these days. What mattered was sticking to from, saying what was expected, making sure he got only the answers he wanted to hear. 'So, how far are you in this new one? Will you have something to show me when I come to New York?'

'That's jumping the gun a bit, isn't it? My agent doesn't even know about it yet, let alone my publisher.'

'Well for chrissakes, get on the ball, Shay!' Then Jared laughed stiffly, scurrying to cover his faux pas when he realized how strident he'd sounded. Calm down boy, he coached himself, or someone's gonna think you're desperate. Then they're gonna guess about the house. Just play it cool. So what if it's up for sale? You could be selling it simply because it holds too many memories of your long happy history with Abby. Nobody's gonna guess that you're going broke here, as long as you play it cool...

It was a speech he'd rehearsed countless times in his head, on those nights when the oblivion of sleep eluded him yet again.

'Since I can just tell there's something perfect in this for Lillie, Shay, why don't I bring her along to the lunch?'

John was beside himself. That was the last thing he wanted right now – to be anywhere near Lillie if she was engaged to Jared Warren. But Jared was racing ahead of him at a hundred miles an hour. 'Are you listening to anything I'm saying, Warren?' The only thing keeping John from shouting was his reluctance to alarm the staff or to be overheard by any of the other patients. He didn't want even a hint of this new heartache coming up in a group therapy session. After all, he was on his way out of this nut house. 'There's no deal yet,' he went on quietly. 'The book's not even halfway done. I have no clue if there's something in it for Lillie.'

'Well, now I've given you something to shoot for! That's exhilarating, isn't it? Or is it just me? I know I'm exhilarated. I know it's going to be another great book, so you keep me posted, Shay, you hear? I want to be the first one you call when you want somebody to read it. Maybe we don't need to bring Lillie in on this so early in the game, but you and me will hook up when I come out to New York. We could meet at the Belle Saison again – food only, I swear. So help me God, no liquids will be allowed anywhere near our table.'

'All right, Warren.' John knew when he was defeated. 'I'll be in touch with you when I can.'

John hung up the phone and sat in the silence of his room, unaware of his heart pounding. All he could focus on was the comfort that eluded him – the comfort of booze. Is there anything on earth, he wondered, that can come close to that? He longed for the days not so long ago when all that mattered in his world was the movie screen in front of his face and a glass of scotch in his fist.

*   *   *

Jared hung up the phone. He paced his spacious study. Most of the furniture in it was gone, sold off quietly, except for the necessary desk and chair, a small couch and an end table. To explain the sudden lack of furnishings all over the house, he'd told the kids that he wanted to start over when he moved to the new place. 'Less possessions,' he'd said. 'I need less clutter in my life.' To save money, he'd given up his outside office and all but one car. All he worried about now was selling the house, paying off the boat, the pre-schools, the graduate schools, the credit cards, the insurance bills, the funeral expenses...

I need to talk to Lillie, he realized.

It would be prudent to clue her in on the fact that they were officially engaged. That would be a disaster, her hearing about it from someone else. Jared dialed Lillie's home phone but she didn't answer. He tried her on her cell. She didn't answer that, either. He left a message, brief and to the point.

'Honey, it's me. Let's do dinner tonight. I want to go somewhere nice, private, quiet. You know, romantic. Call me when you get this and wear something pretty.'

There would have to be a ring to make it really official. Jared headed to the other side of the house, to Abby's old room. Somewhere in one of those drawers was a diamond ring that had once belonged to his mother. Finding it was the first order of business, recognizing it would run a close second. He would have to be very careful. What if he gave Lillie Abby's old engagement ring by mistake? He might not notice the difference but his daughters would, in a heartbeat.

111

Abby's room was dark, the shades were drawn. Jared hadn't been in here since before his wife had died. There was no real essence of Abby in the room, only the lingering reminders of her illness, an illness that had consumed her long before she'd actually surrendered to it. Jared thought of it as the Sick Room, not really as Abby's room. That room had been upstairs, the one they'd shared together for over thirty years, the room he still slept in, the room that three of his four children had been conceived in. Once Abby's illness had progressed beyond hope, when she was primarily bedridden and could only be moved in a wheelchair, they'd relocated Abby's world to a room on the first floor. It looked out on the front yard with its exquisite landscaping, as well as the long front drive. Abby could watch life through the large picture window, in all its comings and goings.

Jared noticed that none of the family photos were left in the room. They'd been Abby's favorites. He figured the kids had taken them as mementoes of their mother. All that remained on top of the dressers were bottles of pills and jars of ointments and creams, unused nursing supplies and rolls and rolls of sterile gauze.

Jared pulled open drawers and rummaged through closets until he found Abby's jewelry case. It was the same one she'd had all through their marriage, originally belonging to an aunt or a grandmother. The outer leather was worn smooth with time. Inside, it was a riotous mixture of colorful costume pieces and pieces of gold and valuable gems. Jared found two diamond rings and was surprised to discover how well he knew just which ring was the ring he'd selected for Abby when they'd gotten engaged. If he'd been asked to describe it blind, he wouldn't have been able to do it. But seeing it now, holding it, the ring was as familiar to him as if he himself had worn it throughout their marriage.

Now he recalled their engagement day perfectly. It had been in the late fall. They were both still living in New York City, this was back when Jared was trying his luck at directing one-hour movies for television – when the medium was in its infancy and not taken too seriously by the powers in Hollywood. Yet for Jared, television was a chance for steady work. He was given a free hand and the shows he directed were hard-hitting, creative dramas. They quickly caught the country's imagination and Jared suddenly found himself with an excess of cash for the first time in his life. He knew he was headed for the top, that it was just a question of time.

He bought Abby an engagement ring on credit in a small expensive shop on Fifth Avenue, then sprang for dinner at the Russian Tea Room. Of course Abby had known something was up – they usually dined at coffee shops. She wore the same simple black dress she always wore because she didn't have others to choose from, but she wore her hair up, and she'd borrowed a string of pearls and a black cloth coat from her mother. It had a fur trimmed collar and made the then twenty-year-old Abby look sophisticated and grown-up.

When he proposed to her over dinner and she accepted without pausing, without even a moment's hesitation, it was the happiest night of Jared's entire life. It beat even the thrill of winning his first Oscar because his engagement to Abby had been about promise and hope, there'd been nothing contrived or political about it.

Jared left Abby's ring in the jewelry case and pocketed the ring that had been his mother's. That was the ring he would give to Lillie. It was graceful, tiny, understated; it would probably fit Lillie's slender finger and she'd never suspect he was giving it to her because he couldn't afford to buy a brand new one. But once they were officially engaged, once the announcement made the rounds of gossipmongers and entertainment news channels, his future, for the time being, would be back on solid ground. The success now aimed at Lillie would spill over and become Jared's success, as well.

* * *

L illie's small designer handbag was beeping discreetly in her lap. Someone had left another message on her cell phone. She hadn't even heard it ringing. She'd been lost in conversation with Darrel Jeeves, a director who worked primarily in New York. He'd flown out to Los Angeles just to meet with her. After an hour of lighthearted banter at the most visible table in Arie's, the trendiest new restaurant in town, Darrel was finally getting around to pitching Lillie his project.

'It's sophisticated, smart, subtle. There's humor, not over the top, just enough to keep it flowing, to give it movement. I know you'd be perfect for the part of Reina. She's born and raised in New York, the finest schools, a good family, etc. She's married to a rich guy who works in television but she's starting to question things, her life, her choices, yahdah, yahdah, yahdah. The usual, "is my life too superficial"? She suspects her husband is having affairs with other women, younger, professional, blah blah blah. The twist is that she accidentally kills one of her husband's lovers – poison – at a dinner party she's throwing, and that's where the comedy really kicks in. Turns out the poison was meant for her. You see, her husband is trying to dump her without the added cost of alimony.'

Lillie was losing interest in the pitch. She was more curious about the phone message beeping in her handbag. Darrel was a hot, sought after director with a proven track record, but she couldn't picture herself as Reina, at least not yet. She didn't want to be in a lousy marriage, poisoning anybody, regardless of whether or not it was meant to be a comedy. She wanted something with a little more love in it.

She took the script anyway. 'I'll read it. I'll think it over,' she promised him. And then she cut the meeting short. In the front seat of her racy red convertible, the bright L.A. sunshine beating down on her, she played Jared's message. It sounded like he had a project, too. Something was definitely up.

Before returning his call, Lillie stopped in at her favorite boutique on Rodeo Drive. Jared was in the mood to be romantic – a rare mood for him these days. Lillie decided it called for a new dress. Something he hadn't seen her in before. She chose a sheer black lace cocktail dress. It was off the shoulder with a flattering empire waist, and it set her back more than two grand. But she wasn't worried. She could afford it.

Understandably, Jared hadn't been himself since before Abby had passed away – since the strange night of the Awards, frankly. Lillie had been patient, though, and it seemed as if now he was finally coming around. With a blissful smile on her face, she dropped eight hundred dollars on a new pair of shoes to go with the new dress, and then five hundred dollars more on a handbag to go with the shoes.

When she arrived back home, she called Jared.

'Good news!' he barked at her. 'John Shay's got a love story this time, and a part in it that's perfect for you!'

Lillie couldn't believe it – this was good news. 'Jared, honey, how did you find out?'

'I got it straight from the horse's mouth. We'll talk more about it at dinner. I'll give you all the details. But it's off the record for now, if you know what I mean. I can tell you the title, though, The World I Could Give. Now how does that strike you? Of course, it's just the working title. We'll probably change it.'

'The World I Could Give.' Lillie repeated the title again. Something about it struck a chord with her. The words resonated in her mind, like a memory fleeing or a barely recalled dream; it moved her. 'Can you at least give me a clue what it's about?'

'No,' Jared replied. 'I can't – I won't. Not right now, later. Besides, I have something else I want to discuss with you at dinner, too. You got my message, right? Wear something pretty. Not that you don't always look pretty, sweetheart. Just that tonight I want things to be a little extra special. Memorable, you know.'

'Sure, honey. I just bought a little something. I think it'll fit the occasion perfectly.'

Excited by the prospects of working on another John Shay project, Lillie frittered away the remainder of the afternoon, daydreaming about an epic love story. This time, she told herself, she'd make an effort to spend a little time with John, to get to know him finally and not be so absorbed in her work.

She congratulated herself on her intuition. I knew there was a reason I didn't want to work with Darrel Jeeves right now, she thought. Maybe I'll make a trip to New York anyway. I'll drop in on John and see how the book's shaping up – if he'll let me.

Lillie couldn't deny it, she had hoped she'd be the one John would have called first when there was news that another novel was on its way to completion. Their phone conversation had been brief, yet to her it had sounded genuine. Now it seemed as though John's novel had been much farther along than he'd let on over the phone. But the truth was that Hollywood was still predominantly a men's club. Perhaps to a man like John Shay, Jared seemed more like a player than Lillie did. She would have to give that idea some thought; how to appear more like a player – someone in the industry who could get things done. True, she was only twenty-eight, but at least she had an Oscar to her credit. She was determined to make that count for something.

CHAPTER SEVEN

A t eight o'clock that evening, Lillie and Jared met at the bar in Salvatore's.

Jared's face lit up when he saw her make her entrance in the black lace dress. She was wearing the diamond earrings he'd bought for her, too – he was still paying on those diamonds; he'd probably be paying on them for the rest of his life. 'Honey, you outdid yourself. You look fantastic.'

Although she didn't come out and say it, secretly she agreed. 'I feel fantastic,' was all she admitted to.

Salvatore's prided itself on catering to the strictly A-list crowd, a crowd who was not easily impressed with anyone beside themselves. Still, all eyes were on Lillie Diver and Jared Warren as they were led through the dining room to a secluded table in a romantic corner. The room was buzzing.

Jared ordered a bottle of the restaurant's best champagne. 'We're celebrating,' he explained to the waiter, confident that the waiter would pass the information along.

'So, what is it?' Lillie asked when the waiter was out of earshot. She was unable to contain her curiosity a moment longer. 'You have an announcement to make, I can tell.'

'It's not an announcement. It's a proposal.'

'A proposal? What, a business proposition? Is this about John Shay?' She grew more excited by the minute.

'No, it's about you and me. It's a proposal.'

Lillie looked at him blankly, waiting for him to continue.

'You know, marriage?'

'Marriage?' She still didn't follow.

'You and me, Lillie. It's time for us to get married.'

When it finally penetrated Lillie's brain, what it was Jared was actually saying, she was stopped cold. It was hardly the type of marriage proposal she had always envisioned. 'You make it sound as if you have an agenda for the evening and that was the first item on your list.'

Jared laughed uneasily. 'I'm sorry, sweetheart. It came out all wrong. I was going to at least wait until the champagne was poured.' He fished in his pocket for the ring and held it out to her. 'This was my mother's,' he said. 'I want you to have it. If it doesn't fit, then we'll go to plan B.'

In silence, Lillie took the ring and slid it easily on her finger. Funny, she'd never thought of Jared as having had parents. He'd always seemed as if he'd been born a parent himself.

'It looks good on you, sweetheart. I know it's a simple ring, but you have very delicate hands.'

'It all seems so sudden. I mean, I've been waiting for this moment for six years already, but it still seems sudden. What is your family going to think? Abby's only been gone a month – barely.'

'My kids know I want to make some changes. To be honest, I even have the house up for sale.'

'You're selling the house? After all these years?' This was another shock. She'd taken it for granted she would live there one day, long after Abby was gone, as the second Mrs. Jared Warren. She knew that Jared loved that house in Bel Air.

'It was a great house to raise the kids in, to do the whole family thing, but all that's behind me now.'

'Behind you? But what about us? I want to have kids, too, Jared.'

This was something he hadn't counted on – an unexpected astronomical expense, raising another kid in Bel Air. He had grandchildren he couldn't afford, for chrissakes. 'Well, we'll cross that bridge when we get to it. Besides, wouldn't you rather have a house we could call our own – a place to start fresh, no ghosts? Maybe even your house – what's wrong with your place?'

She had never considered it. It was a nice house, the one she'd bought in the Hollywood Hills, but to her, it had never been more than a stopping off place, the place where she'd decided to live while she waited for her relationship with Jared to become permanent. 'I guess it would be okay,' she admitted reluctantly.

The waiter came back with the champagne. As he poured it, Lillie stared at the ring on her finger. It was a lovely ring. It suited her. This unexpected sentimental side of him touched her. 'I love it, Jared,' she said. 'I really do.'

'So your answer is yes, then?'

'Of course it's yes. It's been yes since the day I met you. I love you, Jared. You know that.'

'I'll tell you, sweetheart, sometimes I don't know anything.'

*   *   *

John had more trouble than usual getting to sleep, but he was determined to deal with it. He refused to let his progress get derailed. He'd find a place in the farthest recesses of his heart,

119

store away this awful news and never dwell on it again.

But how would he finish the book that way? His love letter to Lillie – he couldn't leave it hanging like this, unfinished, like a wide open wound. He had to rescue it from the call of oblivion, it was still a worthy project. He had to ignore this urge to abandon it. This wasn't the end of the world. So what? A movie star he'd become infatuated with was engaged to be married. It happened all the time and thousands of deluded fans were left a little heartbroken and then life went on. Lillie was a dream that had gotten him through a few very tough months. But that's all it had been – a dream.

Still, what a comforting dream it had been. And it had given birth to a very promising novel. He could sublimate it somehow, couldn't he? He knew he had it in him. He could take this jarring news from Jared Warren and turn the book into something even more stirring than what he'd originally intended. Because now he had the pathos of an aching heart to add to the mix. After all, if anyone could take a heartache and turn it into a work of art that could sustain the imaginations of generations to come, it was Johnny Shay.

But art aside, it was a bitter disappointment.

Granted, he barely knew Lillie Diver, had only met her on a handful of social occasions. Still, she hadn't seemed the type to marry a man like Jared Warren. She was above his calculated callousness, wasn't she? There was more to her than business, whereas Jared Warren was nothing but business.

Maybe she saw a side of the legendary director that outsiders weren't able to discern. That happened often enough in relationships.

Still… Lillie Diver and Jared Warren together in holy matrimony? Nothing about it made sense to John, but then he was reasoning with his heart and his heart was nothing if not flawed.

She's half my age anyway, he tried to console himself. What would a woman like Lillie Diver want with a man like me? Most of my life is behind me, my success. I've been there and done that. She has her whole life ahead of her. Her world is just getting underway.

But wait, that didn't make sense! John turned over restlessly in his bed and punched his pillow. Jared Warren is even older than I am!

What was it about that guy, he wondered, that held such an attraction for a woman like Lillie? She had youth, success, money, beauty. But obviously, there was still a missing piece, a piece that she thought a man like Jared Warren could give her. John had to get to the bottom of it. He'd put his fertile imagination to work and then take what he'd learned and put it in his book. He would make love to Lillie that way; by painting a portrait of her life and making it perfect, fill in that missing piece, give it grace and rhyme and meaning.

The way God would want life to be lived, John decided; if God didn't have to leave the living of life up to mere mortals, that is.

As he drifted to sleep at last, John realized he was no less infatuated with Lillie Diver than he'd been before. It would take more than an engagement to cut off his feelings for her, as irrational as they might be. He'd take his love letter of a book, and write it with even more determination. But now instead of an invitation to love, it would be a gift to Lillie, and a wish for her happiness. Marriage could still be that for people – a gift of happiness. For a time, it had been just that for Amanda and him. And some day, when he got over this childish fixation with a movie star, he'd find somebody to love and it would be that way for him again, too.

* * *

More champagne, sweetheart?'
'No, honey, I'm driving. And so are you, remember?'
'Lillie, you're so practical.' Jared put the half-empty bottle

back in the ice bucket. 'So what do you say? Should we go to your place and finish celebrating?'

Lillie tossed her napkin onto the table. 'No,' she said. 'I want to see your place. I've never been there, Jared, and I've always wanted to see it. Now that it's up for sale, I guess I don't have much time left, do I?'

'It's not too impressive anymore. I've sold off most of the furniture, everything I didn't absolutely need.'

'You sold your furniture?'

'I'm trying to streamline my life, honey. I look on it as starting over.'

They left in their respective cars and drove out to Jared's house in Bel Air.

Abby's death must have cut him to the quick, Lillie thought as she followed closely behind Jared's car. Why else would he suddenly want to get rid of everything? He was trying to erase the reminders, the memories. He can't take it, she decided; all the heartache.

Lillie had never seen this side of Jared before. She wondered if it was the best time for him to be getting engaged. He wasn't thinking clearly yet.

'So we're engaged,' she said softly to herself. 'That doesn't mean we have to get married right away. I've waited six years already. I can wait a little longer.'

The two cars pulled up the long front drive and at the end of it, Jared's huge house loomed in darkness. It seemed strangely unlived in to Lillie, Jared hadn't left a single light on.

'Well, here we are at last,' she announced good naturedly, getting out of her car. 'The fabled mansion in Bel Air.'

Jared unlocked the front door and escorted her inside. He switched on the light in the foyer. It was an impressive crystal chandelier and it shone down on a marble floor, but there wasn't a stick of furniture around. It made the foyer seem enormous.

He led her into the living room where there was a couch, a table, and a single upholstered chair, all of them dwarfed by the cathedral ceiling. A fieldstone fireplace took up the entire length of one wall, and a built in wet bar took up another. What appeared to be a breathtaking picture window was hidden behind closed drapes. The room felt cold and cavernous.

'Are you planning to move out tomorrow, or something? This is kind of creepy, Jared. It doesn't feel like anybody lives here.'

'Nobody does, really.'

'What do you mean, honey?'

'I have the study, I work in there. And then I have my room upstairs, but I don't sleep. I have terrible insomnia these days. Truthfully, I can't wait to get out of this place.'

Loss, that's what this is, Lillie realized as she looked around the lifeless room, a terrible emotional loss.

And she'd been too self-involved to realize the scope of it. How foolish she'd been. She'd occupied her hours, her years, with the endless waiting, forgetting that he was a man who'd been married to the same steadfast woman for thirty-five years. He'd probably only become attracted to Lillie out of despair and denial, not realizing he was already grieving for Abby, even while her actual death was still six years away.

Why hadn't she been able to see it until now? She'd been too involved with her own heart, her own career. 'Jared, I'm so sorry. Should we go to my place? I guess I didn't understand what you've been going through, but I think I do now.'

He sighed and smiled. 'It's okay. We're here already. Why don't I show you around?'

'Are you sure you want to?'

'I'm sure.'

He gave her the grand tour of his near-empty house. The formal dining room that had once held a table large enough to comfortably seat twenty-two. The kitchen, twice the size of her own, with two built-in refrigerators and a stand-alone freezer. A breakfast room, complete with bay windows and an upholstered window-seat looking out over the pool area. The legendary gym – at least he hadn't sold off any of his equipment yet. He showed her his study next, where allegedly great deals were made. It was a handsome room with a fireplace and another built-in bar. They went past the Sick Room. That door stayed closed. The spacious, carpeted family room still had a large television set in it but not much else – another fieldstone fireplace along one wall. Lillie could almost feel the family that had grown up in that room. How many childhoods had been spent in front of that TV set, counting the children and now the grandchildren? Even as an empty room, its grandeur was a far cry from the apartment Lillie had grown up in Mountville.

Then there was the upstairs. Six bedrooms, each with its own private bath. Most of the rooms were empty. Jared's room, however, still had a full bedroom suite and a king-sized bed.

'So this is it,' Lillie said almost reverently. 'I've always tried to picture it, your bed, the place where you sleep at night.'

'Or don't sleep, as the case may be.'

'Oh, Jared…'

'Come on,' he encouraged her, taking her hand. 'Let's at least sit down on it. We're supposed to be celebrating our engagement, remember?'

'Are you sure you want to go through with this?'

'Go through with what?'

She sat down next to him a little reluctantly. 'The marriage, Jared. Are you sure you want to do that? I mean, wouldn't you rather just stay in this magnificent house, get your furniture back, grow old with your family around you? And we could just take it slow. We could go on like before.'

'Not on your life, kiddo. I have no intentions of sitting around, growing old.'

'I didn't mean it like that. You had so much here with Abby. Something doesn't feel right, letting it all go like this. It's obviously been your show place. You've prospered here for such a long time.'

'And it's time to move on, Lillie. I couldn't be happier letting this place go. I want to sell it, don't you see that? I need the change.'

'You can make changes without having to get married right away.'

'Don't give me a heart attack, Lillie!'

The abrasiveness of his tone startled her.

'I've been planning on this,' he went on, nearly shouting. 'I want to marry you. I want us to be together. For chrissakes, it's gone on like this too long. Weren't you always the one harping about getting married? Harping about Abby? Well, here we are, free to get married. After all this, don't tell me you've changed your mind?'

She didn't want to lose her temper. He was going through a tough emotional time. 'I just, well, I didn't want you to feel pressured, that's all. I see now that maybe I was being unfair and I was pressuring you. Of course I still want to get married.'

'Good. Then that's settled. You want to make love?'

Lillie couldn't believe her ears. 'Do I want to make love? Right now? Are you serious?'

'Of course I'm serious.'

'Isn't that switching gears a bit? Doesn't it feel a little awkward?'

'You wanted to come here.'

'I know, but I wasn't expecting it to feel like a tomb – I'm sorry,' she added quickly. 'I didn't mean it to come out like that.'

Jared suddenly sounded tired. 'Apology accepted, honey, don't worry. It is like a tomb around here. Come on. Let's go downstairs. We'll get a drink, we'll relax. We'll see where it leads us. If you feel like making love, we'll make love. If you don't, then we won't. How does that sound?'

'Much more sane.' Lillie followed him back downstairs.

In the living room, Jared summoned the enthusiasm to build a fire in the fireplace. 'It's for effect only,' he assured her. 'In southern California, I've very rarely needed to light a fire to keep warm.'

Then they turned out the light and had a drink by the fire, both of them privately wondering if they would in fact make love. It had been a month since they'd last been together.

'By the way,' he began, noticing Lillie's face – by the firelight, it looked even more exquisite. 'You were right, that comment you made earlier over the phone; that is the perfect little outfit for this occasion. The night Abby and I got engaged, she sensed it was coming. Did you guess you were getting engaged tonight?'

'No. In fact, it was the furthest thing from my mind. I thought we would be celebrating something to do with John Shay.'

Jared felt a twinge in his gut. It reminded him to keep track of the lies he'd told. The twinge was a survival skill – one that had become quite keen as his career in Hollywood had evolved. 'Yes,' he said. 'John Shay. The new novel, the love story.'

'The World I Could Give… I wonder what it's about? How much has he told you, Jared? I'm dying to know. I've got such a good feeling about this.'

'Well, you know, I'm not at liberty to say. I made a promise. I take it he's still negotiating with the publisher or something. I don't think the book is finished yet.'

'And he called you to tell you about it! He's home now, back in New York?'

'No, he's still in that place, whatever it's called. He's got another month or so to go.'

'You're kidding? He's still in the Lindegaard? And he called you from there?'

'Well, he called collect, so of course I knew it was important.'

Lillie sipped her cognac and gazed into the fire, her anticipation growing. 'And he said there was a part in it for me? Jared, he must have told you something about it! I'm going crazy, tell me.'

'Give it some time, honey; he made me promise. Look, why don't we wait until the book is done and then we'll read it over together – this part that was meant for you.'

'I can't wait that long, at least give me a hint!'

'My lips are sealed and that's final, sweetie.'

In the back of her mind, Lillie decided she would call John Shay herself. She'd wait a few days, maybe she'd even wait until he'd been released and sent home – she'd play it at least a little cool. She could get his number in New York. She knew plenty of people. She'd find a way to get in touch with him and then feel him out for details. She'd just have to wait another month.

'Now, where was I before you took me on that little John Shay detour?' Jared asked. 'I think I was telling you how beautiful you look tonight.'

'Yes, I believe you were.'

'Would you like another cognac?'

'Not yet. I still have plenty.'

'Well, I'll bring the bottle over here. In case we don't feel like getting up later.'

As he walked over to the bar, she sensed what was on his mind now. He wanted to make love to her, here in front of the fire. Something about him just didn't add up tonight. He seemed unpredictable, and that was very unlike Jared Warren. Maybe grief was doing it to him. Grief did so many unexpected things to people. When her mother died, Lillie knew she was grieving the loss, but she didn't realize until years later how crazy it had made her behave. That whole fiasco with Sam Kincaid, she'd done that out of grief. If only she could wipe that slate clean. But if it hadn't happened, she wouldn't have run away to New York the way she had – suddenly deciding to become an actress, of all things. And who knows, maybe she wouldn't even have her career now.

'A penny for your thoughts,' Jared said, sitting down next to her on the carpet. He poured her a little more cognac and took some for himself.

'To be honest,' she said, 'I was thinking about grief, about when my mother died.'

'Well let's move right off that topic, shall we? There's never a shortage of time for grieving in life. And never enough time for making love.' He kissed her while the taste of cognac was fresh on her lips.

Lillie slipped off her shoes and got more comfortable, cuddling up to Jared. 'I've missed you,' she said. 'It's been hard having to stay away.'

'I know, but it's all behind us now. We can bring our relationship out in the open.'

'As if we were ever fooling anybody,' she said quietly.

'Who cares, honey? We tried. We made the best of it and now our turn has come.'

Our turn, Lillie liked the sound of that. With a little faith and perseverance, things had a way of working out in life, didn't they? Her career had taken an important turn, she had the freedom to make the kind of choices she couldn't have dreamed of making a year or so ago. And even though that was an exhilarating feeling, the thing she'd longed for most in life had finally come to pass, too. She and Jared were engaged. Soon enough, she could give up acting altogether and raise the family she really wanted. Jared was the one who loved the industry with so much passion, not Lillie. It wasn't going to bother her a bit to take a back seat to his career, to let him go out and keep making all his money since it seemed to be what he thrived on, while she'd concentrate on making a real home for the first time in her life.

'Is it terrible to say that I feel so incredibly happy right now?'

'Why would it be terrible to feel happy?' he asked.

Lillie put her arms around him. 'I feel like my happiness has come at Abby's expense.'

'Don't think that way. She was ill before I even met you. You had nothing to with it.' Jared lightly brushed Lillie's hair from her face. The diamond earrings glinted in the firelight. They would have to find a project soon, he told himself; a real blockbuster. There wouldn't be time to wait on John Shay to finish some nebulous novel. It would be better to get something going right away.

Lillie slipped her off-the-shoulder dress farther down her shoulders, down her arms, letting her breasts come out, exposing them to the firelight.

'Perfect,' he said quietly. 'You've got the prettiest tits in Hollywood, you know that? We could make a fortune off those tits alone.'

'Jared! What thing to say.' Lillie laughed in spite of herself.

As if her tits were suddenly too perfect to last, Jared abruptly pulled her closer, right up to his face, taking one of her breasts in his mouth as if he might devour it. He sucked on it roughly, trying to drain at least a drop of his salvation from it.

Lillie mistook this minor assault for a rush of lust, not for the desperation it actually was. She responded to Jared's rough advances with passion. Hiking her expensive new dress feverishly around her hips, she straddled his lap; letting him devour her, holding his head close, her fingers digging into his silver hair.

As he twisted her tender nipple with his mouth, she felt on fire for him. The bulge growing in his lap was jammed up against the crotch of her silky panties. She pressed her mound hard against him, riding the bulge, urging him on.

Jared's tired back soon ached from the weight of her in his lap. He laid back on the carpeting instead and fumbled with his zipper. 'Are you ready to fuck?' he said coarsely.

'I'm ready to fuck,' she baited him in reply.

When his cock was standing out straight from his open fly, Lillie pulled aside the soaking crotch of her panties, and then lowered herself down on him.

His cock slid straight up and filled her. She let out a whimper, her hole stretching around the cock to accommodate him.

The view was fantastic. Jared contented himself with a few well placed thrusts of his hips, otherwise he let Lillie do the work. He watched her supple, half-undressed body writhe to the furious rhythm of fucking, her gorgeous tits dead center in his vision. He watched them bounce and swing and tremble, the length of his cock delving repeatedly up that snug, hot passage hidden in the center of those undulating hips.

She leaned down over him, her tits in his face, the stiff nipples grazing lightly over his skin.

Her ass lifted slightly. It was perfect for grabbing onto now. Jared held on tight and he worked his cock vigorously in and out of that tight, mysterious hole. He never got tired of having his cock up in there. Her tits in his face taunted him. She smelled so pretty. He grabbed her ass more firmly and fucked her hole with all his power.

Oh God, she was crying out. God. There was a rhythm to her cries, it matched the rhythm of his cock. He fucked her harder, feeling like the head of his fat cock was punching up into her voice box; his cock was hitting her button, 'Oh! Oh! Oh!' the cries kept coming out like little stabs of sound. She was steadying herself on her elbows. Her arms surrounding his head, her soft fat tits pressed against his face as her cries increased. Now she was whimpering, 'Yes, yes, yes!' and he felt the trigger in his balls, the trigger that unloaded the rush of fire through his cock.

'Shit,' he cried, realizing in a burst of sobering consciousness that he'd forgotten to put on a condom. 'Up, up, get up,' he said urgently. 'I'm coming.'

And he let himself shoot all over the front of his unzipped trousers, hoping to God that there wouldn't be another mouth to feed anytime soon.

*   *   *

Hours later, Lillie and Jared lay entwined together upstairs in his king-sized bed. The cognac had gone to Lillie's head and she was drifting sweetly to sleep.

Jared, however, was wide awake, his mind chasing its proverbial tail, as it always did these days. Thinking, always thinking, and resisting the urge to scream.

CHAPTER EIGHT

From a secluded table at Salvatore's straight to God's ears; the news of a diamond ring having passed between Jared Warren and Lillie Diver at an intimate champagne dinner was all over the tabloid news by the following day.

Lillie drove herself home mid-morning, and then Jared sat in his study alone, waiting for the phone to ring. And ring, it did. He let his voice mail answer every call, not wanting to appear too eager, not wanting to seem as if he were sitting by the phone.

In lieu of having a family to break the good news to, Lillie called Eduardo and announced her engagement. He was suitably impressed, gushing in his characteristic way, 'My princess! At last, the final act of the fairy tale we have all been waiting for! And who do we suppose will be doing our hair and make-up at this larger than life wedding?'

Eduardo was off and running with plans, ideas, advice. He seemed blithely indifferent to the fact that the happy couple hadn't set a date yet.

When Jared retrieved the first batch of voice messages, he was dismayed to learn that most of them were from family members who were saddened, outraged, or hurt by both the suddenness of this momentous decision and by being left out of the loop.

The message from Gracie, in particular, cut like a knife. She was obviously crying. 'Mommy hasn't been gone a month and you're already getting married again? To some girl who's barely older than I am? And I have to hear about it on the car radio? Daddy, what's the matter with you? How could you do this to us?'

With any luck, Jared hoped he would never have to actually explain why he was doing it. Methodically, he deleted all the messages that had nothing to do with work.

By evening, a call came through that perked his spirits. It sounded right up his alley. The actor, Jake Brown, had a promising action vehicle with no director attached yet and a leading female role that would be ideal for Lillie. It would make a great summer movie. This would give Jared and Lillie time to take that extended vacation together on his boat, and maybe even get married while they were at it, then be back in California in plenty of time for pre-production on the film. Most important of all, Jared knew the production company who'd signed on to the project. They were a solid company with a good track record. The budget was likely to be huge.

Jared picked up the phone to call Lillie. 'How about that vacation I promised? Are you up for it?'

'You mean on the boat?'

'I mean on the boat. I'll round up a small but able crew and we can be off, just the two of us. Perhaps we can put in at a few key ports and throw little engagement parties here and there. How does that strike you?'

'Like heaven,' she replied excitedly.

Jared hoped that he sounded suitably romantic and not as if he were trying to escape from disapproving family members, or shielding Lillie from the imminent announcement of the deal he was negotiating for them with Jake Brown. He would discuss that with Lillie onboard the boat, when he had her undivided attention.

'We can fly to Miami tomorrow. From there, I can make a few calls, get the crew together and have the boat ready to hit the open seas by the end of the week. Is that 'whirlwind' enough for you, sweetheart?'

'As they say, I started packing the day we met, my love.'

* * *

John Shay flew into JFK with very little fanfare. Selena was back at school and Amanda was kind enough to make the trip in from Connecticut to meet John's plane.

She was waiting for him outside of the customs area. 'It was the least I could do,' she said. 'After all, I was the one who set you off on this grand journey to Copenhagen.'

They collected his bags at the baggage claim area and then Amanda began the long trek out to John's Long Island estate.

'I'm more than halfway done with a new novel,' he told her in the car.

'John, that's wonderful news. I'm so happy to hear that.'

'It's a love story. A bit of an epic, I'm afraid.'

'Those are the best kind.'

When they reached John's house, Amanda helped him bring his bags inside. She introduced John to the caretaker she'd hired in his absence, and then they did a quick trip to the grocery store together. Signs of spring were everywhere.

'I hope you're going to be okay, John. It'll probably feel funny being back at the house again. If you need any help, any recommendations in finding a counselor or something along those lines, let us know, okay? And don't be surprised by the bar, John. I had everything cleared out. Not that I didn't trust you to do it on your own, I just thought it would be more merciful to have it done while you were gone. You should consider having that bar turned into a second kitchen or something. Anything to keep you from thinking about booze every time you want to watch a movie or entertain people.'

As usual, John thought she was being very decent, but he spared her the sentiment. 'I've got the novel to think about,' he said. 'I should be all right for now.'

'Well, I sure hope so. Don't forget to call Selena at school and let her know you got home safe, okay? She's waiting to hear from you.'

'I won't forget,' he promised her.

She had a long ride home ahead of her, so she left after they had a quick bite to eat.

Steve Swenson was the caretaker Amanda had hired. He was young, capable, smart; he had the air of a park ranger about him. John liked Steve Swenson on sight and decided to keep him on at the estate indefinitely. This way, John could concentrate solely on finishing the book.

The house did feel strange. Everything about the place seemed almost too familiar, as if maybe he were revisiting it from a past life rather than simply returning home from a few months overseas. There were still traces of Jacqueline in some of the rooms. John wondered what had become of her, why she'd left so abruptly. He figured he'd had a lot to do with it, yet he doubted he'd ever remember what it was he'd actually done that had prompted her to leave in such an apparent hurry.

John's body was still on Denmark time. The sun had barely set when he felt like collapsing. He made a quick call to Selena at her school in Connecticut. Then he took a shower and got into bed.

One day at home without a drink, he told himself.

He switched off the light, and then fell into a deep sleep.

The following day, John called a temp agency in search of a typist who could enter all his many scraps of paper that comprised his new novel into a file on his computer.

The agency sent over a young girl who was soon going to graduate from the local high school. Her name was Trina. Quiet and serious, Trina was the fastest typist John had ever come across. And she was good at translating his chicken-scrawl handwriting into words that actually made sense.

Trina's career goal, once she graduated high school, was to become an Administrative Assistant, she'd said. John didn't think she'd have any trouble succeeding at her goal in spades, and he told her so.

It took Trina less than a week of working after school to complete John's file. On her last day of work in John's home, the quiet, serious Trina became uncharacteristically bold.

'I know who you are,' she confessed to him. 'You're John Shay, that writer. I've read some of your books.'

John was impressed. He wasn't aware that anyone under the age of thirty-five read any of his novels anymore.

'You won an Oscar for that movie Lillie Diver was in, didn't you?'

'Yes, I did,' he said. 'Are you a Lillie Diver fan?'

Trina flushed. 'Of course, who isn't? She's so beautiful.'

'I doubt she can type as fast as you can, though.'

Trina laughed. 'You've met her, I bet?'

'Yes, a few times, but I can't say I really know her.'

'I think this new book you're writing would make a great movie.

And Lillie could be in it. She'd be perfect for the role of Ruth, don't you think? It would be ten times better than Master of the Storm. Not that I didn't like that, because I did. It's just that this new one you're writing is so much better and it could easily be for Lillie Diver, don't you think?'

It was John's turn to feel flushed. 'Yes,' he admitted. 'I suppose so.' He suddenly felt transparent. Out of the mouths of babes, he warned himself.

'I have friends who went all the way to Mountville to see where Lillie grew up. Everyone in Mountville knows her. And you know what? She was kind of poor. The place where she lived was really run down. My friends took pictures of it and I saw them. Not the inside, because people are living there, but the outside of the building. They took pictures of that.'

John found Trina's conversation quite interesting. 'Mountville, huh? That's pretty far north, isn't it?'

'Yes, they get an awful lot of snow up there.'

John made a mental note to research Mountville. Maybe he'd make his own pilgrimage there and get some clues into Lillie Diver, who she really was, get some ideas for the book.

A few days later, after John had had time to acclimate himself to being back home, free from the constant monitoring of staff members and security guards, he told Steve Swenson he was going to take a little day trip.

'It might turn into an overnight trip,' he went on. 'I'm driving all the way to Mountville. I need to do some research for my new book.'

Steve assured him that he had everything under control. After all, he'd been managing the estate on his own for close to four months already. 'Take your time,' Steve said. 'Everything here will be fine. And hey,' he added. 'Don't forget, I'll be here around the clock. Don't hesitate to call if you need to, you know? Like if you're feeling like taking a drink alone up there in Mountville or something.'

As John went upstairs to throw some things into an overnight bag, he wondered just what kind of a caretaker Amanda had hired for him, but he let it go. He preferred to continue thinking of Steve Swenson as a friendly park ranger type, not as an alcoholism crisis counselor in disguise.

It was a good five hours of non-stop driving before John made it to the Mountville city limits. 'Mountville Welcomes You!' a sign read, followed by, 'Fasten Your Seat Belts – It's the Law!' Underneath that, another sign was tacked to the same metal pole: 'Fine for Littering $100, Keep Mountville Beautiful!'

The town had a pronounced New England feel to it. Small, neat streets laid out on a grid that ultimately led to the town square. Dotting the distance, the spires of churches from various denominations could be seen peeking up through the hills and the tops of trees. Spring was coming a little more slowly to Mountville than it had to Long Island. Green buds were in abundance, but nothing was yet in bloom.

John drove through the streets of the city proper, taking in the small shops, watching the people. He made a note of where the library was, but kept driving, past the railroad tracks – that old-fashioned reminder that there was a less desirable side of Mountville, just like in any other town.

Here, John found brick and clapboard buildings that were given over to decay. There was an old boarded up movie house that had probably never had a heyday. There was a run down school with a crumbling concrete schoolyard. If Lillie had indeed grown up poor, he wondered if this is where she might have gone to school. This was clearly the only poor section of tiny Mountville.

He drove back toward the center of town, looking for an office of public records. When he found it, he discovered that it was only open on Wednesdays from noon to five. This being Thursday, he made do with the local library.

A classic Greek revival structure, the library had one state of the art computer, but most of the old town records were still on micro-fiche. The librarian set John up in a small dark room. It smelled musty and reminded him of a schoolroom from the nineteen forties, or even earlier.

Scrolling through the micro-fiche, under the name of Diver, John quickly discovered that Lillie's mother had been named Sarah but was called Sally and that she had died from a prolonged illness in the county hospital when she was just forty years old.

A local newspaper article from seventeen years before that, announced the birth of Sally's daughter, Lillie. Strangely, there was no mention of a father's name.

Why had Sally done that? John wondered. If a baby had been born out of wedlock, especially back then, it was unusual to announce the birth in the local papers. He decided that for some reason, Sally had wanted the town to know about the birth of her baby girl.

There was nothing else on the micro-fiche about the Divers and John wondered what even smaller town Sally had probably come from.

He left the library and made his way two streets south to the town's only hotel. There, he booked himself a room for the night.

The hotel, not to his surprise, was outdated to the point of being almost charming. His room was modest but comfortable. There was a phone, a TV, and a private bath, but beyond that, there were no amenities to speak of.

The nights that far north were still quite cold. By eight o'clock in the evening, the steam heat was hissing up through the radiator.

John lay on the bed and thought about Lillie growing up poor in an isolated town like Mountville. He would make inquiries about her the following morning. Doubtless everyone in town would be willing to tell an anecdote about their local girl-made-good, especially a star as famous as Lillie Diver had become.

Early the next morning, John ventured to a nearby coffee shop for breakfast. He could tell immediately that he was marked an unwelcome stranger when he stepped foot through the door. The few people drinking coffee at the counter had probably been doing just that for decades and were accustomed to recognizing everyone who frequented the small establishment. They eyed John uneasily.

He sat down and ordered two eggs with toast, bacon, potatoes and a cup of black coffee. He decided it would work against him if he let on that he was a writer, so instead he passed himself off as an overly zealous fan of Lillie Diver's who'd come to town in search of stories or memorabilia relating to his all-time favorite movie star.

It did the trick. The locals who had started out tight-lipped and unfriendly became talkative to the point of overload. John wasn't sure if he could keep all their stories straight. But he was given directions to the cemetery where Sally was buried.

'She was an out and out drunk, y'know, sad to say. She didn't start out that way.'

'Not-a-toll,' chimed in another. 'She was a real beauty in the early days.'

'But drinking drove her crazy. That's why they locked her up, y'know. At that county hospital over on the Wahassee Highway, ask anybody, they can direct you there if you want to see it.'

'A gothic monstrosity, that hospital is.'

John interrupted the gaggle of gossipers. 'Lillie's mother was an alcoholic?'

'As bad as they come, son, sorry to say.'

'The kind that doesn't know when enough's enough.'

'Even when the money's gone,' another put in. 'I heard she sold Lillie's winter coat one Christmas just to get her hands on another bottle of booze.'

'And they had her committed for it, for her alcoholism?'

'Well, y'know son, folks back then, at least around here, couldn't go to those fancy places you find nowadays – rehabs, they call 'em – unless they had piles of money.'

'The kind of money that only Kincaids have around these parts.'

The scenario wasn't lost on John. Perhaps that's why Lillie had called him all the way from California the night they won the Oscars; she knew a little about lonely alcoholics going crazy.

Then John was told where to find the apartment building where Lillie had lived when she was growing up, and the school she had attended. Judging by the rough directions he was given, it was indeed the area of town he'd driven through the day before.

He wondered how to broach that most delicate question now, why there had been no mention of who Lillie's father had been in her birth announcement.

'What about Lillie's father?' he ventured. 'Is he still living, or has he died, too?'

'Now that's a good question, son.'

'As far as we know, there never was any father.'

'Clearly, she had to have a father,' John joked.

'If she had one, he didn't settle in Mountville.'

'In the old days, if there was a war on,' someone pointed out, 'and an unmarried woman turned up pregnant, why, they used to say the father was killed in action.'

'That was some action,' someone else remarked.

The comment was greeted with snide chuckling.

'Sure was. That Sally Diver was a real looker in those days.'

As the conversation degenerated into mean-spirited innuendo, John took the opportunity to pay for his breakfast. He thanked everyone for being so helpful, and then set off on his sightseeing adventure.

He found the local cemetery easily. He strolled leisurely through the winding paths, reading the various tombstones until he came upon Sally Diver's. It was a small, plain stone marker, with the dates of her birth and death etched in it. She was proclaimed a 'loving mother' and that was the end of it.

John looked upon the stone sadly. He really was a lucky man, wasn't he? He had not only the financial resources, but a family, estranged as they were, who'd cared enough to get him the best possible help. Not everybody got that lucky in life.

Then he wondered about the mystery of Lillie Diver's father. Was he buried somewhere in this cemetery, too? Was he thriving somewhere, miles away? The pieces began to fall into place in John's active imagination.

'The missing piece, in fact,' John said aloud. 'Jared Warren is a father figure. That's what their relationship is all about.'

*   *   *

Jared's private yacht was an impressive ship, still it was dwarfed by many of the other yachts off the coast of Miami. The years when he could afford the biggest and the best were at least temporarily behind him, but that didn't mean the Bonnie Anne skimped on interior luxury.

The main salon boasted an elegant dining area, an entertainment grouping that converted into extra sleeping quarters, and a lounge that comfortably seated six. The galley was better equipped than the average person's kitchen and it had an adjoining bar stocked with some of the finest cut crystal barware. There were five separate cabins and three heads – or bathrooms; all of it, save for the bathrooms, paneled in cozy, fine-grained wood veneers.

The three man crew slept in the cabins closest to the navigation room. Jared had secured a percentage of his expected earnings on the Jake Brown project in order to ready the ship and adequately pay the crew.

For years, Lillie had been hearing about the luxurious Bonnie Anne, but that hadn't prepared her for just how impressive a ship it was.

The master cabin that she shared with Jared had a queen-sized bed with matching side tables, a small separate lounging area, and a built-in vanity set that managed to feel more chic than some of the hotel suites she'd stayed in on dry land.

It didn't take long for Lillie to feel right at home.

They spent their lazy days above deck in the balmy breezes, relaxing in the sun. Their evenings were spent either gazing up at the breathtaking expanse of stars, or below deck in the intimacy of the salon with the lights kept low to enhance the already romantic atmosphere.

Privately, Lillie passed the hours dreamily planning her future in her head. Now that the time had come and she was actually engaged to be married, she found herself curiously disinterested in having a big wedding. An intimate affair, or even a quick trip to a Justice of the Peace in some out of the way town, was more to her liking, regardless of how Eduardo would respond to the idea. She knew she was too famous now to have anything less than a circus if they opted for a full-blown wedding.

Late one evening, moored off the coast of South Carolina, the water lapping rhythmically against the side of the Bonnie Anne while Lillie and Jared sat together under the quiet stars, Jared broached the subject of the wedding. He had been entertaining his own private musings about the event.

'I was thinking we should pull out all the stops,' he said. 'Go for broke, make a memorable splash out of it. After all, this'll be your first wedding.'

'My first wedding? You say it as if I'm likely to have more than one.'

'Well, let's face it sweetheart, I'm no spring chicken. Who knows, ten, twenty years from now, you may find yourself in the position of getting married again. But that's down the road. Let's not get sidetracked by morbidity.'

'Jared, I would much rather have a private ceremony, something that we can really enjoy together or with your children. Don't you think it would be more meaningful that way, after everything you've been through over the last few years?'

Jared didn't want to touch the subject of his children. They weren't likely to want to attend any wedding, be it tasteful or ostentatious. 'What have I been through,' he asked her, 'that countless other people haven't had to endure? Sadly, it's part of life. It shouldn't keep us from enjoying the time we have together, don't you think? Abby had a nice funeral, a big send-off, I didn't pinch pennies saying goodbye to her. But now that door's closed. Our wedding will have nothing to do with Abby's illness. It's not a time for mourning.'

He had a point, but still… 'I just don't want it to turn into a circus, honey. I want it to have meaning.'

'So we'll have a private ceremony, heavy on the meaning, and pull out all the stops at the reception. We'll compromise. How's that sound?'

She didn't answer. He seemed hell bent on having a full-blown media frenzy of a wedding. She wondered why; what was the attraction in it for him? After all his years in Hollywood, did he still crave attention? Maybe it had simply become a way of life for him; everything was planned with the media in mind.

She resolved to bring it up again later. There was no date set for the wedding yet, anyhow.

A feature film was in production in the movie studios in Wilmington, North Carolina. Jared and Lillie knew many of the cast and crew working on location there. So as they moved slowly up the coast, Wilmington was the spot they chose for hosting the first of several engagement parties they would throw onboard the Bonnie Anne.

Without batting an eye or mentioning it to Lillie, Jared went deeper into debt for the party, banking on the upcoming Jake Brown project to tide him over.

It was a lively affair. Everyone from the Wilmington studios attended. From the film's Executive Producers, to the costumers and set designers, down to the decorators and day-workers, they all made there boisterous way out to the Bonnie Anne on smaller boats. The yacht's upper deck had been strung with white lights, and a string quartet had been hired to lend the festivities an air of class. Champagne had been brought in by the crateful, and two extra cooks had come aboard to assist the Bonnie Anne's chef.

It wasn't a crowd known for its decorum or restraint. Regardless of age, race, or sexual preference, the primary aim of everyone in attendance seemed to be to consume as much free champagne as possible and then get laid. But it wasn't a desperate crowd. The movie that was in production had all the earmarks of a hit and the filming was going well; spirits were high.

'I hear you're attached to the upcoming Jake Brown project,' one producer said to Jared over a glass of champagne below deck.

'I saw that script. I'm surprised Lillie went for a role like that, especially after the stellar job she did on Master of the Storm.'

Jared hedged his bet. 'Every script has room for improvement,' he insisted. 'Overall, we think it has a good feel. Lots of action, perfect for summer.'

The producer looked skeptical.

Maybe these parties are a bad idea, Jared thought privately. I'm going to have to speak to Lillie tomorrow about the Jake Brown script, before she gets wind of it from someone else.

In the meantime, Jared made certain to stick close to Lillie's side through the remainder of the party, keeping the conversation on anything but future film projects.

The following morning Jared and Lillie slept late. They took a light breakfast on deck. The fresh air and sun helped eased them over the first hurdle of the post-party hangover.

'Lillie,' Jared announced with a good dose of false bravado, 'I've got great news, honey.'

'And what's that?' Lillie asked, taking a sip of coffee and putting on her best face, hoping to mask the queasy feeling in her belly and the pounding in her head.

'We're in negotiations for the next project.'

Lillie was floored. 'How on earth have you managed to be in touch with John Shay while aboard ship?'

'It's not with Shay. It's a quick action picture. We can fit it in while Shay puts the finishing touches on the novel.'

'An action picture?'

'Yes,' Jared said. 'With Jake Brown.'

'Jake Brown?' Lillie was incredulous. 'He's a martial arts guy. What would I be doing in a movie with Jake Brown?'

'Surprising your fans, stretching your limits, opening new horizons for yourself; how's that sound?'

147

'Not on your life,' Lillie replied in a tone that surprised them both. 'Jared, you can't be serious? I'm not going to make an action picture, least of all with Jake Brown. Every single female role in a Jake Brown film is a throw away. It's the type of part an actress takes on her way up, not after she's just won an Oscar.'

'But this is the lead female role. And it's got an unusual twist to it.'

'I don't care. I don't want to work with Jake Brown. I want to do a love story. You know that. And I want top billing.'

'But I'm telling you, this script is different. I know you're going to love it.'

'I'm not going to love it. I'd sooner do the Darrel Jeeves movie in New York than a ridiculous, over the top Jake Brown vehicle.'

Jared felt his blood pressure skyrocket at the mention of the famous director's name. 'What Jeeves movie in New York?' He began to quietly panic; was she seeking out projects that didn't include him, that wouldn't have him on the payroll? Was he supposed to just sit alone in some rented room and twiddle his thumbs in abject poverty while her career soared in New York?

'You were busy with the funeral, Jared. Darrel came to L.A. to pitch me a project. It's some sort of a murder comedy thing. He wants me for the lead. It's not a bad role, but I want to do the Shay script. I'm willing to wait, in fact.'

'Well, I'm not willing.'

Lillie stared at him in disbelief. 'Well, then go ahead and make the Jake Brown picture. You don't need me for that. I don't mind sitting it out and taking a little time off while you work.'

'It's not that simple!' Jared snapped.

Lillie tried to chalk up this strange behavior to both their hangovers. 'Why is it not that simple?'

'It just isn't. I don't want to discuss it now. I'm not feeling up to it. But I'm asking you to take a look at the script. I've got it in the cabin.'

'You brought it along? What does that mean, Jared? That this negotiation has been underway since we left Los Angeles?'

'Something like that,' he muttered. Then he stood abruptly. 'We'll discuss this later. I think I need to alone now.'

Lillie tried to finish her breakfast, to at least eat a piece of toast, drink her coffee and her tomato juice. She felt worse now than before, only this wasn't because of the hangover.

What is going on with him, she wondered. Since Abby died, he's been acting so strange.

Lillie stared out at the endless Atlantic and then remembered, that, no, Abby's death had been a coincidence; Jared had been acting strangely since the night of the Awards. Since the moment he came backstage to congratulate her.

It's almost as if he were trying to live my career now instead of his own.

Then a black thought surfaced in her head. What if he only wants to marry me because I won an award and he didn't? Because my success makes him more bankable?

But she brushed it off as quickly as the thought had come.

That is just plain crazy, she told herself.

*   *   *

Jared lay on the bed in the master cabin. How was he going to reconcile this? He had already accepted a percentage of his fee from Jake Brown's people. They'd cut him a check in good faith and he had already over extended his credit again. He had to do this project, had to complete the negotiations and convince Lillie to get on board.

John Shay was somehow the key to this whole mess. If he could somehow get to Shay and have him convince Lillie that the script for The World I Could Give was still a long way off, not before the end of the year, say; that she had plenty of time to do something fun like an action picture...

Who am I trying to kid now, he cautioned himself. God only knows how much of that book is actually written, or if it'll even get published. There's no script, no deal, yet.

Jared would have to make contact with Shay. Find out if he was back in New York yet and then meet with him, nail him down, get that project. And if there wasn't any project, Jared would have to pull one out of thin air and convince Shay to script it. Otherwise, he might lose Lillie to the likes of upstart directors like Darrel Jeeves – New York intellectuals who didn't have the balls to move to L.A. and jump into the fray with both feet, like everybody else.

If there isn't a project, I will pull it out of my hat, he repeated to convince himself. I've done it before, God knows how many times. I'll pull a project together with Shay somehow, keep Lillie, and get my career back on track. I can do this. I've done it before and I can do it again.

If I can just convince her to do the Jake Brown vehicle first...

For hours, Jared's thoughts chased themselves in vicious circles. He lost track of the time, of Lillie, of everything but his desperation. Twice, she came to the cabin to check on him, but he shooed her away, feigning a headache, claiming he needed sleep.

Lillie paced the deck, knowing for sure that something wasn't right. She'd look over the damn script if it was going to make him feel better. She could at least do that much, but as soon as they were ashore again, she was going to try to contact John Shay herself. She wanted that project. If Jared was losing his grasp on things, what was to keep him from blowing the negotiations with John Shay and then ruining it for her in the process?

Lillie went into the master cabin a third time. Above deck, the sun was beginning to set. The entire day was shot. 'I'm sorry to disturb you,' she whispered, 'but I thought I'd take a look at that script now.'

At the sound of her hopeful words, every knotted muscle in Jared's anxious body began to relax. 'Thanks, honey,' he said, sounding as casual as he could. 'I think I set it over there some-where. Check on the table.'

CHAPTER NINE

Spring had sprung riotously all over John's Long Island estate. Apparently, Steve Swenson had a whole handful of green thumbs. He quietly tended to the landscaping while John stayed in the study and labored lovingly over the novel.

It was shaping up surprisingly well. Since his informative trip to Mountville, John had been able to infuse the character of Ruth with elements of realism that gave the whole story an added dimension, bringing it to life.

John's agent had read the first several chapters and she'd responded with pronounced enthusiasm.

'You've got another winner, John,' she'd gushed. 'I think that little respite they gave you in Denmark did you a world of good. You're writing better than ever.'

The agent's initial meeting with the publisher left her feeling even more jubilant. With her commissions on John's books alone, she'd lived comfortably for many years and it looked like the trend would continue.

'It's not too soon to talk subsidiary rights,' she reminded him.

'You know this is going to be a movie.'

'I want Lillie Diver again,' he said.

'Perfect,' she concurred. 'I'll work on it.'

While the agent's sub-agent went in search of Lillie Diver, John resumed work on The World I Could Give. It had blossomed into an intimate look at a young woman's spiritual search for her father. Just how intimate the novel longed to be, only John himself could attest to. Frequently, he found himself removing entire passages that he felt had inadvertently revealed his own needs too blatantly – passages that bordered increasingly on the pornographic.

It had come to that, John's infatuation with Lillie. It had gradually evolved into a carnal desire. Lust was all over his thoughts of Lillie these days, try as he did to keep it all in perspective. His character, Ruth, was a product of his imagination, he knew that. He understood it. Still, he couldn't help but get lost in his desire for Lillie and confuse the flesh and blood woman with the character he'd created in his head and that he manipulated with his own words.

At night, he went to bed in a state of heightened arousal. His body peculiarly exhausted from having lingered on the precipice of lust for another entire day – a lust he succumbed to only in his vivid imagination.

Some days he'd purposely let his writing go off on debauched tangents, sending his character Ruth into the depths of his own lust, using his mind to undress her, caress her, penetrate her – in lieu of the real thing, of having Lillie in his arms to explore.

John couldn't bring himself to entirely delete these passages. He removed them from the manuscript, but filed them away in a folder he'd labeled 'L.D.' A folder that served as his wish list, his own private world of sexual fulfillment.

At night in his head, he relived each erotic detail of the adventures he'd created for Ruth during the day. Not since he'd been a teenager, had he spent so much time jerking off. Perhaps it was partly because of his newfound sobriety, it was an unfamiliar condition for John's body to be in, night after night. He felt more responsive and alive than he could remember having felt for a very long time. His sexual urges were no longer deadened by a flow of booze slogging through his veins.

Yet strangely enough, all this fervent sexual activity in John's mind didn't motivate him to go in search of actual feminine comfort or companionship. Why should he bother? All he wanted was Lillie in his life. He knew she was a fantasy, still everyone else paled in comparison. His 'girl du jour' days were over. He could no longer settle for second rate; he'd rather be alone than have sex without love. And he'd rather do without love altogether if he couldn't have a life with Lillie.

As he lay in his bed in the dark he wondered, how am I going to overcome this madness?

Especially once Lillie and Jared Warren had gotten married – how would he stand it when the day came that she legally belonged to another, to a man John had only the slimmest respect for?

He tried to believe that there was a side to Jared Warren that was redeemable. He loved Lillie too much to allow that she might err in her judgment, that she could be vulnerable to the vagaries and blindness of love like anyone else. Lillie might only be twenty-eight, but she'd endured and overcome hardships, hadn't she? She'd succeeded in a business that ate people alive. John was certain this had afforded Lillie wisdom beyond her young years.

She must know what she's doing, he tried to convince himself. There must be a very good reason why she would want to marry a crafty weasel like Jared Warren.

But the pep talks didn't make it any easier for John to sleep at night. Either his hard cock pestered him for constant attention, or his soul ached for the companionship of a woman who could never be his.

These equal parts of heartache and lust fueled John's creativity, day in and day out, until the first completed draft of The World I Could Give was plopped down on his agent's desk. She read it, enthralled, in just one sitting.

It struck her as a resounding success.

'Lillie Diver is apparently lost at sea, by the way,' she told John over the phone.

'What does that mean?'

'She's off on some romantic excursion with Jared Warren, on his yacht. As soon as she reaches dry land again, we'll pitch her the project. Unless you'd rather go through Warren himself, get him attached first?'

John relented. 'Either one of them is fine. They're engaged, you know. They're getting married – to each other, that is, if you can believe that.'

'Yes, I read that somewhere, some tabloid story.'

'Well, I got it straight from the horse's mouth.' He kept any further opinions on the proposed nuptials to himself. He didn't want to appear overly opposed to the marriage; he didn't want to give himself away.

* * *

Off the coast of Cape May, another engagement party was thrown by Lillie and Jared. This one smaller and more intimate, the guests staying aboard the yacht overnight and continuing on to Atlantic City the following day. There the happy couple and their guests took time out on dry land to toss their money away in the many casinos.

When the timing was right, Jared slipped out to the boardwalk alone. Here, to his relief, his cell phone was finally working. Without delay, he called whoever he could think of who might have a home phone number for John Shay. Four phone calls later and Jared had the number he needed.

It was nearing seven o'clock in the evening. The phone call came when John was sitting down to eat his dinner.

'Shay? It's Jared Warren! I'm glad to hear you're back in the States at last.'

'Yes, I'm back. I've been back for several weeks. How are you, Warren?'

'Very well, thank you. And how about yourself? Any good news for me, Shay?'

'If you mean about the book, my agent's been trying to reach you. Apparently you've been out at sea, with orders not to be disturbed.'

'Please, Shay, you could have disturbed me. I've been counting the days until I heard some good news from you.'

'Counting the days? I thought you were on some celebratory voyage with Lillie Diver.'

'I am, Shay, I am. But you know me, always thinking ahead. Got something I can look at?'

'Not just look at, Warren. The rights are available as of now.'

Jared's bowels lurched. 'Shay, listen to me. I can be in New York the day after tomorrow. Why don't we meet? You know I'm serious about this deal. Don't go courting anybody else, you hear me? And there's something in this for Lillie, right?'

'Nobody but Lillie.'

For the first time in weeks, Jared felt like the world was beginning to turn his way. 'Well, that's very good news, Shay, very good news, indeed. Listen, let's meet face to face, you and me. We'll talk a little, compare notes. Then we'll bring Lillie in on it. In fact, we're throwing another little engagement party on the boat in a couple days – we'll be docked off the Hamptons there, probably not far from you. You're invited, of course.'

John didn't think he could stomach it, a party celebrating Lillie's engagement. But at the same time, how could he refuse? How could he turn down a chance to see her, regardless of the reason? 'I'd be honored to attend,' he said.

'Who're you kidding, Shay? We're the ones who'll be honored. So listen, day after tomorrow, can you get into the city so we can meet? The same place we met the last time, it had good luck for us. And bring a copy of the book, Shay. Is that doable?'

'It's doable.'

'Say around five-thirty?'

'Five-thirty it is.'

Jared clicked off his cell phone and went back inside the casino. Alone at his dinner table in New York, John felt uneasy.

If I didn't know better, he told himself, *I'd say that guy sounded more desperate than usual. Something's up*, he decided. *I wonder what? I guess I'll know soon enough.*

* * *

On the top floor of the casino, Lillie sat in the VIP lounge with Alexa Pruitt, one of her guests from Cape May and a long-time confidant. In the anonymity of the noisy, crowded lounge, Lillie confided in her. 'The script was absolutely abysmal, Alex. I don't see what Jared sees in it. I gave it the benefit of the doubt for his sake, you know? But I just don't see why he would need me – or even want me – to be on a project like this one.'

'You're right, honey, it doesn't make sense. To go from something classy like Master of the Storm, to a backseat bimbo part in Shanghai Outriders is nothing short of ridiculous. You simply can't do it.'

'Unless maybe Jared has plans for turning it into a real spectacle, you know? Groundbreaking special effects, or something?'

'Are you trying to convince me or yourself, Lillie? Because I'm not buying it.'

Lillie had been afraid of that, afraid that if she bounced the idea off someone who was emotionally uninvolved with Jared and level headed about the industry, the whole concept would seem even more like a bad joke than it already did.

'Do you think he's losing his taste? His sense of what the audience wants?'

'No,' Alexa replied flatly. 'He's no fool. There's an audience for every Jake Brown picture. It's just that it's not your audience, Lillie, and it never will be. I'd say he's after the money on this one, and your career goals are taking a back seat.'

'I had a sick feeling you were going to say that.'

'Hey, you wanted me to be honest, right?'

Lillie gave Alexa's hand a quick, affectionate squeeze. 'Of course, I did. I really did. I just hate to hear you say what I've been afraid to even think.'

'Are you sure you want to marry this guy?'

Lillie bit her lip. 'That's another weird thing. He wants a huge wedding, a real media free-for-all, and all I want is something simple and private, something with meaning.'

Alexa studied her cocktail glass.

'What?' Lillie asked her. 'What is it? What are you thinking?'

'Truthfully?'

'Truthfully.'

'I'm thinking this guy is going off the deep end. He just buried his wife of thirty-five years. I'm not saying he doesn't love you, honey, but something doesn't sound right. He's jumping into things without thinking them through. He built an impeccable reputation, a commercially and critically successful career, on making all the right moves. He's not doing that now. You'd be smart to postpone the wedding for as long as possible. I'm not saying to break it off with him. Just postpone things until he's back to normal. Otherwise, you might find yourself in a marriage that's falling apart before the ink on the license is even dry.'

With that sixth sense lovers have for each other, Lillie looked up and spied Jared coming across the crowded lounge. He had a smile on his face. Something she hadn't seen in weeks. It gave her courage.

'Sweetie,' he called out to her. 'Hold onto your hat. I've got great news!'

'What is it?' she asked, putting on her best face again.

He turned to Alexa first. 'This is off the record, doll.'

'My lips are sealed.'

'I'll have a copy of the new John Shay novel in your hot little hands in two days. Can I deliver, or can I deliver?'

Lillie was elated.

'I just got off the phone with him,' he continued. 'He assures me you're the only actress he wants for the project. And I'll give you a little insider's scoop. He's been holding the rights until he heard back from me.'

Lillie and Alexa exchanged a quick glance. Maybe, just maybe, Jared was getting back on track.

'So we can forget about the Jake Brown thing?' Lillie asked.

'Are you nuts?' Jared replied. 'We can do both. There's plenty of time! This is only May. In fact,' he went on, pulling out a chair for himself and sitting down at the small table, 'after we wrap Shanghai Outriders, there'll be just enough time for the wedding and then we can move on to the Shay project.'

Tactfully, Alexa tried to feign enthusiasm for Jared's compact agenda, but Lillie knew that Alexa was just as appalled as she was and she began to feel distraught.

'See how it all works out?' Jared went on, nearly congratulating himself for being so clear sighted. 'Now, what are you gals drinking? Let's have a round on me.'

CHAPTER TEN

Very late that night, Jared and Lillie boarded the small boat that would ferry them back to Jared's yacht. Their party guests were staying on at a hotel in Atlantic City and then flying off to Bermuda the following day.

The yacht was dark and peaceful when Lillie and Jared returned to it, and the crew, sound asleep.

In the privacy of the master cabin, Lillie finally spoke her mind. 'I've read the script, Jared, and I don't like it. I gave it a fair shot, but I don't want to do the Jake Brown picture.'

Jared began to undress. 'But I'm already attached.'

'So, stay attached. I'm not telling you not to do it. I'm just saying that I'm not going to do it.'

'But you have to do it, Lillie,' he said dismissively.

'What do you mean, I have to do it?'

'I've already given them my word.'

She was stunned. 'How could you give your word on something that's my decision to make?'

Jared continued undressing calmly, as if he were talking about something trivial, like having ordered her something off a menu without asking her first.

'Look on it like a package deal, honey. Where I go, you go.'

'That's insane. We don't have any kind of package deal.'

In a pair of royal blue silk pajamas, Jared sat down wearily on the edge of the bed. He was too tired to put up a front any longer. Besides, he knew he held the wild card; the project Lillie really wanted – John Shay's next script. 'Listen, I already took a percentage of the advance. That's how I was able to pay for this little pleasure cruise. I gave Jake's production people my word that you would get on board. We start shooting in late June. It'll be a quick shoot, a no-brainer for you. By late August, it'll be over and we can be looking forward to the wedding.'

'Jared! What are you saying?'

'Listen to the words, honey; you understand English, don't you? I'm telling you I'm going broke and I need to make this picture. But I don't get the project if you're not attached, too. It's simple. You're worth more to the picture than I am.'

Lillie needed to sit down, she needed to make sense of this; he was going broke? 'But it's a stupid picture, a stupid part. Any other actress in town could do it with her eyes closed. It's not a smart career move for me and you know that. I don't see why you can't bring in some other up and coming actress that will satisfy them.'

'You're not listening to what I'm saying,' he said. 'They could care less about me. I'm not on the picture if I can't deliver you. And I've already taken a percentage of my fee, can't you understand that? I don't have the funds to pay it back.'

'My God,' she said softly, putting it all together at last. 'The house, the furniture... Jesus, Jared. And that talk about moving in with me... you were serious weren't you? You want to live in my house because you're broke, as in, really broke.'

'That's correct, I'm broke. I can't even afford this boat anymore otherwise I would just live here and not bother you. But what else am I supposed to do? Where can I go? Move in with one of my kids? And let them know that the long happy futures they assumed were in front of them are in jeopardy now?'

The boat seemed suddenly too cramped and the air impossibly close. Lillie wanted to get away from him, to escape this conversation, but they were moored off the coast of the Atlantic Ocean, drifting too far from civilization. 'Do you hear what you're saying?' she said. 'You're not talking about this like you want to marry me, Jared. You're talking about it like you need room and board.'

'That's not true, and you know it. I love you, Lillie. I told you we would get married just as soon as I was available. I'm following through on my promise,' he explained patiently. 'You're not just a convenience to me. I love you. But I do happen to be going quite broke.'

Lillie wished she could believe him – this talk of love – or feel some compassion. She wanted to feel anything except how she despised him at this very moment. 'You're lying,' she said. 'You're lying and you don't even know it.'

'How can you say something like that?'

'Because of the goddamned Jake Brown project, that's how!' she shouted. 'You would never have tried to pimp me off on some piece of crap movie like Shanghai Outriders if you really loved me, if love was what motivated you, and not your own pathetic fear and greed.'

Everything had become crystal clear and Lillie felt like her brain would snap. This explained everything, Jared's crazy behavior. He was broke and panicking and he'd lost faith in himself. But why had he turned on her? Used her, instead of confiding in her?

Jared saw the ugly dawn of recognition on Lillie's face. He went to her, grabbing her in his arms. 'Listen to yourself,' he begged her. 'Listen to what you're saying. Nothing could be further from the truth, Lillie. You're just disappointed and upset. Let's try to be reasonable here, not turn on each other. We can't just throw everything away after all we've been through for the last six years.'

For the first time in their relationship, Lillie didn't want to be in his arms. She pulled away. 'You lied to me,' she said. 'It almost doesn't matter why; but you lied.'

Jared searched his brain frantically for something he could offer that might woo her back to him. 'Put yourself in my position, for chrissakes. Think of how it feels to be in my shoes. You're young and you're on your way up. There's not much you have to worry about. But me? If I can't stay employed, my hand folds in a hurry. There are hundreds of younger versions of me yapping at my heels. I'm sixty-two-years-old, Lillie. In Hollywood, that's like being next in line for the embalmer. I have too many mouths to feed at home, too many kids to put through school, too many medical bills, funeral bills... Jesus, Lillie, give me a break!'

He was falling apart at the seams. He seemed two breaths away from begging her to spare him a dime and she couldn't stomach a sight like that. Jared Warren had been her hero, her mentor, her father figure – her lover. She was engaged to be his wife. She couldn't stand to see her idol fall. 'I'm going to another cabin!' she snapped. 'Maybe I'll be able to discuss this in the morning, but I can't promise you anything.'

She grabbed her nightgown from the dresser drawer and then left him alone in his master cabin – the master of nothing but a sinking ship.

*   *   *

Alone in the guest cabin, Lillie went through the motions of getting ready for bed – as if she would sleep. But when her weary head hit the pillow, she couldn't hold back the tears. Everything she'd planned for, waited for, dreamed of for the last six years with Jared were unraveling and she was helpless to stop it.

Was their entire relationship built on lies? Was she seeing him now for who he truly was, or was this just some passing craziness brought on by too much grief?

If this was just grief, she had to make up her mind here and now if she would stand by him until it passed. Really, what did it matter if he was broke, or if they lived together in her house? Nothing – if they were truly in love. She could go on working; she could be the breadwinner for a while. She didn't mind. She'd never been afraid of work. And working to help maintain a home with someone she loved? That was easy; she could do it with her eyes closed. She could even pay back Jake Brown's people, extricate Jared from that embarrassing problem if she had to, she wasn't proud. She and Jared had the John Shay project to work on anyway…

But was Jared worth her effort? Did he really love her? If he did, how would she know for sure? If he'd been able to mislead her so easily and tell her all these lies already, how would she ever know when he was telling her the truth?

And then the worst question of all came to her; did she really love him? Was the hate she was feeling now just anger? Would it pass? Would she be able to go back to seeing him through the eyes of a lover? Or would there be nothing left for her to feel but pity and contempt?

Whatever the answers were, she knew she would have to make some painful changes. The first being putting off the wedding indefinitely, if not breaking off the engagement entirely.

When her heart had cried itself out, she was exhausted. Somewhere around dawn, Lillie finally fell to sleep.

At noon, Jared himself brought a breakfast tray to Lillie's cabin.

'Sweetheart,' he woke her quietly, placing the tray on her bed. 'I'm sorry I'm waking you. I just couldn't stand it another minute. I want to make this up to you. I don't want to fight.'

Lillie dismissed the food with disinterest. 'You look tired,' she said. 'Did you get any sleep at all?'

'Not much. All I could think about was how wrong everything was going, and I kept trying to figure out what it was I could have done to stop it in the first place. And if I could figure out what that thing was, could I still do it? Could I still stem the tide of disaster? Lillie, I don't want to lose you. But I don't know who I am without my career.'

For the first time in her life, Lillie thought he looked defeated and old, as if one night had aged him twenty years. She felt sorry for him. She'd been around long enough to know that if anyone in the industry saw him as he looked right now, he'd never be hired again. He was an old man. Was this who she wanted to be starting a new life with, sharing a home and raising a family with?

'Jared, I think we need to call off the engagement until we can think clearly about what we want.'

'Lillie, don't do this. Don't turn on me.'

'I'm not turning on you. I just can't think straight. I don't know what the hell's going on between us. Until yesterday, I thought we were headed for some kind of paradise. Now it seems like the best we can hope for is to cut our losses and move on.'

'You're not leaving me, Lillie, and that's all there is to it. I won't let you give up. We'll fix this problem – I'll fix it. I promise you that. This is just a temporary set back. I've been down before but never for very long. You just don't know me well enough yet. You've only seen me on the upswing.'

How many upswings did a man have in him, she wondered. Wasn't artistic inspiration a well that eventually ran dry, or was it a limitless spring of possibilities? She recalled the stories of the great directors, the few who had made Hollywood what it was, who'd put it on the map in its golden days. Even great men like those had been kicked to the side when their creative wells had run dry. They became pitiful drunks, endlessly reliving their glory days from the confines of cheap, booze-infused dreams, surviving alone in rented rooms, dying in poverty and obscurity.

Was that going to happen to Jared? Was that his destiny, too?

Her heart ached for him, he looked so defeated. She didn't want to think of him coming to a wretched final scene. She knew she could resurrect him, or his career at least – she had the 'youth' and the 'bright future.' She wasn't all that naïve. He hadn't won the Oscar but the picture had still been a great success. He was broke and panicking, that's all. Those problems were fixable, for now. She could still help him get quality work.

But if all he had left of his career was her bright future, what would she have?

'Let's not make any rash decision right now, Lillie, please. At least promise me that. Give us a chance. Don't throw it all away.'

'But things are different now. And it's your fault.'

'I can make it better, Lillie. I can. Just tell me what it is you want. What is it going to take to get us back to how we were just yesterday?'

Yesterday? She remembered yesterday. It seemed hopelessly far away now. 'I just don't know, Jared. It doesn't seem possible.'

'You're being dramatic, that's all. You need time to relax and think. Then you'll come back around.'

'No, I'm not going to come back around. If it's going to work between us, it's because things are going to change. For one, I'm not doing the Jake Brown project. That's final. And I don't want that crazy wedding. I don't want any wedding at all, in fact.. Not yet, anyway.'

'Not yet?' Jared turned this cataclysmic news over in his mind. No marriage, no movie, no money. But the ring was still on her finger. It's not like she was throwing it back at him. There was still hope. They could stay engaged indefinitely – he could get a little mileage out of that. And there was the Shay project. When it came right down to it that might be all he needed to get back on top. He had to secure Shay, and then he could parlay that into other projects eventually, with or without Lillie.

'All right,' he said. 'I won't rush you. We don't have to set a date yet. We can take our time and just enjoy this idea of being engaged. That's safe enough, honey, isn't it? And I'll back out of the Jake Brown deal. I'll give him his money back somehow. I can always sell this boat. Then all we'll need to worry ourselves with is getting the Shay project off the ground. Does that sound better, honey, something safe and manageable? Is that what you want to hear? And of course, those three magic words: I love you. I do, you know.'

Curiously, there seemed less magic in those three little words than ever before. But Lillie knew he was trying. He was making an effort. She couldn't just dismiss it. 'Okay,' she finally relented. 'That works for me... for now.'

CHAPTER ELEVEN

There was no moon in the sky and the warm spring night outside John's balcony seemed to lay like a blanket of tranquility over the earth, or at least over Long Island.

He stood in nothing but his boxers, looking down over the peaceful darkness that had settled around his estate. Twenty-eight days at home without a drink, he told himself. It felt like some kind of landmark occasion. In that time, he'd completed his best novel to date. Twenty-eight days. It seemed biblical somehow, or spiritual; like a cycle of the moon, maybe?

What he knew for sure was that today he'd felt the renewal. As if every fiber of his being had finally dried out; as if the alcohol had receded from him completely and every cell in his brain had felt the rush of sober consciousness.

He felt invigorated and in control, hopeful. For no tangible reason, it had been a great day.

Tomorrow he'd take the train into the city and meet with Jared Warren at La Belle Saison. The last thing John really cared about was another Hollywood version of a story he'd created. But what did matter, what mattered most of all, was getting a copy of the new manuscript to Lillie. As if her reading it was what would give it credence, or bring it home, or complete its special purpose.

'My God, who am I trying to kid? It's a love letter to her and I want her to read it, to recognize herself, to dump this weasel Warren, and to fall in love with me.'

He sighed doubtfully at this declaration and went back into his room. The lights were off and the moonless night made the room especially dark. It was the first night since he'd been home that was mild enough for sleeping with the balcony doors open – there would be fresh air all night and the sound of birds in the morning. Everything felt promising for a change.

Is it spring that does this to a person, he wondered; even to a person like me who's forty-eight years old, for chrissakes? Or is it love that's doing this to me, making me feel so hopeful?

Either answer suited him just fine.

He got in bed and, as always, when his head hit the pillow he thought of Lillie. His cock stirred. God, he was horny.

That Jared Warren is a lucky son of a bitch, he thought.

John pictured the two lovers entwined in passion on Warren's yacht. Night after night, no one to betray their secret lusts as they went at each other; nothing around for miles but the wide open sea and a canopy of timeless sky.

John was downright envious.

His cock in his fist, he surrendered as he always did to the pictures of Lillie blossoming in his brain. He tried like hell to cancel out all thoughts of Jared Warren, and instead, put himself in the old bastard's place.

What would that feel like, having the real Lillie Diver, the flesh and blood woman naked, next to him in bed every night? Was she at that age yet, he wondered, where sex had become the great goal of an evening? Where her body was insatiable for intercourse?

John knew that happened to all women eventually. He recalled fondly a woman or two, women he'd been intimate with over the years, whose bodies had been in the throes of that sexual peak.

Always pleasurable, he decided; sometimes sex became a sport of endurance. He wondered if he'd ever get to go that special distance with Lillie Diver anywhere else except inside his head.

Still, whether or not his lust would ever be requited, John loved this feeling. His mind was a wide open book where he could script any fantasy he pleased. He firmly believed his erotic imagination had been God's greatest gift to him. God's second greatest gift had been putting Lillie Diver on the planet at all.

He settled more comfortably into his pillows. The first order of business tonight was to get Lillie off that boat. Get her far away from Jared Warren, to someplace only John would know about, where they could be utterly alone and uninhibited.

For some reason, his mind chose an old hotel he'd once visited in Spain, on the Mediterranean coast in a small town not far from Barcelona. He'd been with Amanda when he'd stayed there in real life, but tonight he was going there with Lillie.

It was a romantic place, that old hotel. The lobby in particular, had been breathtaking. Designed to resemble a Spanish town square, a working fountain stood at the lobby's center. Exquisite tile mosaics were everywhere – on the fountain itself, the floors, the walls. He and Amanda had taken the vacation in a last ditch effort to save their crumbling marriage. It hadn't worked, but throughout his brief stay there, John had wished he could be enjoying it with a woman he felt passionate about.

Now he was in that hotel with Lillie. In the quaint guest suite, it was evening and Lillie was naked in the deep feather bed.

Never having seen her naked in real life, John could only imagine her body in vague detail; her tits, her hole, the curve of her ass. But her physical attributes weren't what mattered, ultimately. His desire for her came from an ethereal place, a place where sex was energy. It fed on its own lust and multiplied. The more John hungered for her – wanting to have his cock in her, or his arms full of her, his nose taking in her smell – the more the sexual need intensified.

Yes, she had a beautiful face and yes, her flesh was what he wanted to feel, it's what drove him in his fantasies. The hope that finally one day he would connect with her, body and soul. Mount her in her most vulnerable position and find that she was offering herself to him; that what he wanted was what she wanted; to have his cock in her, to be in his arms, their hearts beating close, their quick breaths drawing from the same unfathomable space.

These were all elements of his desire. But what held him truly captive was something more that came from his heart, not his cock. A love that was born in him had created him, and he recognized it emanated from her. That was it, love, a love that recognized itself at home in the other, the most magnetic pull of all.

That was why he couldn't look at another woman with any interest anymore; they simply didn't exist for him. His cock was limp and useless when it came to other women, because his heart wanted to recognize itself and couldn't find itself there.

In that fantasy bed in the old hotel, John mounted her in the missionary style. Her legs wrapped around him, her breasts soft and full against his chest. With his cock going in deep, there was no way to be closer to her than this. Perhaps to kiss her, to have their mouths locked on each other while his cock pushed in and filled her hole.

He needed her that close.

He tugged his cock unmercifully, letting the lust feed on itself, until the pictures in his head dipped down to the next level. Where it wasn't so much bodies coming together as sex organs distinct in themselves, thick, stiff, engorged, swelling, longing to feel satiated. She held her thighs wide to reveal the purplish-red swell of pouting lips, the dripping hole slightly open.

His cock pushed into it then, the thick head forcing its way into the opening, stretching the hole, until the slippery muscle hugged his shaft, let it push all the way up and disappear.

These were the visions that filled his head now; the cock connecting with the hole.

He turned her over in every position, to ensure his cock was in the hole. Her hole. His cock. Going in, filling her. Sliding out, pushing in. Hard, deep, thick. Images sucking him, pulling his cock. Sloshing and pumping. Sucking and sucking. Until her mouth, that fabulous mouth. Those pouting lips, slick and red. A new hole to push, to poke, to fuck. The tip of his cock kissed the lipsticked flesh and the lips parted, taking him in. He fucked her mouth like it was any other offered hole. Like she didn't need it for breathing or eating, like her mouth was made for fucking. Expressly for fucking. Just fucking. For sucking in cocks and letting them fuck.

And this was how he came, spurting all over his stomach. Alone in his room, in the dark, in his bed. His cock shoved into his tugging fist, his mind overflowing with vivid pictures – a pretty mouth riding a stiff dick, making him come all over himself.

Then he passed quickly into a dead sleep. Ten minutes later, he awoke to the thought of two lovers. They were naked, entwined in a bed somewhere in that old hotel on the coast of Spain.

Amanda, he told himself vaguely, pulling the blankets up over himself.

Then he thought, no, it was someone I loved more than her.

But before he could quite recall the dream, he'd drifted back to sleep.

*   *   *

John drove himself to the train station. He parked his car, bought a round trip ticket for Manhattan, and then waited on the platform in the bright sunshine. It was another glorious spring day. He had on a lightweight jacket. A hint of summer blew in on the warm breeze and tousled his hair.

True to his word, in his briefcase, he had an unbound copy of The World I Could Give for Jared Warren. Carrying it now, John felt nervous and excitable. Like he'd felt in the old days, in the beginning, when he'd delivered the final draft of his first novel to his agent, knowing that he had written a gem, but not so confident that anyone else on earth would recognize that fact.

It felt good to be nervous for a change. It gave John a fresh perspective. It wasn't that he hadn't felt his other books were special – in his eyes, they were all his children. It was simply that he felt more invested in this one. He'd written it sober, for one thing, and in the throes of infatuation and lust.

The train arrived right on schedule. It was midday, long past rush hour and the train was nearly empty. John took a seat by the window. He loved riding trains. He loved to watch the world go by.

As a boy, John had grown up with his family in New Jersey, not far from the Princeton University campus where his father had been a professor and where John had ultimately gone to school. There they'd had the 'Dinky,' a one-car train that took them to Princeton Junction, where they could catch another train that took them all the way to Pennsylvania Station in New York.

His first ride alone on that New York-bound train marked the day John Shay felt his independence. He'd been all of fifteen years old back then. That fine day had sealed John's love of trains.

To him, they symbolized freedom, even more so than the automobile would. New York City had always mesmerized him when he was a boy. Taking the train there on his own and being in the city alone, was both a fright and a thrill for him. First, he got lost in Pennsylvania Station. Then, once he'd managed to find his way to the street above ground, he lost his sense of direction and wandered clear to the Hudson River, hoping he was heading toward midtown, too intimidated by the rush of people to stop and ask for directions.

These days when John reached Penn Station, he rushed through it blindly, knowing his way up to the street by heart. But he never lost that sense of being a boy, enthralled by the big city. As an adult, he had a difficult time being too far away from New York.

It was a perfect afternoon for strolling through midtown. With time to spare, John headed leisurely across town, then north to La Belle Saison hotel. Walking along the streets and avenues in the bright sunshine, he felt confident and sober. Still, he couldn't ignore the tiny voice at the back of his brain, reminding him that he was not just on his way to a business meeting, he was on his way to a bar.

When John stepped into the hotel's famous lounge, he was struck by the comforting, familiar ambiance of it. He couldn't help but be drawn to the exhilarating sight of the long, sleek and polished maple wood bar. At this hour of the afternoon, there were very few customers and only one bartender working, not anyone that he recognized.

'Shay!' A voice called out. 'Over here.'

John figured that by now, he would know that voice anywhere. He spotted the silver hair immediately. Jared Warren was sitting alone in an enormous booth along the back wall. His stature seemed dwarfed by the emptiness of such a large table, but he seemed oblivious to it; he had a big smile on his face.

'Do you always have a goddamned tan?' John asked, scooting into the booth.

'Always,' Jared assured him. 'What are you drinking, Shay? I'm drinking scotch.'

Jared glanced down at the glass on the table and felt something squeeze like a fist around his heart. Since when did Warren drink scotch? And what about that meal we were supposed to have? 'I'll have a club soda with lime and plenty of ice.'

Jared waved to the one waiter on duty. 'I'm not ashamed to say it,' he told John. 'I'm very excited to see this new book.'

'You are?'

'I am, Shay. I get a good feeling about it, sight unseen. A club soda with lime and plenty of ice,' he told the waiter. 'And before I forget,' he continued to John, 'you must come to our little soiree aboard the Bonnie Anne tomorrow night. I know it would kill Lillie if you missed our celebration.'

'It would?' John tried not to seem too interested in Lillie's opinion of him. He had a healthy skepticism for every word that came out of Jared Warren's mouth. 'And why would it matter so much to her? We barely know each other, Lillie and I.'

'She's all gung-ho about working with you again, Shay. You know you helped her get a goddamned Oscar with the last one. I guess it would be a sign of good faith if you put in an appearance at the party.'

The waiter set John's club soda in front of him. John took a tentative sip, momentarily hoping for the warm taste of scotch on his tongue, to match the distinct aroma wafting up from Jared's glass. But the drink in his glass was tasteless, nothing but empty bubbles. He shifted his attention elsewhere. He didn't want to think about scotch. 'It was a nice surprise when Lillie called me in Denmark,' he said.

'Yes, I heard that you two had a quite a little chat. The wires were humming.'

Is he serious, John wondered; or fishing for something?

'Actually we didn't talk long. It was barely dawn in Copenhagen. It was just a quick congratulations, you know – business.'

Jared nodded his head. 'Yes, I know, business, and speaking of business, can I see the book?'

John retrieved the unwieldy manuscript from his briefcase. When he slid it across the table, Jared grabbed it like he was afraid it would disappear.

'Are you planning to read it now?' John joked, a little taken aback by it.

'No, you know how Lillie is. She likes to have first crack at a book. I just like having my hands on it.'

At last, Lillie and his book; John felt an excited kick in the heart, like a schoolboy with a hopeless crush. He tried to keep his face a blank, though. He was mindful of keeping his heart to himself. The man across from him was the man who made love to Lillie at night, the man who had the world in his hands. John played it cool. 'So, you and Lillie are engaged.'

'That's right. We're engaged. And we want you to come to our party tomorrow, don't forget.'

'I won't,' he said. 'So when's the wedding?'

'Don't worry. You're invited to that, too.'

'I didn't ask that. I was just wondering when it was.'

Jared thumbed absently through a few pages of the manuscript. 'No date yet,' he said casually. 'We're still concentrating on getting some projects together.' Then he packed the manuscript safely into his own briefcase. 'You know my wife just died, Shay. It wouldn't look right to rush into a wedding. And the kids are not exactly in my court on this one, they think Lillie's too young for me. I need to give them some time to adjust to the idea.'

Why was he being so decent, John wondered. It wasn't the Jared Warren he'd worked with back in L.A., the man who let nothing like a little human need get in the way of anything. 'I guess that's a testament to Lillie's virtue that she's willing to step aside for your kids; that she's willing to wait. Not many women would be so patient. I don't suppose it's really any of my business, but it does seem like you two have been sort of an item for a long time.'

Barely aware that he was doing it anymore, Jared unleashed his self-conscious pack of lies. 'Look, Shay… Lillie and I, that whole affair?' he explained. 'We both knew we weren't really fooling anybody, everyone knew we were hopelessly in love from the day we met, like a couple of kids. To be honest, Lillie wasn't much more than a kid herself. You know how that is, you get a little older and the young ones come running. You gotta beat 'em off with a stick sometimes, right? But I had my wife's feelings to think about. Mind you, my marriage was over long before I met Lillie Diver. But my wife found out she was ill at the same time that we were deciding to get divorced. Under those circumstances, a lot of things changed. Why put the kids through a double whammy like that? Or put Abby through it, or me, for that matter? Abby and I decided to stick it out, for the sake of appearances, if nothing else. She had her own room, her own separate life. To the world, and to our kids, we went through the motions of staying married. When I met Lillie, I told her straight out about Abby and the illness. Luckily, she understood the need for certain pretenses. She'd make a good First Lady, you know? She's good at standing on ceremony, at keeping up appearances. Lillie comes from quite a classy background, I don't know if you're aware of that.'

'No, I wasn't,' John remarked in genuine surprise. Who is

Warren trying to impress with this lie? 'I had figured she was just a small town girl, humble beginnings and all that.'

'Lillie? No way. She comes from good New England stock, the best, money, education, all of it. Can't you tell by just looking at her?'

'I suppose, now that you mention it.' John was curious to see just how far this charade was going to go. 'You know, I went to Princeton.' he offered. 'It's sort of a tradition in my family – my father, my grandfather. I never suspected Lillie was from a similar mold. What school did she go to? It was Ivy League, too, I take it?'

'I don't really remember.'

'But she comes from money?'

'Yes. Not me, though. I come from right here, New York City, strictly working class. I attended the city university for awhile, did theater projects and such, but then I cut my teeth in television, the early days, when almost anyone could get a job in TV. Abby was right there by my side through all of it. The lean years clear up through the successes. She went to secretarial school, worked in an office and made more money than me, most of the time. In those early days, I mean. Unlike you and Lillie, I came up the hard way,' Jared went on. 'I really had to work my ass off. Nothing was handed to me, no Ivy League connections like you two have. But once I got a shot at directing movies for television, the whole world opened up for me. I got that call from Hollywood that everyone hopes for and then I went from one killer project to the next. I've had a great career, a long, long, great career, without the help of a family name or any kind of family money.'

John stared at him, fascinated. It almost felt like watching a train wreck. What was going on with this guy? He was trying to prove something, make some kind of point, but John didn't know what.

'I'm ready for another drink,' Jared announced. 'How about you?'

'No, I'm fine. But you go ahead.'

'How's it going, anyway? The drinking thing, is it under control?'

'So far, so good, I've been sober for four months now, twenty-eight-and-a-half of those days right in my own unsupervised home.'

'Good, Shay, that's real good.'

Jared ordered another scotch from the waiter. 'This time, make it on the rocks.'

John's stomach lurched. *Is it my imagination, or is he trying to unravel me?*

He took another sip of his club soda. He was going to stay calm. There was nothing outside himself, nothing he could ingest, he reminded himself, that could make his world any better than it already was.

When the new drink was placed in front of Jared, he said to John, 'You probably remember, I never used to drink this stuff.' He rattled the ice in his glass for emphasis before taking a sip. 'I was always more of a vodka or champagne man. But lately, life's lessons have gotten a little tougher and scotch has become my beverage of choice. I suppose you know all about things like that.'

'I suppose so,' John replied vaguely. He had to steer clear of this subject of drinking. Nothing would be worse for him right now than to start romanticizing his life-long relationship with scotch.

'Coming from money, Shay, the privileged class, I suppose you were raised to appreciate the finer things, like, top shelf liquor. You can spend a cool fortune on good scotch, you know. Me, on the other hand, I grew up thinking that an extra dry martini was a successful man's drink. Turned out gin made me feel nuts, so I switched to vodka. Abby was the one who clued me in on champagne. You want to spend a fortune on something to drink? You can drop a bundle in a hurry on a good bottle of champagne.'

'I know,' John replied, beginning to fidget in spite of his resolve.

'Lillie loves champagne, you know.'

'No, I didn't know.'

'She sure does. Won't touch anything else. She's got expensive taste in just about everything. It was instilled in her at a very young age, as you can maybe relate. I keep telling her, she's going to break me one of these days. She's a tough gal to bank roll. But who cares, as long I keep on working, right?'

'I imagine she does okay in her own right. And if her family has all that money, like you say…'

Jared cut him off. 'Tell me something, Shay. What gives with you two, anyway?'

'What are you talking about?'

'This little game you've got going on. I know what's up, I'm not stupid.'

'You've lost me, Warren. What's happening here?'

'I'm talking about you and Lillie and this goddamned book.'

John was speechless. 'What do you mean?'

'I mean, you couldn't care less if I directed this project, you just want to make sure Lillie gets a hold of it. To you, I'm just a messenger.'

John took a deep breath. How could this be happening? What was with this guy? How could he know anything about it? John sifted quickly through his brain, trying to latch onto even a shred of a drunken memory. Had he said something to Jared Warren when he'd been on his little holiday bender? Something sickeningly revealing about his feelings for Lillie that he had no recollection of now?

'You two have your little Oscars,' Jared went on blindly. 'And you think you can write your own tickets now, that you don't need an old guy like me. But let me tell you something, Shay. I understand Lillie Diver. I know how to make her look like roses on that screen. It's my eye, my vision that's made her who she is. You try to cut me out and you're making a big mistake. You think a guy like Darrel Jeeves could have made Master of the Storm?'

'What does Darrel Jeeves have to do with anything?'

'Nothing, because he doesn't have balls, Shay, and you need to have balls to work with a woman like Lillie, solid gold, diamond encrusted balls.'

'Really?'

'Yes, really. She doesn't respect a man who can't put her in her place once in awhile. She's got a father thing, as I'm sure you know. It's nothing to be ashamed of, a lot of successful girls have that, they want a man who takes control. I've always been happy to play that part with her. I have no problem with it. I know how to show her a firm hand and then when to back off. It's like our roles were assigned to us from day one. When I first met her, she was nobody. And I mean, nobody, Shay. She'd never been in a picture. She'd done a couple of print ads, nothing more. Not even a commercial. Not even a walk-on on a Soap, for chrissakes. She was just a scared kid on her own in New York.'

'But from an Ivy League school,' John pointed out. 'With plenty of money and connections, like me.'

'That's right. And another thing about that girl, she barely knew how to fuck. And I'm not exaggerating. I never saw a girl so ill-equipped in the bed department in all my life. It was almost laughable the way she tried so hard to get me off. She didn't have a clue how to make me come. And then trying to act so sophisticated, like she'd been in a producer's bed in the Waldorf before. But a sweet kid, you know, she was sweet.'

'And I think you're drunk, Warren. What the hell are you talking about? I don't want to hear this crap. Listen to yourself. She's going to be your wife, for chrissakes. Shut up and get a grip.'

Jared stared down at his glass of scotch. It was nearly empty. He couldn't remember drinking it. 'How do you stand this stuff?' he said. 'It goes right to your brain.'

'I know. Maybe I better put you in a cab. Where are you staying?'

'On the boat over by 72nd Street.'

John shook his head. 'I assume a man as worldly as you, knows not to drink scotch in the middle of the day on an empty stomach?'

'Can it, Shay.' Jared fished in his pocket for his wallet and with noticeable impairment, took out a fifty dollar bill and tossed it on the table.

'You're not seriously leaving a fifty for two scotches and a club soda? Come on, Warren, let me get you in a cab. I'll go with you to the marina myself.'

Jared glared at him darkly, obviously drunk now. 'You think I can't look out for myself, Shay? I grew up in this town. I started out nobody and made it all the way to the top. I don't need you or Lillie Diver to look out for me. I can take care of myself. I always have.'

'I know and I'm impressed. But you've got my manuscript in your briefcase and while you're out there taking care of your drunken ass, I don't want you leaving my book behind in some goddamned public cab.'

* * *

On the train back to Long Island, John tried to make sense of what had happened. None of it had been his imagination. Jared Warren had been trying to derail him, purposely enticing him with scotch. Then trying first to intimidate him with some weird, make-believe concoction about Lillie's impressive past, and then, when that hadn't worked, trying to take her down a few pegs in John's esteem.

What a despicable thing to do, John thought; especially to someone he supposedly loves.

The best explanation he could come up with was that Jared Warren was threatened by this Oscar nonsense. So what if he hadn't won this time? He already had two to his credit. Not many people in the industry could say that. And John's own Oscar? It was practically meaningless to him, since so many other writers had had a hand in that script.

John stared out the window at the scenery rushing past him as twilight spread out over the sky. Then it finally came to him. 'He thinks he's old,' John said quietly to his reflection in the train window. 'That's what this is all about. He thinks he's old. He's feeling his mortality. I bet his wife's death aged him twenty years. He's probably afraid now that he's washed up. He's afraid of being alone.'

CHAPTER TWELVE

Lillie was appalled by Jared's obvious condition. He was unsteady on his feet when one of the crew helped him out of the smaller boat and back on board the yacht.

'I take it you haven't eaten yet,' she said. 'What happened, did you drink your dinner?' Then she remembered who he'd been meeting with and felt doubly appalled. 'What happened to John? I hope he's not in the same shape you're in?'

'Why all this concern about Johnny, sweetie? I'm the one you're engaged to, not that swine. He's out of your league, anyway. He comes from a decent family.'

'And what is that craziness supposed to mean?'

'It only means that his mother took the time to get married before she got knocked up, that's all.'

'Jared, stop it, you're drunk!' Lillie glanced nervously at the chef who was standing in the gangway, awaiting the dining instructions.

'I guess we should eat as soon as possible,' she told him apologetically. 'I don't think he's had a thing to eat since breakfast.'

Jared plopped his briefcase down on the deck. 'There it is, honey, at long last, your next claim to fame. I had to consume an ocean of scotch to pry it out of his grubby paws.'

'Since when do you drink scotch?'

'Since Shay insisted that he didn't like to drink alone and I didn't know how to refuse.'

Lillie took Jared by the arm and helped him over to the stairway. 'So John was drinking to? I'm disappointed to hear that.'

'Don't be so surprised, honey. I've been trying to tell you that guy's a loser. He's on his way down. His tricks are played out. I wouldn't be surprised if this new book is nothing but trash. When I saw the shape he was in, I almost didn't bother to take the damn thing. But you had your heart set on it.'

Lillie guided him carefully down the stairs. When they reached the bottom, she said, 'Why don't you go lay down? I'll have them bring the food in to you when it's ready.'

She went into the lounge with Jared's briefcase and sat down. This was disheartening. She had been excited about this new book for a couple months already. For some inexplicable reason, she'd had high hopes about it, sight unseen. It was equally disturbing to her that John had fallen off the wagon so quickly. She knew that sobriety could be a tricky thing for some alcoholics to endure for long. But she hadn't thought of John Shay in that category – like the kind of drinker her mother had been.

She pulled the manuscript out of Jared's briefcase and set it on the table. She read the title page out loud. 'The World I Could I Give, by John Shay.'

It still gave her belly a quick tumble. Something about that title spoke to her in an intimate way, one that she couldn't put her finger on.

'Well,' she announced to the manuscript in front of her. 'Ready or not, here I come.'

Several hours later, she lay stretched out on the bed in the guest cabin, still avidly reading, consuming the text. She felt entranced, addicted, and even a little ashamed. She identified with the illegitimate-born Ruth and her search for her father. Lillie felt she recognized herself in the character, in her less than desirable upbringing on the wrong side of town, in the lies she wove to conceal the truth about her past, and in her sometimes pathetic sexual advances toward older men. That had been her life.

But the author treated it all with compassion as if to prove the old saying that 'to err is human'. Lillie considered John Shay's talent for forgiveness something along the lines of the divine; God-given, a world apart from other writers.

How on earth can a man who writes like this be a drunk? Lillie simply couldn't make sense of it. In fact, childish as it seemed, she felt like she was falling in love with him, based solely on the contents of the book, on how he expressed the beauty of life with all its mysteries and seeming unfairness.

It would make a spectacular movie, she realized. And she knew that she'd been born to play this part. Even more so than Master of the Storm, this would be her defining role. Jared was worried for nothing.

Lillie kept reading. The pages flew by her fingers in a timeless world. She lost track of the fact that it was just a manuscript she was holding the characters were that alive on the page.

Toward the end of the book, she suddenly stopped reading and set the manuscript aside. She was overcome by a flood of disconcerting memories from her own past. In particular, what she'd gone through when she'd found out about her father, about his wealth, his power, and the illicit nature of his relationship with her mother.

In those days, Lillie knew next to nothing about sex. And her mother's drunken ramblings about the strange life she'd lived at

Montecito's did little to clear it up. But Lillie absorbed enough of the innuendo to grow increasingly curious about sex and her parents' strange and lurid appetites. Until Lillie obsessed about it, the shameful things her parents were doing together.

After Lillie's mother had died at the county hospital, Lillie was on her own. She was seventeen when she had to drop out of school and start working as a waitress. It was a small but respectable restaurant on the good side of town. And it held an added attraction, a thing that both terrified and thrilled her; the Honorable Samuel Masters Kindcaid III – the same Sam Kincaid of the insatiable sexual appetite, her father – was fond of dining there with various upstanding wealthy residents of Mountville.

She would never forget the evening he finally came in to dine. Lillie was told to wait on him and his dinner guest, and to make sure he got the check.

Lillie observed him warily from the safety of the waitress station. He had a fine head of sleek silver hair, every strand of it in place. He dressed impeccably. But he was old. Lillie was sure he had to be close to sixty. When it was clear she would have to go over to his table and actually speak to him, to take his order, it felt like her legs would go out from under her.

Up close, he smelled rich and successful. She felt utterly intimidated.

Sam Masters cocked an eyebrow when she timidly approached him. He looked her up and down and then obviously approved of what he saw. 'You're new,' he said, with a keen interest but not smiling. 'I haven't seen you here before.'

'I just started a couple weeks ago.'

He glanced at the name tag pinned to the breast pocket of her uniform. 'Well, Lillie,' he said. 'Don't be so timid. It doesn't become a girl as striking as you.'

Then he proceeded to place his order, and his guest placed his order, and Lillie left the table. But throughout the meal, Sam Kincaid kept a roving eye on her. Whenever she tried to sneak a surreptitious glance his way, with a jolt, she'd find him looking at her.

When his dinner was over and he was on his way out, he sought her out personally and handed her the tip. It was a ten dollar bill. Far above and beyond what was considered a generous gratuity. 'I'll ask for you next time,' he told her. 'I come here often.'

Fascinated with him, this man who was secretly her father, Lillie counted the days until he came to the restaurant again. True to his word, he expressly asked for her when he did return. However on that night, barely a word passed between them. And whenever Lillie stole a glance at him, he wasn't paying her the least attention. He left another big tip, though, and gave her a quick smile on his way out the door.

It continued like that for several months. When Sam Kincaid would come in to dine, he'd ask for Lillie and sometimes he made small talk with her and eyed her up and down, and sometimes he didn't. But he always left a big tip.

Until one night, when he was on his way out of the restaurant, when he came over to hand Lillie the generous gratuity, he stood unusually close to her and in a quiet voice said, 'Can I ask you a personal question?'

Lillie felt flushed. He was looking her in the eye. Suddenly he didn't seem old at all. He had beautiful eyes. She found them enigmatic. These were the eyes her mother had looked into when Lillie was conceived, she realized. Sam Kincaid may have been close to sixty but he was still decidedly handsome. It was unnerving.

'How old are you?' he went on. 'I ask because you seem so young and yet I've noticed you're always here working, so you must be out of high school.'

'I'm eighteen,' she lied, not wanting to admit to a man as important as he was, that she was a drop-out.

'Eighteen?' He repeated it thoughtfully, as if now considering something very important that had hinged on this answer. 'I see you don't wear a ring. You're not married, are you?'

'No,' Lillie replied shyly.

'What does a girl like you do when you're not working?'

'I go home,' she said.

'You go home? Don't you go out on dates at all?'

'No, not really.'

'A pretty girl like you? That's hard to believe.'

Lillie knew she was blushing but she couldn't help herself.

'Would you like to go out with me sometime?'

'On a date?' She was astonished.

'Sure, why not? Do you think I'm too old for you? We don't have to get married, you know. It's just a date. I can buy you some dinner, we can have a conversation. You're a very pretty girl and I like to be in the company of very pretty girls.'

Without thinking twice, Lillie said, 'Okay.'

Then Samuel Masters Kincaid III smiled back at her, and said, 'Okay.'

The date didn't take place until several weeks later, leaving enough time for Lillie's childish daydreams to become thoroughly fixated on Samuel Masters Kincaid III. She had fantasies of confiding in him about who she really was and him being overjoyed by this news and taking her in as his flesh and blood, welcoming her in to his life, his world.

Since she knew he liked pretty girls, she made a special effort to look as pretty as possible when they met in the lobby of the very staid and very expensive Elmont Hotel. She had to take a bus clear into the next town to get there.

His face lit up when she walked through the hotel's front door.

'Well, I must say, you clean up real good,' he said, cocking that eyebrow again and eyeing her almost salaciously. 'You should stay out of that waitress uniform from now on. It doesn't suit you. You're a very pretty girl, Lillie. Listen,' he said, 'I have a suite of rooms upstairs.'

And then he said something about privacy and ordering up a nice dinner and having some champagne already on ice.

'Do you drink champagne?'

'Sometimes,' she lied, never having tasted it once in her short life.

Then she followed him up in the elevator to his suite of private rooms. Again, she noticed the aroma of his cologne. It smelled like wealth, he smelled like a rich man.

It was at that point that she should have told him, that she should have said what she'd been practicing over and over for nights on end. 'I'm Lillie Diver, I'm your daughter. You're my father. Sally Diver was my mother. You knew her at Montecito's.' Instead, she said nothing. She was too overwhelmed by his presence, too overcome by his blatant flattery to think straight. His suite of rooms was so impressive, ten times larger than the tiny apartment she'd lived in all her life. And he was handing her her first glass of champagne. She would wait until later in the evening to bring up more personal topics. For now, she would have her drink and enjoy herself.

After just a few sips of the champagne, she put the glass politely aside. It wasn't as sweet as she'd expected it to taste. She wasn't sure she liked it.

'The night is young,' he said. 'You're not ready to eat yet?'

Frankly, she was famished, but she was too timid to admit it.

'Good,' he said then. 'No places to rush off to, that's nice for a

change. What about your champagne? You've hardly touched it.'
He took her glass and added a splash more to it. He sat down next
to her and handed the glass back. 'You are a very pretty girl,' he
said again. 'You remind me of a girl I knew a long time ago.'

'Really?'

'Yes, really. We had some very good times together, me and that
girl. Tell me,' he said, running a finger lightly up her arm. 'Are you
interested in having a good time? Do you ever do things like that,
a pretty girl like you?'

She stared at him, clutching her glass of champagne. It was at
that moment that she was in over her head – or perhaps that
moment had come months ago, when he'd first come into the
restaurant and she hadn't told him who she was.

'I could always make it worth your while, you know. I've got
plenty of money. You wouldn't have to wait tables anymore, that's
for sure. A pretty girl like you should not be waiting tables. You
should be out enjoying your youth and having a good time. Do
you even know what I mean by having a good time?'

Her voice faltered. 'I think so.'

He smiled that salacious smile again. 'You do? Tell me what you
think it means. I want to hear you explain it.'

Now she was caught. He'd finally pinned her. She had only a
vague clue what he meant. But she knew it had something to do
with sex and what had gone on at Montecito's in those years before
she was born.

'Doing stuff for money? I don't know, kissing?' she offered, her
heart pounding wildly now. She'd changed her mind about everything and wanted to leave.

He seemed to find her answer amusing. 'You can't really be that
innocent, Lillie. Come on, talk to me about sex. I've got plenty of
money, what do you like to do?'

She didn't reply to that. Her thoughts were now on the door and how to get out of it. 'I have to go,' she said. 'I've changed my mind.'

He sighed and looked disappointed. 'It doesn't surprise me. I'm too old for you, I know that. But it was worth a shot. Girls like you have always excited me.'

She put down the glass of champagne and got up to leave. She was trembling, ashamed of herself. She was such a fool. He'd mistaken her for a pretty whore, that was all, a girl just like her mother. It had been nothing more extraordinary than that.

He followed her to the door. 'No hard feelings, right, Lillie?'

Lillie turned to him and replied in a hollow voice, 'No, no hard feelings.'

'Good,' he said. Then his hand grabbed the back of her neck, pulling her face up close to his. His mouth was on hers. He was kissing her, trying to slip in his tongue. She squealed desperately into his kiss, shoving him away from her.

Then she ran and ran and ran, down all those steps, down to the lobby and out the hotel's front door, where she found a taxi waiting and she jumped in, too horrified to wait out in public, out on the street for the bus back to Mountville.

Reliving those troubling memories, Lillie saw now that it hadn't really been fair to blame herself all these years. It wasn't really as if she'd seduced her father into kissing her. So what if she'd made that extra effort to be as pretty as possible for him? It didn't make her a whore. And so what if she'd been too nervous to identify herself, to let him know who she really was? She'd only been seventeen years old; a drop-out, a waitress, trying to survive on her own. And Sam Kincaid had been nearly sixty, she was afraid of him. The world was his oyster and had been for his entire life.

She almost felt sorry for him now. His only crime had been that he wanted whatever attracted his fancy and he was more than willing to pay for it. Like everyone else on earth, sometimes he got it in spades, and sometimes it fled off in the night.

* * *

I t was dawn when Lillie finally re-focused on John's manuscript. She picked up the remaining chapters and read the book to its harrowing conclusion. It was a spectacular novel. Lillie had no other words for it. It would be another winner, a best seller; there was no doubt about that.

She switched out the light beside the bed but she was too keyed up to close her eyes. She lay there alone, thinking, thinking, thinking…

How does a book do that, she wondered; draw a map of a person's life, a total stranger's world, and reclaim everything? Sublimate it somehow, make it beautiful?

It had something to do with love, she was pretty sure about that. She wished she could talk to John Shay right at that moment, get to the bottom of who he was. Find out how his brilliant mind worked, how it was that he did what he did. He was more than just another drunk writer, Lillie was sure of that. And now she wished she'd had the foresight to have invited him to their upcoming party.

CHAPTER THIRTEEN

B y the time Lillie woke and came above deck, she discovered that they'd long ago left the Hudson River and the 72nd Street Marina and were now out on the open sea again, heading up the coast to the tip of Long Island. By evening, they would be docked once more and hosting another elaborate cocktail party in honor of the engagement.

Jared was awake already and appeared to have been so for some time. He was finishing a pot of coffee and soaking up the bright sun, although it was much cooler up here in New York than it had been down in the Carolinas.

'I read the book last night,' Lillie announced. 'I finished it in one sitting. It's a marvelous piece of work, Jared.'

Jared looked up at her. 'And good morning to you, too.'

'Good morning,' she added. 'It's a fantastic book. It's hard to imagine the guy could ever be the loser you make him out to be.'

Jared sat up in the chaise lounge. He drank his coffee. 'So what do you propose I do now? If we want the rights to this hot little property, I'm going to have to put up or shut up.'

Lillie sat down in a deck chair and gave it some thought. Finally, she said, 'Would you like a loan, Jared? Enough to pay off Jake Brown's people then secure the rights from John Shay? Eventually you'll sell the boat, the house, you'll pay me back. Is that what you had in mind? A loan?'

Jared made no reply.

'You know, Jared, you could still do the Jake Brown project and I could just buy the rights from John myself.'

'And then do what?' he said darkly. 'Become a producer? Find another director?'

'I didn't say that.'

'No, you didn't, sweetie. But I can hear the words coming out of you anyway. They're practically screaming at me.'

'Why would I want to do a thing like that, Jared? We've always worked well together. You have a good eye for John's work, you understand the visual scope of it, I know that.'

'But?'

'But, what? There is no but.'

'Yes there is, Lillie. It's called 'time and money,' two things I have very little of right now.'

'And what's that supposed to mean? You're not exactly over the hill yet.'

'Maybe not yet, but by the time I can get my side of the finances in order, I will be. I think you're shrewd enough to know that. I have a fairly clear idea of what your game is.'

Lillie was dumbfounded. 'What my game is? I don't play games with you, Jared. I never have. That's not my style.'

'No? What about that night in the Waldorf, what game were you playing then?'

'That night in the Waldorf? When?'

'You just think about it. I'm sure it'll come back to you. In fact,

I was just reminiscing about it yesterday. With John Shay, over cocktails. We were talking about all the silly young women in the world, how they throw themselves at older, more successful men, leeching off them, all starry-eyed. He talked about having to beat them off with a stick – those were his exact words. Shay may not be as old as I am, but he's no spring chicken, either, my dear. He's been around the block. He knows what the young ones are all about. You, for instance; I told him how you were a classic text book case. Poor white trash trying to pass yourself off as sophisticated, doing everything you could think of to keep me from kicking you out of bed. It was a career you were after then, and that's what you're still after. You're just better in bed now, that's all, in fact, much, much better in bed. You learn fast, don't you, Lillie? You don't have to be taught a thing twice.'

'Are you losing your mind?' she snapped. 'How dare you speak to me like this, and talk about something so personal, something about our private life, with a total stranger?'

'He doesn't strike me as a total stranger, Lillie. You two have met on a number of occasions, if I recall correctly. And there were the midnight phone sessions, you said so yourself, involving God-only-knows what. I'd hate to think they compared in any way to the phone calls we used to have, because your mouth, Lillie, is irresistible when you want it to be.'

'Shut up, Jared! Just shut up. You're crazy, you know that? You have no idea what you're talking about. You're losing your mind.'

She got up from the deck chair and headed for the lower deck.

'Lillie, wait!' he called out to her. 'Don't leave. I didn't mean it. I'm sorry. I don't know why I said that. Don't go.'

But she was too hurt and angry to stop. She kept on going, locking herself in the guest cabin. It had become her sanctuary from him. She tossed herself down on the bed and began to cry.

It was really happening, she realized in sick horror, this was no joke. Jared was losing his mind. The man she'd loved, idolized, worshipped, given herself to so willingly all these years, was clearly going off the deep end and she had no clue what do to about it. And here she was stuck out at sea, of all places. Who could she turn to? The crew? Not very likely. They couldn't wait to get back on dry land and start gossiping about all they'd been privy to aboard Jared Warren's yacht and she knew it. But was going to have to do something and she didn't know what. The thought of abandoning ship became a very appealing notion.

'Lillie, honey.' There was a knock on the door. 'Please, let me in. Let's talk. I'm so sorry about those things I said. Truly, I don't know what came over me.'

'I know what came over you,' she shouted out at him, not budging from the bed. 'You can't stand the thought that I have my whole future ahead of me and you can't get your greedy hands on it!'

'Lillie, please. That's hateful.'

'And what do you call the things you said? I'd call them worse than hateful.'

'Honey, please. Do we have to shout at each other like this through a locked door? Won't you please open up so we can talk about this calmly? I said I was sorry. I meant it.'

'Go away!'

'Lillie!'

'No!'

'Don't be so childish. I can go get the key, you know. This is still my boat. Don't make me have to do that.'

Lillie sobbed even harder. Why was he always treating her like a child?

Because I am a child, she cried in anguish. I'm always a little fool when it comes to men. When am I ever going to grow up, get a grip on my life and start feeling like a grown up, like I'm worth something?

Then she thought painfully of John Shay and she wanted to disappear. What had Jared really said to him about her? She felt humiliated.

Men and their drunken little one-up-manships. Why did they always have to impress each other at the expense of a woman's dignity? Comparing notes about their little conquests; she felt disgusted and ashamed.

Jared was back. Lillie heard him sticking the key in the door. Then he opened it.

'Come on, now, Lillie,' he said. 'Let's be adults about this.'

'I have nothing to say to you.'

'You have plenty to say to me.'

'I do? Well, I can't imagine you'd want to hear about it. It wouldn't be very flattering.'

'You can start by having a little gratitude, you know. You can start by thanking me.'

'Thanking you?' She was incredulous. 'Thanking you for what?'

'For giving you a career, for one thing, a career that's made you rich, that's made you a household name. You can thank me for sticking by you, guiding you, showing you how it was done. You can thank me for giving you a goddamned job – how about starting there?'

'I've never been ungrateful for any of that, Jared, and you know it. But what's going on now is not about any of that.'

'Oh really, what is it about, then, in your lofty opinion?'

She glared at him through her tears, weighing her thoughts carefully. 'It's about your ego running out of control, if you really want to know. It's about Abby dying and you getting older, and over extending yourself and not believing in your talent anymore. This isn't about my ingratitude.'

He looked like his knees were going to buckle. Her words had hit him hard. He sat down slowly on the bed. 'Just give me another chance,' he said quietly. 'Don't leave me. Give me some time to sort this out, to pull myself back together.'

She wanted to, she really wanted to. But how could she handle this? Her hero had become so pathetic.

* * *

By the time the boat reached the marina in Long Island, it was too late to cancel the engagement party. So Lillie did her best to seem on top of the world – like someone announcing an engagement might seem. But she wouldn't go anywhere near Jared.

The people invited to this particular party were heavy hitters; a lot of money people were on board. Producers Lillie had worked with over the years and would likely work with in one capacity or another for the duration of her career – however long that would be. Even if she stayed with Jared at this point, Lillie couldn't afford the luxury of putting her illustrious career on hiatus to start a family. She was going to need all the money she could get for a long, long time.

So Lillie spent the evening doing what she was starting to do best, giving an Oscar worthy performance, acting like the ultimate classy hostess for as long as she could stomach it. When the party was in full swing and her presence was no longer even noticed, she tucked herself unassumingly in the background and let the party go on around her.

This crowd was one that was much more secure in its idea of

itself anyway; it didn't need a hostess at the helm. The smells of wealth and achievement were everywhere. The champagne flowed and flowed and flowed, until several partygoers, young women in particular, began reveling shamelessly; stripping out of their evening clothes and splashing naked into the yacht's small swimming pool. The guest cabins below had been quickly besieged by A-list honchos partaking of various hedonistic indulgences and all of this excess in honor of Lillie's so-called engagement made Lillie feel a little ill.

She walked out to the deserted bow of the ship with a glass of champagne, unaware of where Jared might be and not even caring. Alone with her thoughts, staring out at the gently lapping sea and the twinkling lights of the quiet marina – a sharp contrast to the boisterous world surrounding her on the boat – she passed a good portion of her own party in solitude.

'Lillie?'

It was a voice behind her – a man's voice. She turned around. 'Hello,' he said.

'Why, Mr. Shay.' So he'd made it to her party without her invitation.

'John,' he insisted.

'John.'

'Am I intruding?'

For a moment, they stared uneasily at each other. 'No,' she finally said. 'You're not intruding.'

'I'm sorry to get here so late, although it looks like the party hasn't suffered without me.' He indicated the reveling skinny dippers by the pool, whose rowdy numbers were growing. 'Truthfully, I had a hard time making up my mind about coming at all, that's why I'm so late. I'm still new to this sobriety thing and I figured a party like this, well, you know. It might bring out the worst in me.'

She raised an eyebrow doubtfully.

'I've only been sober for four months,' he went on. 'But I suppose that now is as a good a time as any to start holding my own in these types of situations.' She looked at him as if he were speaking ancient Greek. 'You know – wild parties?' he explained. 'Social gatherings?'

Who was he trying to kid? 'Has it really been that long since you've had a drink?' she baited him.

'Yes, four months. Twenty-nine days of it right in my own home.'

'Is that right? So how did your meeting with Jared go yesterday?'

'Well,' he said, 'to be honest, it wasn't the most encouraging meeting I've ever gone to, but at least I gave him the new book. That much was accomplished.'

'You know, Jared was pretty drunk when he got back to the boat.'

'I know. Since when did he start drinking scotch anyway?'

'Since never,' she replied in disbelief, wondering where this charade was going. 'I've never known him to drink scotch – of his own accord.'

'Well, he can't handle it. That much is obvious. Two drinks and I had to pour him into a cab and get him to the marina. You got the copy of the new book, though, I hope?'

Lillie was thrown. Two drinks? Now she was wondering what had really happened at the meeting, if Jared had lied about that, too. John Shay didn't seem like some lush who'd fallen off the wagon. He seemed strikingly sober and in control.

The silence grew uncomfortable. John tried to remain detached, but he wished he had a drink to at least hold on to. This conversation isn't exactly going great guns, he thought; it was a mistake to come. I should have waited until she'd read the book, waited for her to get in touch with me. I'm making a fool of myself over a movie star half my age. Look at her; she's young, gorgeous. She's got the world on a string. She's having the time of her life these days and she should be. A woman like her isn't going to drop everything to read some lousy book.

'I did get the book,' she finally said. 'In fact, I read it, the whole thing, last night in my cabin.'

His heart began to pound with hope again; she'd read it. 'The whole thing? Well, I guess I'm flattered. Should I be flattered? You know, you've got a strange look on your face.'

'I wish…' Her nerve faltered for the slightest moment. She wanted to tell him what she really thought, how much she'd loved it, loved him; how the book had made her feel about her life, what it had taught her about herself. 'I wish we could be somewhere a little more private,' she said.

'I see.' He still felt confused. 'So, is that a good thing, or a bad thing?'

She didn't answer. She seemed to be looking to him for assistance of some kind. He stepped a bit closer to her. 'Lillie, are you all right?'

She was hardly all right; her world was falling to pieces. She didn't know truth from lies anymore. 'I'm glad you came, John,' she said.

'I'm glad you invited me.'

'Oh, yes, well…' Jared again. Why was he doing this to her, weaving this web of craziness around her? 'I'm glad you're making so much progress with the drinking thing. You've written a wonderful book. A truly wonderful book. I loved it.'

John wanted to kiss her, he felt that grateful. But he kept his cool.

'I hope you'll let me buy the rights to it,' she went on.

'But what about Jared and his production company?'

'I don't know about Jared,' she answered distractedly. 'He's been acting a little strange.' She took a sip of her champagne.

'I know.'

'You do?'

'Yes. I wasn't going to mention it, but he was talking about all kinds of crazy things yesterday.'

Oh god, Lillie thought in despair, feeling exposed, remembering Jared's ranting earlier about the Waldorf. 'I sure hope he didn't say anything crazy about me.'

'No,' he assured her, lying to protect her from the ugliness of it. 'We didn't talk about you. But he does seem like a very unhappy guy.'

'Unhappy?' she scoffed bitterly, motioning to the debauchery going on around them. 'But look at all this, look at the life we're living. How could anyone be unhappy with this?'

'Lillie, what's going on?'

She took another sip of champagne. 'I've been thinking of going ashore, spending a little time away from this crazy boat. If I did, do you think you might have time to meet with me somewhere?'

'Of course I would. I'd be happy to meet you anywhere.'

'I'd really like to talk about your book. Some place a little more sane, you know, a little more quiet.'

As if on cue, the boisterous crowd by the pool turned the pandemonium up a notch and a stark naked couple began screwing their brains out, in plain view of everyone.

Lillie was mortified and quickly looked away. 'Jesus, John, I'm sorry. I usually don't throw parties quite like this one.'

'Don't worry about it. I've been to plenty of parties before.' He neglected to add that he'd behaved like that at parties before and that watching the rowdy action was making him want to do it again – right there, with her.

John felt his resolve to stay sober beginning to crumble. He was getting a killer hard-on. He hadn't counted on a free sex show, for chrissakes. He couldn't take his eyes off the spectacle. It made him want to throw Lillie down right there and screw her brains out, too, just like the couple by the pool. And he knew from experience that a single scotch on the rocks could help him be very persuasive with a woman…but she wasn't that kind of woman! What was he thinking? And then all of his hard work from the last few months would be shot to hell. 'I think it might be better for me to go,' he said abruptly.

'Go? But you can't go! You just got here. How am I going to endure this insanity if you go?'

The crowd growing around the screwing couple was cheering them on wildly. Even for Lillie, such a lurid spectacle within the tight confines of the yacht had become impossible to ignore.

'This place is really making me want a drink,' he continued.

'But I can make sure you don't drink.'

'Under the circumstances, I think I'd be safer at home, Lillie. Trust me.'

'Then take me with you,' she insisted.

'You can't leave your own engagement party! People will talk.'

'And which of these fine people will even notice I'm gone?'

She had a point. Still, John knew it was a bad idea. How could he leave the party with her and then not tell her what he was feeling, what it was he wanted to do with her? And even if she turned him down flat, leaving a wild party like this and taking off with the engaged hostess would only lead to a public showdown with Jared Warren, and the tabloids would love it. A scandal like that died a hard death in the public's insatiable imagination, and then who would take their efforts to make another picture together seriously?

'Come on,' he decided. 'Let's go down below and find a place where we can talk. Come hell or high water, I promise I'll stay sober.'

He grabbed Lillie's hand and led her through the crowded gangway, trying to keep his eyes off the free sex show as they squeezed past the pool. They maneuvered the narrow stairway to the lower deck with difficulty; there was a line of guests trying to come up as another line of guests was trying to go down.

Below deck turned out to be much worse, simply because there was less room. There was music playing and lots of loud conversation. People were crammed into tight groups that overlapped each other; smoking, snorting, drinking. John had a very difficult time filtering it all out, keeping his eyes off temptation, when everywhere he looked held another testament to excess. And as for the closed-off sleeping cabins, John got the distinct impression that a wide variety of sexual activities were underway all around him. He thought he would go crazy just from his own overly active imagination.

Lillie banged on the door of the guest cabin that had become her little sanctuary. 'Sorry to disturb you,' she called out. 'But I need this room now.' Above the music, there seemed to be a shuffling sound coming from inside the cabin. They waited.

In the crowded narrow hallway, Lillie was standing impossibly close to him. John couldn't take a breath without catching the scent of her hair. How would he endure even a moment alone with her once they were in the cabin, where he knew the bed would be the focal point of the tiny room? 'Lillie,' he said quietly, right in her ear. He was pressed that close to her.

'Yes?'

But he was suddenly at a loss for words. His hard cock ached inside his trousers, wanting to burst out of them. He was close enough to kiss her. She was looking right into his eyes now. He felt that she wouldn't object if he did kiss her. But it wasn't what he wanted. Not here, not like this.

Someone bumped into Lillie then and pushed her flat against him. She was certain that she felt a hard-on in his pants. Awkwardly, she inched away from him, trying not to notice it.

At last, the cabin door opened and three people squeezed out, looking the worse for wear; a man and two women. They were straightening their clothes. Unabashed, they made their way through the narrow gangway heading to the crowded salon area. And then Lillie and John popped into the available cabin. They were finally alone.

She quickly shut the door behind them and turned the lock, then sat down in a heap on the disheveled bed. 'Jesus! What insanity. All this for an engagement I don't even want anymore!'

He wasn't sure he heard her right. 'That's quite a statement. What do you mean by that?'

'Oh, just ignore me. I'm crying at my own party. Sit down, John, please. I know it's a little close in here, but make yourself comfortable.'

He tried to do just that, but the only place for him to sit was next to her on the narrow bed, and being close to her like that made his erection feel like the most noticeable thing in the room. He got the distinct impression that she was trying very hard not to notice it.

'This is where I read most of your book – last night. It was dawn before I'd finished it. I felt like I'd gone to another world.'

He glanced down at the unmade bed. He thought of her lying there, reading his book, the sheets entwined around her naked legs. He thought of all the nights he lay alone in his own bed, jerking off, obsessed with her. It was only making his hard-on worse.

'This is my room now,' she went on.

'You don't share a room with your intended?'

'You mean, don't I sleep with Jared anymore? You're very polite, you know that?'

'I'm just nervous, Lillie.'

She wanted to tell him that it was over between her and Jared, that it was just a matter of time, and that his book had made her want to make love to him instead. But she knew it would sound crazy. They barely knew each other. So she talked about herself. 'I came from a very small town. Just like Ruth, in the book – I don't know if you know that. My parents weren't married, either. My mother was poor, she drank herself to death.'

'I know,' he said quietly.

'You do?'

'Of course I do. You're famous, Lillie. In a lot of ways, your life is an open book.'

'That's funny – that you said it like that. I feel that your book was my life. I feel like I lived it. I guess you get that kind of response from a lot of your readers?'

'I do, sometimes. Yes.'

'So I'm kind of ordinary in that way?'

'Not at all,' he said. 'Nothing about you is ordinary.'

'I don't sleep with Jared anymore,' she finally blurted. 'At least, I haven't been. I don't think I will again. I think our relationship is over.'

John stared at her, trying to keep his expression a blank, hiding his desire to kiss her mouth, to unzip his pants already, to tear off her clothes and get naked with her, to make very good use of the bed. 'I see,' he said.

'Maybe I seem cruel to you, or cold or something. But I don't think he's handled his wife's death as well as he thinks he has. I think if I married him it would be a disaster – a very short-lived disaster, which might be even worse.'

'Maybe,' he said, trying hard to keep his focus on the conversation and not on the pressure building in his balls.

'Are you married? When I called you in Copenhagen, you said that you had a daughter.'

'I do have a daughter. But I'm not married to her mother anymore.'

'I didn't think so. You don't seem married.'

'No. I drank a lot, I gambled, I traveled. I always found reasons to leave my wife at home alone. Not that there were other women, because there weren't back then. But I was in love with my success. It had come easily to me, right out of college. My first novel was a best seller, and all the other books followed suit. It wasn't until my wife left me and took our daughter with her, that I discovered what a hole it had left in my life. Suddenly I was free to live however I wanted to, and no matter how much wine, women, and song I dredged up, it was never enough to fill that hole.'

'And then the long road to the Lindegaard Institute,' she said. 'So did they show you how to seal up that hole?'

'No,' he said. 'They taught me how to live in spite of the hole.'

'In spite of the hole?'

'Yes,' he said, wishing he hadn't used that word, hole. His lips, his mouth, his throat; they felt impossibly dry. The cabin was even smaller than he'd expected. 'I haven't spent much time on yachts,' he said. Was it his imagination now, or had she just moved closer to him? 'So what is it like?'

'What is what like?' she asked, feeling crazy, wanting to be in this stranger's arms. Wanting to kiss him, wanting to be naked, touching him. She couldn't stand it another minute. She glanced down quickly at his crotch. That was a hard-on, all right.

'What is it like to spend so much time on a yacht?' he clarified.

Her eyes darted back to his face. He was staring at her. Her heart jumped. He knew what she'd seen, he knew that she knew: he had hard-on. 'You mean at night?' she said, swallowing hard. God, he was handsome.

'I guess so, sure, what is it like at night?'

She didn't answer. She'd completely lost track of the conversation. So many lurid thoughts were tumbling through her mind at once. She wanted to feel that cock. She wanted it up inside her. She wanted her mouth on it. She wanted to taste him. She wanted to tear off her clothes and make love to him, behave disgracefully, screw like a couple of teenagers...

Tentatively, she reached her hand out and touched his leg.

'Lillie,' he warned her quietly, knowing where she was heading. 'This is a bad idea. You're engaged, remember? I'm assuming that Jared is somewhere on this boat.'

His words jolted her like thunder. Of course, he was right. What was she thinking of? For all she knew, Jared was just outside the door. And as crazy as he'd been acting lately, god only knew what he might do. She forced herself to snap out of it.

'I'm so sorry. I'm acting like the girl in your book now – practically throwing myself at you. I hope you don't think I'm a complete fool.'

'I don't,' he said. 'Believe me, I don't.'

'John, what is it about you? It's like you've put a spell on me or something. The way I'm feeling, it doesn't make sense.'

Their eyes were locked now. Too much had been said. How could he not kiss her? She was so close to him. But if he kissed her, how could he stop there? He could picture it easily, their clothes coming off, fucking her hard. Making her sweat…

But Jared Warren was still out there! What was he doing on this crazy boat? Why had he convinced himself to come to this damn thing anyway?

He tried to explain himself. 'Lillie,' he began, 'you have no idea what you're doing to me right now. I knew this was going to happen, you know. I knew I shouldn't have come here. I don't have enough will power. My lust for booze is paling in comparison to what it is I want to do to you right now.'

That wasn't a good way to explain it! What was happening to him?

'What is it that you want to do to me?' she asked softly. 'Tell me about it.'

Oh god, her mouth was exquisite, especially when she said things like that. 'I have to go, Lillie. I really do. I've got to get off this boat.'

'No,' she pleaded quietly. 'Please just tell me. We don't have to do it just because you tell me about it. But at least I want to hear it. Give me something to think about after you go.'

He pulled her up close to him, like he would kiss her. Her eyes were looking right into his. 'I want to make love to you so badly,' he whispered. 'You have no idea. I think about you constantly. I don't know why.'

'I think that would be so nice,' she whispered back, her breath close, 'making love with you – I'd like that. Let's do that some time soon. Let's make love. Promise me.'

What was prettier, he wondered; her mouth or the words coming out of it? 'You're sure?'

'I'm very sure.'

'But what about Jared?'

Lillie's hand was on his inner thigh, her fingers trailing up it.

'It's over with Jared. I'm going to leave him. I'm going to leave this boat. And then we'll be free to do whatever it is you're thinking about.'

'Oh god, Lillie,' he sighed. Her hand was on his bulging crotch, squeezing it, stroking it.

'I wish we could,' she said. 'I wish we could do it right now. This is making me crazy. I've never been unfaithful to anybody before.'

He forced himself to keep his hands off her, all would be lost if he didn't. 'Let me go, then. I'd better leave right now. I don't want you doing anything with me that you don't feel right about. We can stop right now. We can wait.'

She knew it was the right thing, what he was saying. 'Promise me we'll meet again soon.'

'I promise you.' He let go of her, and with all his effort, got up from the bed, his aching cock straining inside his trousers. 'I'll be thinking of you,' he said.

She got up, too. 'I'm going to see you off. But before we head back out into that madness, tell me something.'

'What?'

'When you're doing all this thinking about me – am I naked?'

'Oh, you are so bad.'

She smiled – it was that gorgeous movie star smile that he'd seen all over the world, all over his dreams. He couldn't say for certain if this wasn't another dream right now – it had all the earmarks of pure fantasy.

They let themselves out of the cabin, unnoticed by everybody. And they squeezed their way up the stairs to the fresh, sobering air.

Picking their way through the thick crowd, they worked their way over to the ramp that led down to the waiting motor boat. It would take John back to shore.

'Listen,' she said before he set off down the ramp. 'I hope you're going to keep your promise. Because I'm going to be thinking of you, too, and I have a fertile imagination. I might wear myself out if you wait too long.'

'Oh God, Lillie…' Then he gave up all restraint and pulled her close, close enough to feel her breasts press lightly against him. He gave her a very quick kiss on the mouth. 'I'll see you soon. Thanks for inviting me.'

'Thanks for coming,' she said. And then she gave him another of her famous smiles.

She watched as he boarded the motor boat. He turned to her and waved. A rush of lust shot through her. What a kiss, she thought; simple as it was. It had sparked her body to life. This was romance, she decided. Her life was going to change soon, she would see to it. It would change in a big way.

John sat down in the boat and watched her grow smaller as the boat took him closer to shore. She was even more exquisite in real life, as a real flesh and blood woman. Everything was going his way, he realized; she was leaving Jared Warren. They were going to spend time together soon; they would make love at last.

The music from the yacht drifted into the distance and the stars cascaded down from the sky, mingling with the winking lights of the marina coming up before him.

He'd kissed her, finally. And he'd felt the fleeting softness of her breasts – he could scarcely breathe from the excitement they'd promised, pressing against him. Wasn't he just like a schoolboy – so excited over the touch of a woman's breasts? But he knew he would remember that moment for a lifetime – that moment when he kissed her; it was like the night stood still.

And I did it sober, he told himself. Who would have ever thought…?

On board the yacht, Lillie turned her attention back to the

party, taking in the full swing of it, all the merry revelers, their faces dancing in the tiny white lights that were strung all over the boat. They seemed happy enough, these wild merry-makers. Music filled the air, dinner had been brought out at last and the supply of champagne was still plentiful. Everywhere she looked it was as if life itself were having a good time. And Lillie was happy to be part of it. Until the man standing next to her startled her back to earth.

'That was some sweet kiss,' Jared said. 'You must have been one hell of an accommodating hostess downstairs in that cabin, judging from the condition you left the bed in, I mean. I take it you showed him a very good time?'

'Shut up, Jared, you don't know what you're talking about.'

'I don't, huh?' He grabbed the back of her neck and pulled her close.

'What are you doing?' she practically shouted, forgetting that it was their engagement party in full swing around them. 'Let go of me!'

'I just wanted to find out for myself if I could smell him all over you.'

'Jared, you disgust me,' she snapped, oblivious to the people stopping to stare at them.

'I disgust you? Please! That's a laugh. At least I'm not fucking my brains out at my own party – with some played-out loser.'

Lillie tried to push him away from her, but he grabbed a handful of her dress. He jerked up the hem of it, exposing the tops of her stockings, then her panties. She screamed, yanking the dress from his grasp and then shoving him away from her with all her strength. 'What are you doing? Get away from me!'

'Just checking, sweetie.'

'Checking for what?' she hissed.

'To see if you put your panties back on. Enquiring minds want to know.'

'I hate you!' she shrieked.

'I'm your future, Lillie, remember that!'

'Not anymore, you're not!'

She pushed her way through the dumbfounded onlookers, trying to make her way below deck, to the privacy of her cabin.

CHAPTER FOURTEEN

The party went on until nearly dawn, most of the guests oblivious to the rift that had permanently torn asunder Jared Warren and Lillie Diver, the party's dubious honorees. Enough extra help had been hired that the yacht was back to normal only moments after the last of the weary partiers staggered down the ramp to be motored back to shore.

By then, Lillie had been locked alone in her cabin for several hours. Her bags were packed. She hadn't slept. But to her credit, she hadn't cried either. She was too worn out for that. She left a brief note for Jared, telling him that she needed some time to think, that she'd get in touch with him as soon as she returned to L.A. On top of the note, she left his mother's diamond ring.

Nearly forgetting, she scooped up John Shay's manuscript on her way out of the cabin, then she went in search of any member of the sleepy crew who might be good enough to motor her to shore.

In a pair of jeans and a white tee shirt, she wasn't immediately recognizable as one the day's hottest movie stars. But then she was in that area of Long Island where just about everybody was famous or worked for someone famous. At the marina she found an attendant on duty willing to track down a car and driver for her at that early hour of the morning.

'I need someone who's available for several days. I'm taking a road trip. I'm heading up north.'

'Up north?'

'To a little town called Mountville. I need to visit my father before he dies. He's in a nursing home there.'

She'd given the impression her father was on death's door, so the attendant at the marina worked doubly hard to secure her the most dependable car and driver he could find.

Lillie overheard the attendant as he spoke anxiously into the receiver. 'For that girl,' he was saying. 'You know her. She's from Hollywood, man. She won that Oscar. Right – the dark hair. That's her, the one who came in on that boat yesterday. Yeah, she had that big party last night. She needs a driver. Her father's dying. No, he's not with her. She needs to go see him. Right, that's right.'

Within an hour, it had all been arranged and a shiny black car pulled into the marina. The stone-faced driver loaded her bags into the trunk and then helped her into the back seat.

Lillie had a long ride ahead of her, time for her to stare out the window and think. She regretted not having had enough time to track down John Shay and tell him what she was doing. But when she got to Mountville, she'd find a way to get in touch with him. After all, it was because of John and The World I Could Give that she was going home at all.

* * *

John opened his eyes to the sound of birds chirping and to the touch of a light breeze blowing in through the balcony door.

He looked around himself sleepily and realized that it hadn't been a dream; he'd been to the party aboard the yacht, stayed sober, and kissed Lillie Diver. And all was still very right with the world.

He wondered when he would hear from her and he tried to convince himself that it might be as early as that afternoon.

Wouldn't that be great, he thought – his cock springing to immediate attention. Then they could make love all evening. Assuming, that is, that she'd found the nerve to break the bad news to Jared Warren.

* * *

For several hours, Jared had been pacing the master cabin like a crazed squirrel in a cage. He was sure that by now it had to be dawn.

Those goddamned people must have gone home by now, he tried to persuade himself.

But what if they hadn't? What if there were still a few stragglers? He didn't want to risk running into anyone. He knew he was losing his mind. How many other people knew it, as well? He wouldn't budge from the cabin until he felt absolutely certain that there was no one left aboard the yacht except him, Lillie, and the crew.

He sat down on the bed and stared at the floor. Listening, listening…Was anybody out there? The music had stopped a long time ago but that meant nothing to a bunch of self-involved freeloaders. They would hang in there until every ounce of free booze and every morsel of free food had been consumed.

He got up and paced the small room again.

The bill for this particular free-for-all bash had sent him even more deeply into the red. Why was it, he wondered angrily, that the wealthier the guests were, the more they expected to get for free?

But in the long run it was worth it. A lavish display of excess created the illusion of success. And in this industry, success bred more success. As long as everyone thought he was on top of the world, then for all intents and purposes, he was on top of the world. And in no time at all, he would be on top of the world again. This was all just a temporary setback. The necessary resources would come together in the nick of time, like they always did. He'd handle the Jake Brown project on his own and then slip effortlessly into the John Shay picture. Sell the house, the boat and move in with Lillie to cut expenses… everything would take care of itself.

He breathed a deep sigh of relief, then sat down on the bed again and listened.

* * *

Miles and miles of highway passed by outside the car window… there was something about freeways that made all the world look the same. Still, Lillie decided, Connecticut is noticeably greener than New York, and it would just get greener and greener the farther north she went.

* * *

John kicked the sheets down; he was starting to work up a sweat. This morning, he was hornier than he could remember being for a long time and that was saying something. It seemed like all he did anymore was jerk off like some lust-crazed sixteen year old. But the anticipation of fantasy finally becoming reality was almost more excitement than his nerve endings could stand.

With his cock in his fist, he had Lillie on all fours in his head and he wondered if she was that kind of girl, the kind of girl who got unbelievably accommodating when she was getting it hard from behind. He would find out. It would be one of the many things he would find out. It would be easy to experiment now with every fantasy because he knew that she was willing. Her lust had been barely containable the night before.

And when was the last time he'd shown that kind of restraint? A gorgeous woman, a woman he was almost in desperate need of, was practically giving it away and he was saying, no, not yet, not like this, let's wait until the time is right.

Never in his memory had he behaved like that. But she was a woman worth waiting for, worth taking the time to do it right.

God, he was hard. The skin on his cock was stretched taut as he tugged himself up and down, up and down, in rhythm to the frenetic fucking he was giving Lillie in his head. Her ass was arched up high for him and her head was thrown back. Was she one of those girls who slammed back hard against a cock when it was slammed repeatedly into her? He wondered about that, as he wondered about the cries she might make while in the throes of insatiable fucking, too. The sound of her voice was so appealing under ordinary circumstances, it stood to reason that lust only made it that much more irresistible.

Knees apart, ass up high, and tits hanging down – that's when any woman was at her finest. A choice ass, he thought deliriously. Lillie was going to have a choice ass, one of the smoothest, roundest, tightest…

He couldn't wait to get her alone and undressed. And in his bed. In any bed. Or on the floor – he pictured it now, Lillie on all fours on the floor. There was something wide open and unfettered about getting a girl naked on the floor.

But there something about having a woman like Lillie ensconced in the comfort of his bed, as well. To reach over and find her there, naked, next to him.

It was becoming increasingly clear to John that the scope of his fantasies could be spread out over the course of a lifetime. He wasn't sure what that was saying about him and all these desires.

He tugged at his cock determinedly now, he was ready to come, he wanted to come. He wanted to feel the searing thrill of his own orgasm pushing up hot through his balls and bursting out of his swollen cock and –

Damn! The phone was ringing. Who could be calling at this hour?

Lillie, that's who, he realized with a jolt. Maybe it was Lillie calling, announcing that Jared was a done deal and she was on her way over.

He grabbed the phone next to his bed. 'Hello?'

'Where is she, Shay?' a voice was screaming. 'I know she's there. I want to speak to her!'

'Who is this?'

'Who the hell do you think this is? It's Jared Warren and I want to talk to Lillie. Right now, Shay. Put her on the phone!'

'But she isn't here. It's only eight o'clock in the morning. What are you ranting about?'

'You haven't heard ranting yet, my friend. Put her on the goddamned phone! She's not going to run out on me like this, least of all, for some loser like you. I won't have it, do you understand me, Shay? I won't have it!'

'You're crazy, Warren. Listen to yourself. You sound like a deranged maniac. Take a look at the clock. I'm not even out of bed yet.'

There was a pause of heavy breathing on the other end of the line. John tried to make sense out of what was happening. 'Are you trying to tell me Lillie left?' he asked calmly, hoping to get something coherent out of Jared besides this crazy screaming. 'Is that what this is about? And for some reason, you think she came here?'

'Cut the crap, I know what you two did last night! I know what the deal was with you, what you did to my woman on my boat. And don't try to deny it, Shay. I saw you kiss her. Everyone saw you kiss her!'

'I may have kissed her goodnight, but that was the extent of it,

Warren. You'd better get your facts straight before you start accusing me of anything.'

'If you don't put her on the phone this minute, I'm coming ashore and I'll come get her. I mean it, Shay.'

'You don't even know where I live. And, besides, she's not here. I swear it. If I do hear from her, though, and I hope I do, I promise to tell her to call home!'

John slammed down the phone, unnerved and bewildered.

So Lillie had left. John wondered what that really meant; had she gone ashore for something, like to run an errand, or had she really done the deed and left?

If so, would she come to see John?

And then it occurred to him, damn, she doesn't know where I live, either. And I have an unlisted phone number.

But she was resourceful. She'd find a way to get in touch with him.

He glanced down at his limp dick. It had all been for nothing, the pumping and puffing and sweating. And right now, he didn't exactly feel like starting over.

* * *

Jared stood in the navigation room, the ship-to-shore phone still clutched in his hand. Lillie's short note lay on the console in front of him. The crew's captain was in the navigation room, too, sleepily dazed; wearing just his boxer shorts, waiting for Jared to hang up the phone and let him get back to bed.

This was the problem with these boat phones, Jared reminded himself, too many people around to eavesdrop on your heartache. But his cell phone wasn't getting a signal out here on the water.

He slammed the phone down finally. 'Thank you,' he managed to tell the captain. 'Sorry I had to wake you.'

'No problem,' the captain replied.

Jared grabbed Lillie's note and left the navigation room and went back to his cabin.

She was really gone. Now what was he going to do? Was it worth it to try and find Shay? It sounded like he didn't have a clue that Lillie was gone. It could be a huge waste of time, a thing that Jared felt he had in short supply.

He sat down on the bed in a daze. Maybe he should at least try to get some sleep.

CHAPTER FIFTEEN

When Lillie reached Mountville, it was mid-afternoon and she was eager to get out of the car to stretch her legs. It had been a very long ride.

Without much difficulty, the driver had found the town's small hotel in the center of town. It was just as Lillie remembered it. Everything she'd seen so far looked exactly the same, and she'd been gone already for eleven years. It seemed inconceivable, as if time had stood still. Yet the sameness of Mountville comforted her.

She instructed the driver to pull the car around to the lot behind the hotel. Nothing would attract attention on the quiet streets of Mountville like a shiny black town car with a driver in chauffeur's garb unloading a passenger in front of the hotel. And Lillie was hoping for as much privacy as she could get right now.

'Why don't you leave your hat and coat in the car, too,' she told him. 'And I can help you carry in the bags. We'll look more ordinary that way.'

Try as they did, there was nothing ordinary looking about the unlikely duo, especially in a town as perennially ordinary as

Mountville. Lillie's driver was an older black man, around sixty or so. Even without his chauffeur's jacket and cap, he carried himself with an uncommon dignity. Whereas, poor Lillie looked worn and bedraggled.

The lobby of the old hotel was as reverentially silent as a library. The only sound was the creak of the hard wood floor as the pair walked across it to the front desk.

With as much nonchalance as she could muster, Lillie asked for two rooms.

The desk clerk eyed her quizzically. Taking in first the casualness of her attire, then stealing a quick glance at her face. Then he did a double take. 'I know who you are,' he said. 'You're Lillie Diver, the actress!'

'Yes, I am,' she admitted. 'And what's your name?'

'Barry Cross.'

'Well, Barry,' she said confidentially, 'it's very nice to meet you. I was hoping for a couple of nice quiet rooms for a little rest and privacy. If you know what I mean.'

'Absolutely,' Barry replied, thrilled to be in on the secret. 'You're sort of traveling incognito?'

'That's right, sort of. I'm here on a personal visit and I'd like to keep it private.'

Barry assured her she would be afforded an unprecedented degree of privacy. He personally showed the pair to their rooms on the third floor.

'If there's anything you need, Miss Diver, anything at all, you just ask me personally and I'll take care of it. And mum's the word,' Barry assured her, before leaving her alone to her peace and quiet.

The room was adequate and comfortable, with no luxuries to speak of, but that was okay for Lillie. She didn't need luxury right now. All she needed was a phone book.

On the small table next to the bed, she found it, the phone book serving Mountville and the surrounding communities. She wasn't sure where to start. Should she pick out one of the few surviving Kincaids at random and then call to inquire about Sam? Or look for the listing of nearby nursing homes and see if a name might spark her memory? She'd only seen the name of the nursing home mentioned once, in a newspaper article two years ago.

It would probably be less intrusive, she decided (coward that she was) if she were to check the nursing homes first. It would be less likely to arouse suspicion and gossip, anyway. And truthfully, the thought of speaking to any Kincaid directly, unnerved her. She might as well still be seventeen for all the courage she lacked in dealing with the likes of those rich folks from the other side of town. Perhaps she had more money herself these days than any of the surviving Kincaids, but money wasn't really the issue. The issue was old memories and the sway they still held over her self-esteem.

Happily, she discovered that there weren't that many nursing homes in the area, and finding the one that was home to Samuel Masters Kincaid III was one of the simpler things she'd accomplished in a long time.

Yet when she inquired about visiting hours, the nurse said, 'Are you a friend of the family? Because Mr. Kincaid does not receive visitors unless they're friends of the family.'

'Well, he and my mother were good friends a number of years ago,' she tried innocently. 'I'm just visiting Mountville and she told me to be sure to stop in and see Sam, to give him mother's regards.'

The nurse hesitated. 'Well, you know he has a problematic memory. He's not likely to remember who your mother even is.'

'That's all right. It would make her feel better just knowing I saw him, even for a minute, and could see for myself that he was doing okay.'

When the Academy gave out the Oscars for lies told to nursing home attendants, Lillie was sure to snag another coveted trophy. The trusting, small-town nurse had been convinced of the authenticity of Lillie's proposed visit in the wink of an eye. Perhaps there simply weren't too many diabolical people in the area of Mountville trying to sneak in and have an unauthorized conversation with Sam.

But her visit would have to wait until the following day, when she would be thinking clearly again. Lillie hadn't slept in well over twenty-four hours. And now the reality of everything that had happened, the gravity of the decisions she'd made, hit her like the proverbial brick wall. Her system crashed. It was all she could do to halfway unpack and then collapse in bed, dead to the world .

* * *

The afternoon wore on into evening and there was still no word from Lillie. John tried to convince himself that she was okay and that this escape of hers to wherever it was she'd gone, did nothing to change the promise they'd made to each other. They were going to see each other soon. He had to believe that.

And besides, it's not as if a woman like her just fell off the face of the planet. She'd turn up again, even if it was back in Los Angeles. She wouldn't stay gone for good.

He sat down to a modest dinner alone and the evening paper. To his chagrin, the gossip page had a regrettable piece on Lillie and Jared's engagement party. It was a blind item, not referring to the 'happy couple' by name, but enough details of a party on a yacht were given for John to know exactly who they were talking about. There was mention of an ugly scene in the wee hours, where the love birds were overheard none-too-discreetly screaming at each other, with each individual bird disappearing to its respective nest for the remainder of the party.

Well, now it was a little clearer anyway, just what had happened that had caused Lillie to run off at the break of dawn. But John felt bad for her, that anything demoralizing had had to happen to her at all, least of all, in public.

*   *   *

Lillie awoke with a start in the middle of the night. Disoriented, she couldn't remember where she was. She was expecting to be in her cabin on the boat, but even in the dark of night, she could tell this was not the boat.

She switched on the bed side light and then it all came back to her.

That's right, Mountville. She'd come home to Mountville. She'd left Jared. She wanted to be with John now.

She switched off the lamp and then flopped back down on the pillow.

And she was going to see her father.

The wealthy and powerful Samuel Masters Kincaid III and the famous John Shay; in her mind, the two men were becoming interchangeable. It was all because of John's book. She wasn't sure what she was trying to prove by making this trip and going to the nursing home, she only knew she had to do it. There was something about her past that she wanted to reclaim. Something about that was going to make her future better. She was certain of it.

CHAPTER SIXTEEN

A hard rain was falling on Mountville that morning. Lillie decided it would be prudent to get an early start for the nursing home, to be there as soon as visiting hours started. She had neglected to pack for rain, though. She had expensive evening clothes, diamonds, designer swimsuits, tee shirts, high heels, and blue jeans, but no rain gear. Not even an umbrella. She threw on another tee shirt and the pair of jeans and figured she'd just have to wing it. Today she wasn't a movie star anyway, and she probably wouldn't melt.

In the lobby, the driver was waiting for her. In fact, it looked like he'd been waiting awhile. He'd had coffee and breakfast and time enough to read the local morning paper.

He stood when he saw her come down the stairs. 'Good morning, Miss Diver,' he said formally. 'It's raining today. Why don't you let me bring the car around?'

It was a toss up. Did she want to risk being recognized and perhaps hounded for the rest of her stay in Mountville, or did she want to go see her father soaking wet? She was already lamenting that she didn't have anything more flattering to wear than the tee shirt and jeans, so she told the driver to go ahead and bring the car around.

As she'd figured, getting into the back seat of the shiny black town car in front of the hotel attracted unwanted attention, even in the pouring rain. Two women scurrying past her on the sidewalk said loud enough for Lillie to hear, 'It's Lillie Diver! What is she doing back in Mountville?'

Lillie assumed that by noon, everyone in town would know she was staying at the old hotel.

The nursing home was a twenty minute drive from the center of town. It was a relatively modern facility, situated in a bucolic setting. A circular front drive outlined an unassuming fountain and plenty of well-landscaped flowers and shrubs that looked idyllic even in the rain.

When she stepped out of the car it finally hit her, what she had come here for and her belly clenched tight. She was going to see Sam Kincaid again, only this time, she would tell him who she was.

Maybe his mind would be too far gone to comprehend what she would say to him, but at least she would know that on some strange level of human awareness, he would finally know his daughter and maybe her heart would have a little peace.

Inside, Lillie approached the nurse's station, uncertain of what lie would come out of her mouth, but she was prepared to come up against the Kincaid family policy of no outside visitors and she was determined to prevail.

A nurse was sitting behind the desk. 'How can I help you today?' she asked politely.

'I'm here to see Sam Kincaid. I spoke to a nurse yesterday about arranging to see him. I don't know if that was you I spoke to? I'm from out of town.'

'No, that wasn't me. I was off yesterday. Mr. Kincaid doesn't usually have visitors, you know, except for his family. Are you a family member or a friend of the family?'

By Lillie's estimation, the nurse looked to be about twenty-five years old. She probably went to the movies on her days off. 'I'm an old friend of Sam's,' Lillie said. 'I'm Lillie Diver. I used to know him when I lived in Mountville.'

For a moment, the nurse was stumped, as if trying to place the unquestionably familiar name and face. But the nursing home wasn't where she was accustomed to seeing this face.

Then it dawned on her. 'You're Lillie Diver!'

'Yes,' Lillie said. 'And you are?'

'Call me Peggy!'

'Hi, Peggy. So would it be okay for me to see Sam?'

Peggy jumped up from her chair and came around to the front of the desk. 'Of course, it'll be okay, Miss Diver. Let me take you to him. His room is down corridor B.'

It was a bit of a trek to corridor B. But once they reached it, it was readily apparent that corridor B was the Park Avenue of the nursing home. There was carpeting in corridor B, and a separate nursing station. The patients' rooms were spaced further apart for privacy and the common area was less a gathering place for geriatric patients, than a plush entertainment room.

'Here's Sam's room, Miss Diver. Please let me know if I can be of any additional help.'

'Thanks, Peggy. I sure will.'

Room 215B. Lillie tapped lightly on the open door before walking into the room. Sam was dressed but sitting up in bed. He looked pretty much the same, only frail now, not so dynamic. His face lit up when he saw her.

'Sam?' she said. 'Is it okay if I come in?'

He didn't say yes but he didn't say no. He smiled at her peculiarly, almost as if he were in shock.

'Do you remember me, Sam?'

'Of course, I do,' he finally said. 'Sally! It's been such a long time. My goodness, you haven't changed a bit.'

'I'm not Sally, Sam. I'm her daughter, Lillie. I'm Sally's daughter.'

'Sally's daughter? I didn't know she had a daughter. Well, sit down, sit down. How is Sally?'

Lillie pulled a chair over by Sam's bed and sat down. This wasn't going to be easy. 'Sally passed away, Sam, a number of years ago.'

'Sally passed away? You mean she died?'

'Yes, Sam, she died – many years ago.'

'And you say Sally was your mother?'

'Yes. You don't remember that she had a baby? Of course, it's been nearly thirty years.'

'Sally had a baby? Sally Diver? Hmm.' He seemed to be giving it thorough and deliberate consideration. 'Sally was the one I was going to marry,' he said, peering off into the distance, as if watching it unfold again on a faraway stage of life. 'That's right. We were going to marry, but the family was against it. That one was Sally.'

'You were going to marry Sally Diver?' Lillie was stunned.

Sam looked at her. To him, she was nothing more than a stranger he was telling an old tale to. 'Yes, Sally and I were going to marry. This was quite some time ago, dear. You probably weren't even born. We were going to have a baby. But the family was against it. You say you knew Sally?'

'Yes, Sam,' Lillie explained patiently. 'Sally was my mother. I was her baby. I'm that baby.'

But the words didn't register. All that seemed to make sense to him were the images from the past. Nothing new penetrated his awareness. He smiled wistfully at Lillie. 'And who are you?' he asked pleasantly.

'I'm your daughter, Sam,' she said, knowing he would not make sense of it. 'I'm Lillie, your daughter.'

He smiled and nodded. 'You remind me so much of Sally Diver. I haven't seen Sally in years.'

*　　*　　*

In the back seat of the car, heading back to the hotel, Lillie resisted the urge to cry. What would be the point in it? She'd gotten a chance to spend some unexpected time with her father. And she was grateful for that. She doubted she would ever see him again. But at least now she knew that Sam had wanted to marry her mother. He hadn't actually done it, which would have changed her whole world, but at least he'd wanted to. That alone should count for something toward her pitiful mother's memory.

It had been a bittersweet adventure. And she found herself eager to share it with John. Funny, how it never once crossed her mind that it would be something she'd want to tell Jared – a man that she now realized she'd been intimate strangers with for six years, strangers who almost married. It was John and only John that she wanted to tell her story to.

In the lobby of the hotel, a small but noticeable crowd had gathered. Barry stood at the front desk trying to look stern, but looking at best, uncomfortable.

Lillie knew from experience that the quickest way to be left alone was to give the people whatever they wanted – sign an autograph, pose for a photo – or they'd still be waiting in the lobby every time she passed through it.

Barry looked positively relieved when Lillie smiled warmly at the small crowd and stopped to sign some autographs and say hello.

'What are you doing in Mountville, Lillie?'

'Are you visiting family?'

'Are you here shooting a movie, Lillie?'

'Can you sign it 'To Dolores, my biggest fan'?'

'How long are you staying in town, Lillie?'

'I work down the street at the coffee shop. Maybe you'll stop in?'

When she'd signed every last autograph and posed for a couple of snapshots, Lillie politely extricated herself and disappeared quickly to her room. For some reason, now she really did think she was going to cry.

* * *

At ten o'clock that night, John Shay's phone rang. For the time being, he'd given up thinking it would ever be Lillie. The best he could hope for was that it wouldn't be Jared Warren again. 'Hello?' he said warily.

'John? I hope I'm not calling too late. I had to pull quite a few rabbits out of my hat before I could come up with somebody who had your phone number! I finally got a hold of it from a friend of a friend in Los Angeles.'

'Lillie! I'm so glad you called. Where are you, in the city?'

'No, I'm in a little town called Mountville. I grew up here. It's about seven hours away by car.'

'I know. I've been there.'

'You've been here? John, nobody's ever been here!'

'Well, I have. You sound happy.'

'I'm more tired than anything. I left Jared.'

'I know. He called here yesterday morning in a rage, thinking that for some reason, you were here.'

Her upbeat tone changed considerably. 'I'm so sorry he bothered you, John. I hope he didn't say anything too crazy.'

'Listen, forget about it. It was nothing I couldn't deal with. When are you coming back?'

'I'm not sure. Not for a few days. But I wanted to let you know where I was, because I'm planning on holding you to that promise you made the other night. I didn't want you to forget. And I also wanted to tell you what I've been doing up here. It's been interesting.'

From what John had already learned about Lillie and Mountville, he was sure it was nothing but interesting. 'You want some company?' he said.

'What?'

'I could drive up there tomorrow. I know the way. But only if you feel like having company. I know the local hotel in the town there. I could get a room.'

'That's where I am, at that old hotel!'

'Well, what do say, Lillie? I could be there tomorrow afternoon.'

'John, would you really come? I think that would be great.'

'Yes, I'd really come. I've got nothing pressing on my 'things to do' list but to keep my promise to you.'

CHAPTER SEVENTEEN

Jared's bags were packed and on deck as the sun came up. He gave his instructions to the crew's captain. The yacht was going back to dry dock in Miami and he was flying back to L.A. There was work to be done. He had a house to sell and a picture going into pre-production – a picture that needed a new female lead, that was all there was to it. Jake Brown's people would have to get over it. He was Jared Warren, after all. He could get pictures made or make heads roll; let someone just try to tell him otherwise. And with any luck, he'd meet a nice fresh young one – a willing girl with a lot to prove – in the First Class compartment on the airplane. Maybe he could even get real lucky and nail her before the plane touched down in Los Angeles.

*   *   *

John said goodbye to Steve Swenson, giving him free rein of the estate again – for several days, this time. He loaded his bags into the car and set off once again for the long drive to Mountville. It was a beautiful morning. The sun was just coming up. If all went smoothly, he would arrive by early afternoon.

And then what, he wondered; what was going to happen next? If it were left up to him, true love would be exploding all over the place.

He liked the idea of the old hotel. It was romantic. It wasn't like the place in Spain, but then there would be plenty of time for Spain. For now, the romance was where the woman was and the woman was in an old hotel in Mountville.

*   *   *

Lillie woke early. She felt excited. It took her a moment to remember why – John was coming!

Today, the sun was shining. After breakfast, she paid the driver for his expenses and told him he was free to go back to New York.

When Lillie approached the front desk to take care of the driver's room bill, Barry Cross seemed dejected. 'You're not leaving us so soon, Miss Diver?'

'No, Barry,' she explained confidentially. 'I have a friend who'll be joining me here later today. I won't need a driver anymore because my friend,' and she said this while laying the innuendo on thick, 'has his own car.'

Delighted to be privy to yet more movie star intrigue, Barry nodded knowingly. 'Mum's the word, Miss Diver. No one will hear about it from me. Will your friend be needing a room?'

'Yes, but I'll let him arrange for that himself when he gets here.'

Mountville could be strangely civilized, Lillie decided with a sense of glee, as she walked out of the hotel lobby to the street. It was good to be a movie star in Mountville.

With a number of hours to kill still ahead of her, Lillie made the short trip to the cemetery. Another bittersweet adventure. She discovered that the money she was sending to the caretaker every month was keeping her mother's grave well maintained.

But that head stone is such a sorry sight, she thought. Maybe it might be better to buy her mother a new one.

But something told Lillie that the head stone was fine like it was, that what mattered was that Sally was remembered for having lived, not died.

Lillie felt a peculiar chill then, as if her mother were right there. 'I won an Oscar,' she told her mother. 'You should have seen me! I wore diamonds and my dress was so tight, I thought I was going to turn blue.'

The feeling seemed to say, I know. I saw. I was there. I drank a toast to you.

What a tiny grave to hold such a big life. Lillie wondered how they'd ever gotten her mother into such a small plot of ground.

By then, I was ready to lie still and behave. I was so tired, Lillie. It took a lot out of me, all that living.

The chill broke through Lillie like a giant wave and filled her, and then just as suddenly as it had come, the feeling was gone.

She walked back to the hotel lost in thought.

But now comes the important part, she realized; deciding what to wear!

* * *

Where is Eduardo when I need him?' Lillie fussed with her hair in the mirror. Next time, she was going to pay more attention to how he worked his peculiar magic on her. For now, she struggled to make herself look presentable but not overly done up, especially since she would be reduced to wearing a tee shirt and jeans again. She could hardly opt for the diamonds and evening clothes in Mountville in broad daylight.

John made the drive north in record time, breaking the speed limit most of the way. It was just after noon when he arrived at the hotel.

The lobby was as quiet and deserted as he remembered it. At the front desk, Barry was on duty.

'Why, Mr. Shay. Welcome back. It's nice to have you with us again.'

John was surprised to be remembered. But then, the tiny hotel probably didn't get much traffic.

'I need a room for a few days, and I'm meeting a friend here. She's already checked in but I don't know her room number.'

'I see,' Barry said, suddenly seeming quite conspiratorial. 'So you're 'the friend.' You'll be in the room on the third floor.' He said this with a distinct emphasis on the words 'third floor.' John got the impression Barry was trying to speak in code. 'Room 305 will be yours,' he went on quietly. 'Right next to 303, which is, you know, 'hers."

John nodded. It was starting to make sense. Everyone behaved a little queerly when a movie star was in their midst. 'Thanks, Barry. Thank you very much. Your discretion is appreciated.'

'We pride ourselves on being discreet, Mr. Shay.'

With a private smile, John took his key and headed for the third floor. Being under Barry's watchful eye would be better than staying at the Plaza.

John let himself into his room, tossed his bags on the bed, took a quick peek in the mirror and then headed over to Room 303.

He wondered whether the flame would pick up where they'd left it when they'd been aboard the yacht, or if they would have to start from scratch getting comfortable with each other again. He knocked on her door.

'In a mere heartbeat,' she answered, looking as fresh as a teenager in a pink tee shirt and a pair of blue jeans. 'Hello, Lillie,' he said, thinking that at least he could pick up where they'd left off without hesitating.

She smiled her famous movie star smile, the one that had written her ticket to fame. 'Why, Johnny Shay. Welcome to historic Mountville, birth place of movie stars and, well, a bunch of other people.'

He was more handsome than she'd remembered. He seemed virile and alive and happy – things she hadn't seen in Jared Warren in a long, long time.

'Would you like to come in? Have you had a chance to eat yet? We could order up. They make a mean cup of coffee and I can vouch for the toast.'

'I might need something a little more substantial,' he said. He felt like he was unable to take his eyes off her. 'You know, this is a good look for you. Sort of that less is more philosophy.'

'Well, in that case, you'll love the look I have in mind for later. It involves a lot, lot less.'

John thought he would burst out of his trousers.

*   *   *

They dined in a small luncheonette that seemed as romantic to Lillie as any exclusive establishment she'd ever eaten in New York or L.A. – it was the company she was keeping now. She was sure she was recognized by the other patrons, few as they were, but no one intruded on their privacy.

'John, I never had a chance to tell you why it was I loved your book so much. It was what inspired me to come to Mountville, in fact. It made me want to come home and take care of a loose end.'

'A loose end – singular?'

'Yes, my father.'

John was immediately intrigued.

'I identified so strongly with your character, Ruth. I had a similar background, the same hindrances of poverty and illegitimacy, and I realized that the things she'd done in her life were similar to the things I'd done – with men, I mean. And all because I was chasing after my father, his acknowledgement of me, that I even existed; his approval. In fact, I think that's what kept me and Jared together all these years. He was successful and about the same age as my father, and only recently I noticed they looked similar, too.'

So John had hit the nail on the head with that one. 'I take it your father's from Mountville. Is he still alive? Is that why you came home?'

'Yes, although he's not in very good shape. He's in a nursing home now and has been for a couple years. He still doesn't know who I am, but at least I spent some time with him. Well – more time. There was a time many years ago when, well…' Lillie faltered. 'But that's what I loved about your book. It helped me forgive myself. It gave me a different way of looking at my life, one that I realized was just as valid as the other way and it made me feel better about myself. Stronger. Oh, Jesus, you probably think I'm being a screwball.'

'No, Lillie, not at all. I'm glad you liked the book so much, and that you got that much out of it. Truthfully, I wrote it with you in mind.'

'You did? Well, I'm sure it's going to make a great movie.'

'Beyond it's ever being a film, I still wrote it for you, not as an actress but as a human being.'

'As a human being,' she repeated quietly. 'I like the sound of that, John Shay.'

After the meal, they walked around the center of town. Lillie reached for John's hand and held it. 'My father was one of the richest men in Mountville,' she told him. 'And throughout my childhood, he ignored me and my mother, acted like we didn't even exist. I was in my teens before I knew who my father even was. By then, my mother was pretty far gone on the booze so I had to piece the story together myself from her late night drunken ramblings. But you know what I learned yesterday? My father really cared for my mother, in his way. He even wanted to marry her when she was pregnant with me. But his family put a stop to it, and I suppose that money weighs more than good intentions, when you're that rich.'

'Lillie, would you like to go back to the hotel now?'

She smiled. 'I'd like that very much; a little love in the afternoon.'

* * *

They went to Lillie's room and locked the door. She turned off the phone and pulled down the shade.

'Do you remember where we left off?' he said, sitting down on the bed.

'I remember it very well.' She sat down by his side, leaned over and kissed him. 'And if I remember correctly, you had something very distracting going on down here.' She reached a hand along his thigh, slid it up between his legs and there it was, that hard-on. She moaned happily, kissing him again.

He was instantly on fire. It was hard for him to believe that all his craziness of the past year could come down to something so simple, so easy. Did it mean that this was just a passing tryst in a hotel room, something of little substance? Or would it turn into a love that would grow and last, that brass ring he was looking for, the prize he could grab onto and hold? Who could say, really? And it was probably better not to know. For now, he had a shot at the one thing his heart had been aching for, and he had a shot at it stone cold sober. For now, that was more than enough.

Lillie was true to her word. In a moment, she was undressed, completely naked. 'So what do you think?' she asked coyly. 'Is less still more?'

He groaned and grabbed her in his arms, pulling her down on top of him. He was too eager to have his arms full of her, her scent filling his head, to stop and take off his own clothes yet.

'You are so beautiful, Lillie. How is it God made a woman as beautiful as you are?'

'It had something to do with lust,' she explained playfully. 'Beyond that, the details get a little sketchy.'

Lust, John thought as he held her in his arms, kissing her now, his mouth fully exploring hers. That made sense. It stood to reason that lust could create a magnificence like her. The intensity of lust had to produce something of equal measure, why not a woman like Lillie?

Her breasts were pressed against his chest and it was then that he felt the urge to undress. To feel her next to him, nothing separating the touch of her flesh from his. When he was out of his shirt, she helped him unzip his trousers. Before they were completely down, she had retrieved his cock, it was out at last. Out in the open, hard, ready.

When she took it in her mouth, the sound of his gasp filled the room. He couldn't remember the last time he'd actually made love sober. It was a delirious feeling and it made him question why he had ever chosen to be drunk. 'God, Lillie.'

Her mouth was hot and wet. It slid up and down his shaft with just the right amount of pressure. It went from an incredible feeling to outright ecstasy in seconds. He slid his fingers into her hair, he steadied himself, keeping pace with her rhythm. In, out... the length of him disappearing between her lips, emerging a moment later. It gave him ideas, fueled his erotic imagination that simple movement, in, out. He wanted his cock penetrating her everywhere, wanted to watch himself disappear in her in every way.

As if on cue, she lay back on the bed. The ivory whiteness of her skin set off by the dark patch of hair, perfectly trimmed, enhancing the contour of her mound. Her legs parted for him. He was torn between wanting to devour her and wanting to feel his aching cock in her at last.

She hiked her knees up, offering it to him, her hole, in whatever way he wanted to take it. It was his choice now. She was open, waiting.

He fell to his knees, pulling her to the edge of the bed, until she was in his face, the perfect symmetry of her swelling lips parting to reveal the inner lips, the open hole.

His tongue licked the inner lips tentatively. She moaned. And that agreeable sound she made, urged him on. His tongue explored her more fully, took liberties. Dipped into the tiny opening of her hole, pushed up into the hood of her clit.

Her continued moans encouraged his tongue to linger there, to caress the stiff tip of her clit. To lick it repeatedly, decisively. He slid a finger up inside her while his tongue kept at its thorough task.

She held her knees tight, keeping herself spread for him, for the caresses of his mouth and for his probing finger. In and out the finger went, leisurely, easily, while the steady tongue on her clit coaxed a wave of pleasure from her that was building to a peak. It was a slow, gentle build – that growing wave. She felt like she could lie there and take in this sweet pleasure indefinitely. 'That feels so nice,' she said softly. 'Just like that.'

But a second finger went up her hole and challenged the sweetness. It pushed her into something more intense, causing her hole to open, the pressure inside her to grow. And the leisurely pace of his fingers now became more like the rhythm of fucking. 'Yeah,' she said, 'yeah…' keeping up with the new rhythm. Wanting to open wide for it, push down around the intruding fingers. 'Yeah,' she said. 'Yes, God that's good.'

With each inward thrust of his fingers, her hole opened, lips parting, revealing her tender clit more thoroughly to his tongue. In a moment, she would come for sure. Her pleasure was near its peak. But she didn't want to come yet, she wanted to ride this pleasure wave. She scooted away from him, retrieving the condom she'd tucked under her pillow and tossing it to him. She turned over, offering herself up to him, wanting to feel the power of his cock now.

John braced himself for the incredible sight of it. Her ass in the air, her thighs apart, revealing her open hole, slick and waiting for him. He fumbled with the condom, slipping it over himself as quickly as possible.

Then he pushed in his cock and the sound of urgent delight she made, as his cock parted the tight passage and sank deep in her hole, worked like an aphrodisiac, his lust tore through him. He wanted to fuck her hard, crazy. Get up inside her as deep as she could take it before she cried, 'God! Oh!' arching her ass up higher, pushing her hole out more to meet the rhythmic pounding.

God she was luscious, every inch of her, he thought. He held tight to her hips and watched his thick cock slide insatiably in and out, in and out, hugged by the tiny lips stretched tight now, riding the intruding shaft.

This was something he could watch for a lifetime, he thought; this gorgeous hole filled with his cock. He pushed now on her ass cheeks, opened the view up wide. Yes, he could watch this easily, this hole he was fucking, fucking. His cock was slick with her arousal. And the more he worked it deep in her, and pulled it out, and pushed it in, the slicker it got. The more she cried out.

God, God, yes, God!

A chanting rhythm. She steadied her knees, her face flat against the bed, her hole offered up completely. He couldn't get any deeper. She was taking his cock to the hilt.

'Fuck me, yes,' she said.

It was all her needed to hear. It pushed his delirium over the edge. The fire shot out of his balls. He was coming now, coming. Every muscle in his body taut from the pressure of the liquid fire pushing through his cock and spurting out. Once, twice, three times.

* * *

Twilight settled on the room. The blue-gray darkness enveloping the lovers entwined on the disheveled bed. Old springs creaking now, squeaking rhythmically, with purpose. John was astride Lillie, her legs wrapped around him, her arms holding him close. They were kissing, moaning into each other as they fucked. Like lovers, they were fucking. Completely entranced by the nearness of the other, wanting to revel in the ecstasy, prolong the feel of desire.

* * *

Nighttime, silence, darkness all around them. John flat on his back in her bed, Lillie straddling his face, her mound riding his amorous mouth. Rubbing and rubbing, her aching clit captive between his lips, probed repeatedly by the tip of his tongue.

She tugged on her stiff nipples, pulling, twisting, urging the orgasm to crest, to overtake her senses.

'Yes,' she finally whimpered, cried, squealed, 'Yes, oh, yes!'

She was coming, writhing on his merciless mouth, the wave consuming her.

'God, oh God, yes, yes...' she sputtered.

* * *

They showered and slept. And then dawn found them stirring early, eager to check on reality, on any changes the daylight might bring.

He was there in the bed beside her, hard, wanting her again. And she was ready to accept him. All was right with the new world.

They managed to pry themselves from the bed at last to go in search of breakfast, seeing that dinner the night before had completely escaped them. They'd been too consumed by their own lust to stop and consider the equal pleasure of food. Now they were both famished.

In the lobby, Barry greeted them with his customary discretion. And outside the lobby, another beautiful day was underway.

'I can't remember the last time I went through a marathon like this has been, John, maybe never.'

He smiled feeling that he, too, had outdone himself in the lust department.

They went back to the modest luncheonette they'd visited the day before, and as they ate, John wondered just how long their little escape from the world would last. When would he be back in New York? When would she go back to L.A., and then what?

He was no good at this part, at pacing himself when it came to wanting to be with a woman. When he had questions, he wanted to know where he stood. But he didn't want to frighten her away. She'd just come off of a six-year relationship that had ended in an engagement and then a sudden rupture. He was going to have to find a way to sit back and let life happen. He'd written the book that had brought her to him. He couldn't write the script for her whole life, as well.

'What would you like to do this afternoon?' she asked. 'Try out your room for a change?'

'Lillie,' he said, unable to stop himself. 'When are you planning to go back to L.A.?'

She studied her cup of coffee. 'I guess it depends.'

'On what?' he asked, trying not to sound too hopeful.

'On how long it takes us to get down to business.'

'What business?'

'The World I Could Give,' she said. 'In case you're forgetting, I want to make that picture. And I intend to live that part until it's in my blood.' She smiled at him playfully. 'What better way to study the role than by getting it straight from the horse's mouth. You stud, you.'

'Lillie, you're terrible.'

EPILOGUE

One year later… Jared Warren shouted with satisfaction, 'Cut! It's a wrap, gang!'

A good-natured cheer resounded throughout the set. It had been a long shoot, four months, with three different locations. But now they were all back in Los Angeles, home sweet home, where the end of a day's shooting didn't mean another night in a lonely hotel room. It meant a quick ride home and a good night's sleep in one's own bed.

But now it was over, all of it behind them. The World I Could Give would officially be in post-production tomorrow.

Another cheer rang out from the crew as an enormous decorated sheet cake, alight with sparklers, was wheeled on to the set.

Everyone was there for the final day of shooting. From the costumers, to the designers and decorators, people who were usually a day ahead of the set. Even the Executive Producers of the film were on hand, the team from Jake Brown's project the year before. They congratulated each other on their good fortune and they congratulated Jared. 'Great job, Warren,' they said. 'It's gonna be a winner.'

'Would I ever steer you wrong?' he boasted. 'How many years have I been in this business? I'll tell you, too many.'

It had been a tough year, but a fruitful one for Jared Warren. Shanghai Outriders had been a modest success. But the deal he'd cut with Jake Brown's people to put up a major portion of the funding for the John Shay project had paid off in spades for every-body and gotten the project on the fast track. The book itself had barely had time to crack the best seller list when the production was already underway.

Of course, there had been the delay of the weddings. That had put everybody's life on hold. Jared married his starlet from Shanghai Outriders, who was three months pregnant with his sixth child, in an elaborate wedding at his palatial digs in Malibu, while Lillie Diver quietly tied the knot in New York with John Shay.

Lillie and John had opted for a private affair. They were mar-ried by a local Judge in a suite at the Plaza hotel. His parents took the train in from Princeton to attend the happy occasion and Selena came in from Connecticut.

Insiders said that the bride wore white, a Machard original, and that she looked 'positively devastating'.

While, on the plane back to Los Angeles with his new bride in tow, John Shay apparently concurred. He was quoted as saying that 'never in his experience had he seen a more arresting sight than Lillie Diver on her wedding day. I can't believe she was mar-rying me!'

'Word on the street has it, folks,' the reporter went on to state, 'that the whole shebang is on the fast track to sweep the Academy Awards.' But, in all fairness, it was simply too soon to say.